Crimson Shadows

Immortal Descent
Book 1

Eve Newton

Copyright © 2024 by Eve Newton

All rights reserved.

No part of this book may be reproduced in any form or by any electronic or mechanical means, including information storage and retrieval systems, without written permission from the author, except for the use of brief quotations in a book review.

Author's Note

This is a Paranormal Reverse Harem Dark College Age Romance. All main characters are 21.

The guys from Immortal Descent are essentially the bad guys and this book contains adult and graphic content, and reader discretion is advised. This is BOOK 1 of 3. You will come away with more questions than answers... that is what a trilogy is all about ;-)

This isn't a dark, dark read, but there are a few TWs for this book/series. They can be found exclusively on my website. Do check them out for this book, as there are some scenes that require discretion: https://evenewton. com/immortal-descent

Join my facebook group for real time updates on future reads: https://facebook.com/groups/evenewton

Author's Note

Scan Me for Tws

Prologue

Adelaide

Thunder crashes, jolting me awake at the stroke of midnight. I can hear the clock on the mantlepiece downstairs strike the hour.

Happy thirteenth birthday to me.

Rain lashes against my bedroom window, creating haunting shadows on the walls. I've always loved storms; they seem to fit in with the way I see the world, in shades of darkness rather than light, which is weird because my surname, Légère, means light. But tonight feels different. There's a charge in the air that has nothing to do with lightning flashing, splitting the sky before the thunder rumbles, making it feel like the ground is going to part.

I burrow deeper under my duvet, trying to shake off the unease creeping up my spine. It's just the weather. Nothing to be scared of.

But deep in my soul, I know different. I can't explain it, but something isn't right.

I jump when there is a loud, insistent knock at our front door.

My heart rate spikes. Who is that?

I slide out of bed, my bare feet hitting the thin carpet.

The knocking continues, growing more urgent with each passing second.

Curiosity overrides my better judgment. It could be someone in trouble out there in this storm. I creep to my bedroom door and ease it open, wincing at the slight creak. The landing is dark, but a sliver of light spills up the stairs from the entryway below.

I tiptoe to the top of the stairs, crouching low to peer down at the front door.

My mum peers through the peephole and curses, her French accent strong due to her anger. She opens the door a crack, the chain pulled taut as she grips her dressing gown tighter.

"What are you doing here?" *she hisses through the gap.*

A man's voice answers, low and urgent. "Please, I need to see her. You can't keep me away forever."

I strain to see past Mum, but the gap in the door is too small.

"You need to leave," *Mum snaps quietly.* "You can't be here."

"I can, and I am," *the man insists.* "Let me in so we can talk."

A chill runs through me at his voice. It's chilling, forceful. I'm scared.

"Go away," Mum says and tries to shut the door, but the man slams his hand against it, and the chain snaps. Mum gasps and steps back as I stare down, frozen in horror. The stranger in the doorway has dark hair and pale skin. His clothes are soaked through, rainwater pooling at his feet on our tattered and soggy welcome mat.

Mum's voice drops to a whisper, but I can still make out her words. "You can't come in."

The man makes a sound of frustration. "Let me in, Edie, you can't keep me away from her."

"I can and I will. She is protected. She is a child."

"I'm aware," the man hisses. "You are actively keeping me from her, Edie, and this is going to end badly for everyone."

"Is that a threat, Rand? Go to hell where you belong!"

The stranger takes a step forward, but he seems to come up against an invisible roadblock, and I see Mum tense. He curses, but then his face falls. "Please," he says, his voice breaking. "I'm begging you. Just five minutes."

"I said no."

"Damn you, Edie!"

In one fluid motion, Mum reaches for something in the side table drawer near the door. I can't see what it is, and I strain my eyes and crane my neck to get a better look. I should be running, hiding, but I can't move. I'm frozen to the spot. Mum thrusts the object towards the man's face, and he hisses loudly, an unnatural sound that slides over my nerves like nails down a blackboard.

My eyes widen when Mum holds it up higher, and I see what it is. A wooden cross.

The stranger recoils, stumbling backwards, his lips parted, and his teeth bared. For just a split second, I could swear I see... fangs?

I blink hard, sure I must be seeing things. Fangs aren't real. They're the stuff of movies and Halloween costumes. It's not something you see on a random man on your doorstep in the middle of the night.

Right?

"Don't come back, Rand. She is dead to you," Mum says, her voice steely.

She slams the door in his face, the sound echoing through our small, two-bedroom terraced house in the North of England. For a long moment, she just stands there, her forehead pressed against the cheap double-glazed door. I can see her shoulders shaking slightly.

I want to call out to her, to ask what's going on. But fear keeps me rooted to the spot.

Finally, Mum straightens up. She turns, and her gaze travels up the stairs. Our eyes meet, and I see a flash of fear pass over her face.

"Addy," she says softly. "What are you doing up?"

I open my mouth, but no words come out. What can I say? That I saw everything? That I'm scared and confused?

Mum climbs the stairs slowly, her face a mask of forced calm. "You should be in bed, sweetheart. It's late."

"Who was that man?" I manage to ask, my voice barely above a whisper.

Mum's expression tightens for a moment before smoothing out. "No one you need to worry about."

"But—"

"No buts," she interrupts gently, stroking my pitch-black hair that falls straight down my back and kissing the top of my head. "Happy birthday, Adelaide, but you need your sleep. We've got a big day planned, remember?"

She ushers me back to my room, her hand on my shoulder feeling heavier than usual. As I climb into bed, my mind is whirling with questions. Who was that man? What did he want with me? And what did I really see when Mum held up that cross?

"Goodnight, love," Mum says, lingering in the doorway. "Sweet dreams."

But as she closes the door, leaving me alone in the darkness, I know there's no chance of sweet dreams tonight. Not with the image of those impossible fangs burned into my memory.

I lie awake for hours, listening to the storm rage outside and the occasional creak of floorboards as Mum paces downstairs. Every shadow seems to hide a secret, every gust of wind carries a whispered threat as the cramps in my belly get worse. With a groan, I roll over and then out of bed. Creeping to the bathroom down the landing, I feel the wetness between my legs and know that I've started my period. I've been waiting for it, and now it's here.

"Happy birthday to me," I mutter as I reach into the cabinet for the pads Mum bought for me. "Happy flipping birthday."

Chapter 1

Adelaide

The memory of that night of my thirteenth birthday floods through my thoughts. The ticking of the clock on the mantlepiece seems unnaturally loud in the tense silence of our living room. I'm perched on the edge of the sofa, my fingers drumming an anxious rhythm on my thigh as I stare at the man sitting across from me. The same man I saw eight years ago on a stormy night just like this one.

His dark hair and pale skin seem to absorb the dim light of the room. He's dressed impeccably in a tailored black suit that probably costs more than our entire house. His eyes, so dark they're almost black, are fixed on me with an intensity that makes me want to squirm.

"Adelaide," he says, his voice a low, hypnotic rumble. "I know you have questions—"

I resist the urge to snort. "Who are you?" I interrupt, although I have a sinking feeling I already know the answer. I look just like him.

He leans forward slightly, his elbows resting on his knees. "My name is Randall Black," he says, pausing as if to gauge my reaction. When I don't respond, he continues, "I'm your father, Adelaide."

The words hang in the air between us, heavy and suffocating. I glance at my mother, standing silently by the window. Her face is a mask of rigid calm, unsurprised by any of this. She's known all along, I realise with a jolt.

"My father," I repeat, the words tasting bitter on my tongue. "The same father who's been absent for the past twenty-one years?"

Randall has the grace to look uncomfortable. "I know I have a lot to answer for," he says. "But there were circumstances that prevented me from being part of your life. Circumstances that I'm here to explain now."

I'm barely listening to him. My mind keeps drifting back to that night. The night I thought I saw fangs gleaming in his mouth as he recoiled from the cross my mother thrust at him. The memory is so vivid, so real, that I can almost hear the rain lashing against the windows, feeling the chill that ran down my spine.

"Adelaide?" Randall's voice pulls me back to the present. "Are you listening?"

I blink, focusing on him again. "You were saying?"

He sighs, running a hand through his hair. "I was trying to explain why I couldn't be in your life. Your mother wanted to raise you as a human child, keep who you really are from you."

Mum hisses as he says this, appearing to throw her under the proverbial bus for whatever lies are about to be spewed. "Human child," I murmur as my brain catches up. "What else would I be?"

Randall opens his mouth to answer, but a flash of lightning illuminates the room, followed closely by a crack of thunder that seems to shake the foundations of our small, terraced house. I jump slightly, my heart racing. The clock on the mantelpiece chimes 9:00 PM.

Randall leans forward, placing a black envelope on the coffee table between us. My name is written on it in elegant gold script: Adelaide Légère.

"What is this?" I ask, my voice sounding strange.

Randall's lips curl into a smile that I want to say is sinister but isn't quite. "It's your admission acceptance to MistHallow University."

I frown. "I've never heard of it." I glance at my mother again, but her expression remains unchanged.

Randall leans back in his chair, studying me with those unnaturally dark eyes. "You're special, Adelaide. You're what we call a Vesperidae – a being of two worlds. Half-vampire, half-human. MistHallow's mission is to provide education and guidance to young supernatural beings. It's a safe haven for those who need to learn control, for troubled souls who need focus and direction."

His words wash over me as I struggle to process what he's saying. A Vesperidae. Half-vampire, half-human.

The words hit me like a physical blow. I should be shocked, in disbelief. But as the revelation sinks in, all I feel is relief. Suddenly, all the dark thoughts that have plagued me for years, the strange urges and desires I've tried to suppress, seem to make sense.

"I'm a full-blooded vampire," Randall continues as if this is the most natural conversation in the world and not one that has blindsided me despite my ready acceptance to believe I'm not just fucked up in the head. "One of the oldest and most powerful of our kind. Your mother is human, which makes you what we call a Vesper – a rare and uniquely gifted individual."

"So you're a vampire," I say, my voice flat. "A full-blooded vampire who decided to have a child with a human woman. And then you abandoned us for twenty-one years."

Randall's expression hardens. "It wasn't that simple, Adelaide. The supernatural world is complex, filled with ancient laws and customs. Your mother didn't want you growing up in that world."

"You keep blaming her, but all I see are excuses," I snap. "You *had* a choice. If you're this powerful creature, you could've fought harder."

"Not against the witchcraft."

"What?" I look at my mother, who just sighs and shrugs slightly. "You're a witch?"

She shakes her head, apparently dumbstruck.

"Vespers are incredibly rare, Adelaide," Randall interjects on her behalf. "You have abilities that some full-blooded vampires can only dream of. There are factions in our world who would stop at nothing to control you, to harness your power for their own ends."

I laugh, but there's no humour in it. "Powers? What powers? I'm just a normal girl. Well, a normal girl with some serious issues, but still." But there is no denying his words strike a chord deep in my morally grey soul. Automatically, I rub my wrist where thin, silvery scars crisscross my skin. For the first time in years, I don't feel the usual shame associated with them. Instead, it's as if a weight has been lifted from my shoulders. There is a reason for all this fuckery.

"The darkness that you've felt all these years," Randall says softly, "the urges you've tried to suppress – that's your vampire nature. It's been lying dormant, waiting to be awakened."

How does he know all of this?

My throat goes dry. "And MistHallow? What's its role in all this?"

"MistHallow University is a place where young supernatural beings like yourself can learn to control and harness their abilities. It's not just for Vespers or other hybrids, but full-blooded vampires, fae, elementals, and countless other creatures you've only read about in stories." He leans forward again, his eyes intense. "At MistHallow, you'll learn about your heritage, about the supernatural world that exists alongside the human one. You'll develop your powers under the guidance of experienced mentors."

I sit back, my mind reeling from all this new information. Part of me wants to dismiss it all as an elaborate joke or a vivid hallucination. But deep down, in a place I've always tried to ignore, something resonates with Randall's words.

It explains so much. My obsession with blood, and pain and death; my depression and malaise during the daylight hours and night when I come alive; my aversion to being touched because my skin feels too sensitive, too fragile like ancient paper that will crumble if you breathe too heavily near it; my dislike of other people, *humans*, who don't seem to understand me and write me off as the emo goth girl with too much drama, the list goes on.

"Say I believe you," I say slowly, my eyes on the clock as it ticks over to 9:05 PM. "Say I accept that I'm this... Vesperidae. What happens now?"

Randall gestures to the black envelope on the table. "Now, you have a choice. You can continue to live in the human world, ignoring your true nature and struggling to fit in. Or you can accept your place at MistHallow and learn to embrace who you truly are."

I stare at the envelope, my heart pounding. It's tempting, so tempting, to just say no. To pretend this conversation never happened and go back to my normal life. Whatever that is. The choice seems simple. Continue struggling on a night schedule when most of this world operates during the day or go to a place where there are others like me, and I don't have to pretend how fucked up I am, which takes more energy than I usually have to give.

But even as I think it, I know there is no choice. I've never fit in the human world. I've always felt like an outsider like there was something fundamentally wrong with me. And now I know why.

With trembling fingers, I pick up the envelope. It's heavier than it looks, the paper is thick and expensive. I break the seal and pull out the letter inside, my eyes skimming over the words.

"Dear Ms Légère," it reads. "We are pleased to inform you that you have been accepted to MistHallow University for Year 3 of 4..."

I look up at Randall, questions burning on my tongue. But before I can speak, my mother steps forward for the first time since this surreal conversation began.

"Addy," she says softly, her voice thick with emotion. "I know this is a lot to take in, and I'm sorry that it has taken this many years for you to find out. The protection spells on you were strong. I made sure of it. Your father couldn't see you. They broke today, which is why he is here now. You are an adult now, and this choice has to be yours. As much as I wish I could go on protecting you, this has gone on longer than it should've. I know you feel pain living in this world, so you have the choice now to decide what you want to do."

I stare at her, feeling betrayal, yet understanding *her* choices.

Tears shimmer in her eyes. "I'm so sorry, sweetheart. I wanted to tell you so many times, but... something always stopped me."

I look between them, these two people who have shaped my life in such different ways. My mother, always present, always loving, but hiding this enormous secret. Randall, my father, absent for so long but now offering me a key to understanding myself. I can't even deal with this knowledge of what I really am, and I can't show how relieved I am within myself with them both staring at me like this.

I stand up abruptly, clutching the MistHallow acceptance letter in my hand. "I need some time," I say, my voice shaking slightly.

Randall nods, looking disappointed but unsurprised. "Of course. But not too long. The year starts next week."

I don't respond. Instead, I turn and stride out of the living room, ignoring my mother's soft call of my name. I climb the stairs two at a time, slamming my bedroom door behind me with more force than necessary.

In the sanctuary of my room, I sink onto my bed, staring at the letter in my hands. Excitement rushes up as I realise I can leave my dead-end job at the morgue and go and do something amazing. I'd always wanted to go to University and learn as many things as I could, but trying to drum up the energy for day classes was too much for me. Now, with vampires wandering the halls of Mist-Hallow there will have to be night classes, and not just for a couple of hours like at the Tech down the road, but all night on all sorts of subjects.

I read through the letter. It outlines the unique curriculum at MistHallow, designed to help supernatural beings understand and control their abilities. There are courses in magickal theory, supernatural history, meditation and focus.

As I read, I feel that spark of excitement ignite. This is it. This is the explanation I've been searching for all my life.

I may want nothing to do with Randall Black, but this chance to understand myself, to belong somewhere is something I can't pass up.

As thunder rumbles outside my window, I make my

decision. I'm going to MistHallow University. I'm going to learn who and what I truly am.

And maybe, I'll finally find where I belong.

Taking a deep breath, I feel something shift inside me. The darkness that I've always tried to suppress, the part of me that I've always been afraid of – it doesn't seem so scary anymore. Instead, it feels like a strength, a power waiting to be unleashed.

For the first time in my life, I'm not afraid of who I am. I'm excited to find out more.

Chapter 2

Adelaide

Sighing, I know I have to get up and go to work. Reality check central. The morgue doesn't wait.

As I get ready, I can hear muffled voices downstairs—Randall and Mum, probably hashing out years of unspoken tension.

Not my circus, not my monkeys.

Right now, I've got bigger things on my mind.

I shove the acceptance letter under my pillow and grab my bag. Heading down the stairs, I'm waylaid by Randall again.

"Adelaide."

"Not interested. I have to get to work."

"Wait," he says and as I turn to him, he pulls something else out of his jacket pocket.

"What now?"

He doesn't answer; he just holds the white envelope out for me to take. Curiosity gets the better of me, so I take it and open it.

Narrowing my eyes at the black bank card in there, I purse my lips when I pull out the letter that accompanies it.

Then, I nearly choke on my saliva.

"What the fuck is this?" I spit out, eyeballing more zeroes than I will probably ever see in my lifetime of morgue work.

"I've been putting money aside for you since before you were born," Randall says with the gentlest tone I've heard from him yet.

"Putting money aside," I murmur, trying not to panic. There is too much here for me to even contemplate being in possession of. "No thanks," I add stiffly, handing it back.

He doesn't take it. "It's yours. Do with it what you want. Spend it all in one place or don't. I don't care, it's not mine," he states loftily.

"Randall." My mother's voice, sharp and cutting. "This isn't how we do things."

"Well, it's how I do things," he retorts, his gaze never leaving mine. "Adelaide is my daughter, and she deserves to know she has options, especially now."

Ignoring their bickering, I glance down at the black card again. Images of what I picture this MistHallow University to be, flash in my mind—dark corridors filled with secrets, professors who could teach me things my high school science teacher never could, students like me, and they are probably all rich and spoiled and entitled. I have precisely two options. Cut my nose off to spite my face or take what he's giving me and fuck it.

I choose to fuck it.

I've been broke my entire life. If some arsehole wants to give me a few million quid, who am I to stop him? It makes me wonder how much money he has... that leads me to wonder how old he is. Are vampires immortal like in the myths? Am I? Or am I half-immortal? Whatever that could entail, who the fuck knows. I have questions. He can give them to me. He knows this, and he is looking at me expectantly. But right now, I don't want to give him the satisfaction of answering them.

I grip the card tight and shove it in my pocket before either of them can say anything. "Fine. I'll keep it," I mumble. "But this doesn't make us square."

Randall nods once. "Understood."

Without waiting for more awkwardness to unfold, I stride out of the house and hop on my bike. The evening air is chilly, slicing through my coat as I pedal furiously towards the morgue. My mind buzzes with a thousand thoughts about MistHallow—what it will be like, who I'll meet. Or if this is all a dream I will wake up from. I know if that is the case, I will be gutted. It answers so many of my life questions, and I've always been ready to believe that something else exists out there. I didn't think I'd be one of them.

My doubts rise as I pedal. Is Randall legit? What if this is all a big joke? Or maybe he's delusional? Why is my mother going along with it if that's the case?

"Rah!" I growl as all these questions flood my mind. I was so quick to accept it all because it's what I wanted to be real, but now, in the harsh dark of night, it doesn't seem possible.

Does it?

When I arrive, the morgue is dead—it always is. No one really wants to work with corpses in the middle of the night except oddballs like me and the chief mortician, Wesley.

The morgue is eerily silent as I push through the heavy double doors, seemingly more so than usual. The familiar scent of disinfectant mixed with something less pleasant hits me, but I barely notice it anymore. This place has been my sanctuary for the past year, a place where the dead don't judge, and the living rarely venture.

As I'm pulling my hair into a tight bun, I hear a muffled thud from the main examination room. Curious, I head towards the sound.

The sight that greets me as I push open the door stops me dead in my tracks.

Wesley is standing over a body on the examination table. It's not unusual, but this time, the sight makes my blood run cold, and goosebumps skitter over my skin. Wesley's hand is clamped around a wooden object that is buried deep in the dead man's chest.

I watch, frozen in horror, as the body on the table begins to disintegrate. It crumbles away like ash in the wind, leaving nothing but a fine grey powder on the stainless steel surface.

A strangled gasp escapes my lips before I can stop it.

Wesley's head snaps up, his eyes wide with shock as

they meet mine. For a long moment, we just stare at each other, neither of us moving.

"Addy," he finally breaks the silence, his voice strained. "I... this isn't what it looks like."

I want to laugh at the absurdity of his statement, but fear has paralysed my vocal cords. *What the hell did I just witness?*

Unfortunately, I've seen enough episodes of *Buffy the Vampire Slayer* to know what I just saw. A staking.

Wesley takes a step towards me, and I instinctively back away. "Let me explain," he says, holding his hand up.

But as he moves closer, something in his expression changes. He frowns, tilting his head slightly as if listening to something I can't hear. His nostrils flare, and his eyes narrow as they focus on me with an intensity that makes me shiver.

"What are you?" he murmurs.

That breaks the spell of my paralysis. Without thinking, I turn and run, my heart pounding wildly. I hear Wesley calling after me, his footsteps echoing in the corridor as he chases me.

I burst out of the morgue into the cool night air, gasping, aiming for my bike where I left it. Fumbling with the keys to unlock the chain, the doors to the morgue burst open, and Wesley pauses as he looks around for me. My hands are slick with sweat, and the keys fall to the ground before I've had a chance to unlock the padlock.

"Fuck," I mutter. "Fuck. Fuck. Come on."

Wesley sees me and strides towards me. He is in no rush it seems. "Addy," he says as the key finally slips into the lock.

Letting the chain and keys drop to the ground, I leap onto my bike and pedal furiously, not daring to look back.

The wind whips through my hair as I race through the empty streets. My mind is reeling. What did I just see? Was that... was that a vampire? And Wesley? Who is he? Why did he *stake* that vampire?

As I round the corner onto my street, I see a familiar figure stepping out of our house. Randall. I'm glad to see him.

I screech to a halt in front of him, nearly falling off my bike in my haste. "Randall," I gasp, struggling to catch my breath.

His eyes widen as he takes in my dishevelled appearance. "Adelaide? What happened?"

Before I can answer, I hear a car turning onto the road. I turn to see Wesley's old black sedan coming towards us.

Without thinking, I step behind Randall, seeking protection from the man I've worked alongside for months but now feels like a stranger.

Randall's posture changes instantly. He straightens, his presence suddenly seeming to fill the entire street.

Wesley drives towards us, the window rolled down as he stares at us.

It's surreal, something out of a horror film.

Wesley's car slows to a crawl as he passes us, his eyes

locked onto Randall. The tension in the air is suffocating as this scene plays out in slow motion. I hold my breath, half-expecting Wesley to leap out of his car and attack.

But he doesn't.

After what feels like an eternity, Wesley's car accelerates and disappears around the corner. I let out a shaky breath.

Randall turns to me, his face a mask of concern and anger. "What happened?" he demands.

The words tumble out of me in a rush. "I saw Wesley at the morgue. He was... he *staked* someone. A vampire? The body just turned to dust."

Randall's expression turns stony. "Damn it," he mutters as his dark eyes search my face. "Are you all right? Did he hurt you?"

I shake my head, still trying to process everything. "No, I'm not all right! I saw him stake someone, and then it was like he knew about me, about what you told me. He came after me!" I shove my hands into my hair, forgetting it's up in the bun I wear for work.

Randall's expression hardens. "A Hunter," he spits out the word like it's poison. "I should have known."

"A Hunter?" I repeat, feeling like I've stepped into some bizarre parallel universe.

He nods grimly. "They're humans who dedicate their lives to eradicating supernatural beings. Especially vampires."

My head spins. This is too much. Vampires, Hunters, me, Randall...

But the memory of Wesley's face, the intensity in his eyes as he asked, 'What are you?' sends a chill down my spine.

"We need to get you out of here," Randall says, his tone urgent. "It's not safe for you anymore."

"But what about Mum?" I ask, glancing back at our house. "We can't just leave her."

Randall's expression softens slightly. "Your mother will be fine. She is human. They won't, *can't,* touch her."

I shake my head, struggling to process everything. "This is insane. Yesterday, I was just a normal, albeit slightly weird, girl working in a morgue. Now I'm what, some kind of supernatural fugitive?" My voice has gone shrill, and it grates on my nerves. I take a step back and breathe in deeply to bring down the cloak of apathy I reserve for most things.

"Welcome to our world," Randall says dryly. "Now, we need to move. MistHallow is the safest place for you right now."

"But term doesn't start for another week," I protest weakly.

"Officially, but the gates open tonight."

"What?"

He shrugs. "It's a thing..."

"So you what? Either expected me to jump on this without a second thought, or you were going to kidnap me?"

"What? No!" he says, looking a bit miffed. "I mean, the gates open tonight and will stay open for the next week. Then they close. Students are free to arrive as and when they will, but the earlier, the better, I'll admit."

"Why?" I'm intrigued despite the fear still coursing through my veins.

"First come, first served for accommodation."

"And you didn't think to tell me that earlier! I don't want to end up in the fucking basement!" My hands go into my hair again, and I yank the hair tie out, letting my hair cascade down my back, practically reaching the top of my arse.

He chuckles. "You won't end up in the basement, Adelaide. You're my daughter."

"And?" I hiss.

"Forget the basement, we need to move, or this Wesley dick will be back, and this time, he will know what you are. He saw you with me."

I want to argue, to demand more explanations, but the memory of Wesley plunging that stake into that poor man's chest without any chance to defend himself chills me to my soul.

"Fine," I concede, fear driving my decision. "I need to pack and let me at least say goodbye to Mum."

Randall nods curtly. "Make it quick."

I rush back into the house, finding Mum in the hallway, her hands wrapped around a steaming mug of tea. Her eyes are red-rimmed, and she looks up at me with sadness and resignation.

"You heard all that?" I ask.

Mum nods, her eyes glistening. "I knew this day

would come eventually. I hoped we'd have more time, though."

I rush forward and wrap my arms around her, inhaling her familiar scent of lavender and home. "I'm sorry, Mum. I don't want to leave you."

She pulls back, cupping my face in her hands. "Oh, Addy. You have nothing to be sorry for. This is who you are. I've known it since the day you were born. I just wanted to protect you for as long as I could."

"But what about you? Will you be safe?"

Mum smiles, though it's stiff and fake. "I'll be fine, love. The Hunters have no interest in humans, as your father said."

I don't want to point out that they might come after her for information. Maybe that's just in the movies. I really need to get another hobby; I groan inwardly as I'm basing everything about this entire situation on what I stream on fucking Netflix.

But then the reality of the situation hits me like a punch to the gut. "Mum, I'm scared," I whisper.

She pulls me close again. "I know, sweetheart. But you're strong. Stronger than you know. And MistHallow is where you belong. Where you'll learn to be who you truly are."

I nod against her shoulder, trying to memorise everything about this moment - her warmth, her scent, the sound of her heartbeat.

"Go pack," she says softly. "I'll make you some sandwiches for the journey."

I rush upstairs, throwing open my wardrobe and grabbing armfuls of clothes. I shove them haphazardly into my largest holdall, along with my laptop, chargers, and a few treasured books. I grab the framed photo of Mum and me from my bedside table and place it in the middle of my clothes to protect it.

Randall appears in my doorway. "We need to go, Adelaide. Now. The sharks are circling."

I zip up my bag and nod, my heart racing. This is really happening. Randall scoops up the bag as I sling my backpack over my shoulder, and I pause in the doorway, looking back and wondering if I will ever see this place again.

Slowly, I take the stairs, my thoughts a swirl of emotions and turmoil. Am I doing the right thing, blindly walking off into the night with Randall? I don't know anything about him. This could be a trap. Maybe he is a Hunter. I dismiss that thought. My mum knows the details, and she wouldn't let me walk into an ambush. Would she? She has lied to me for two decades after all. Shaking my head, I tell myself to stop. She had her reasons, and if all of this turns out to be true, I get it. I probably would've done the same thing to protect my child. I don't blame her.

No, I blame Randall fucking Black.

I glare at him before I turn to Mum and hug her one last time. "I love you," I whisper.

"I love you too, sweetheart," she replies, her voice thick with emotion. She hands me a lunchbox with sandwiches and crisps stuffed in it, and I smile. "Thanks. I'll ring when I can. Assuming I can," I frown and shoot Randall an inquiring stare.

He raises an eyebrow. "Whyever not?"

Whyever not, indeed.

I follow Randall out into the night, my heart thundering in my ears. A sleek black car idles at the curb, its engine purring softly.

"Get in," Randall says, opening the passenger door for me before he throws my bag in the back.

I hesitate for a moment, glancing back at our small terraced house. Mum stands in the doorway, tears glistening on her cheeks. I want to run back, to tell her I've changed my mind. But the memory of Wesley's face, the intensity in his eyes, his question, and the chase propels me forward.

I slide into the leather seat on autopilot, stashing my backpack at my feet. At some point, all of this will catch up with me, and then I know it will be a case of crash and burn. I just hope the damage isn't too extensive.

As we pull away from the curb, I crane my neck to keep Mum in sight for as long as possible. When we turn the corner, and she disappears from view, I feel like a piece of me has been left behind.

"Where exactly is MistHallow?" I ask, trying to distract myself from the growing ache in my chest.

"Of sorts, in Kielder forest," Randall replies, his eyes fixed on the road ahead. "In the Northumberland National Park. It's... well hidden." He glances at me with a knowing look.

"Of sorts," I murmur. *What the fuck does that mean?*

I have no idea, so I nod, not trusting myself to speak further. The reality of what I'm doing is starting to sink in. I'm leaving everything I've ever known to go to a school for supernatural beings. With a man I've just met who claims to be my father.

Addy, what have you got yourself into?

Chapter 3

Adelaide

The car glides smoothly through the night, streetlights flashing by in a hypnotic rhythm. I stare out the window, watching as the familiar streets of my hometown give way to the unfamiliar countryside. The silence in the car is thick and heavy, with unasked questions and unspoken truths.

Randall clears his throat, breaking the silence. "I know this is a lot to take in, Adelaide."

I snort, unable to help myself. "That's the understatement of the century."

He sighs, his hands tightening on the steering wheel. "I understand you're angry with me. You have every right to be. But I hope you'll give me a chance to explain everything."

I turn to look at him, really look at him for the first time. His profile is sharp and aristocratic. In the dim light of the car, his skin seems almost translucent. It's strange how I can see bits of myself in his features—the shape of his nose, his eyes, his hair, that superior look he gets that I've been accused of getting.

"Fine," I say, crossing my arms. "Explain."

Randall takes a deep breath. "Where to begin?"

"How old are you?"

He snorts. "Wow, okay, going in for the kill. I am one thousand, five hundred years old."

I baulk.

I don't think I have ever *baulked* before in my entire life, but here I am... baulking at him. "Come again," I splutter.

"One and a half kay," he murmurs with a slow smile.

"Jesus fuck," I groan, dropping my head into my hands. "This is like some sort of sick joke."

"Sadly not. I'm old."

"No shit, Sherlock. You're like early Dark Ages old."

"Well, fuck," he mutters. "When you put it like that."

"I can do Maths. I'm quite good at it. You're not old; you're ancient."

He chuckles, and I feel myself relaxing. I'm not sure if it's because I'm starting to truly accept this bizarre reality or if it's just the absurdity of the situation, but I find myself laughing along with him.

"So, you've seen a lot in your lifetime," I say, trying to wrap my head around his age.

Randall nods. "More than you can imagine. I've witnessed the rise and fall of empires, the birth of new technologies, the changing of the world."

"And where do I fit into all this?" I ask the question that's been burning in my mind since he showed up at our door.

He's quiet for a moment, his eyes fixed on the dark road ahead. "You, Adelaide, are something truly special. A Vesperidae—half vampire, half human. It's an incredibly rare occurrence."

"But why?" I press. "Why did you spawn a child with my mother?"

Randall's expression softens slightly. "I loved your mother, Adelaide. I still do, in my own way. But our worlds were too different. She wanted a normal life for you, away from the dangers of the supernatural world, and it's not like we had a choice. Vampires can procreate with other vampires on occasion. Those vampires are also quite rare and very powerful, but mixed-species births are... unique."

"But more of my kind exist?" I shake my head. *My kind*.

"A couple, no more."

"Do you know them?"

"I know of them. A Vesperidae, or Vesper, hasn't been born for several centuries."

I gulp back the enormity of that news as Randall checks the rearview mirror for the hundredth time. "Are we being followed?"

"No, not yet."

"Not yet."

"Your true nature has been found out. They will come." His blunt statement does nothing to calm my growing nerves again as we travel deeper into the very north of the English countryside.

I shiver, staring out into the darkness beyond the car windows. The reality of my new situation is starting to sink in again. But this time, it's not just some fantasy that I wish to be true. I actually know now that all of this is real. I'm not just leaving home—I'm running from danger, from people who apparently want to hunt me down.

"So, these Hunters," I say, breaking the tense silence. "What exactly do they want with me?"

Randall's jaw tightens. "As I've said, Vespers are incredibly rare and powerful. Some Hunters would want to study you and experiment on you. Others would simply want to eliminate you, seeing you as an abomination."

A chill runs down my spine. "Experiment on me? Eliminate me? Jesus."

"Which is why MistHallow is so important," Randall continues. "It's not just a school - it's a sanctuary. It is protected by ancient magicks that keep it hidden from those who would do harm to supernatural beings. That's why I want you there, Adelaide."

I nod slowly, trying to process everything. "And what will I learn there? How to be a vampire?"

Randall chuckles. "Among other things. You'll learn about your heritage, how to control your abilities, the history and customs of the supernatural world. But more importantly, you'll be among others like yourself."

The idea is both thrilling and terrifying. All my life,

I've felt like an outsider, never quite fitting in, and now I'm heading to a place where I might finally belong. But it also means leaving behind everything I've ever known.

I lean back in my seat, letting out a long breath. "This is a lot to take in."

Randall's nod is bordering on sympathetic, but I doubt he has that emotion after so long. "I know. I'm sorry it's all happening so fast. But after what you saw tonight with Wesley, we don't have the luxury of time. I'm glad you have taken this in your stride, Adelaide. It shows me your fortitude."

I think back to the morgue, to Wesley staking that vampire. A shudder runs through me. "Staking, beheading, fire? All these things can kill you?"

"Me? No. You? Yes."

"Am I immortal?"

"Yes and no. With your human side in control, you will age."

"And if my vampire side is in control?" My voice is hushed as I didn't even realise this was an option.

"Then you will be like me."

I swallow back the whimper that nearly escaped. *Be like him*. Ancient, jaded, a bit frightening. Is that what I want for my life?

"So, what can kill you?" I venture.

"Not much."

"But something?" He is being too evasive for my liking now. I want answers.

He sighs. "I'm not being deliberately obtuse, Adelaide. It's unknown."

"Untested?"

He smirks. "You could say that."

"Is that why Wesley didn't stop earlier?"

"It's likely," Randall says grimly. "But Hunters are relentless once they've identified a target. But don't worry, you'll be safe at MistHallow."

We lapse into silence again as the car speeds through the night. I watch as the landscape changes, becoming wilder and more rugged. We're heading deep into Northumberland National Park now, the roads becoming narrower and more winding.

I sink back into the leather seat, my mind whirling with everything I've learned. The countryside whizzes by outside, dark and unfamiliar.

"So, tell me more about MistHallow," I say, breaking the silence that's fallen between us. "What's it like?"

"It's quite unlike anywhere else you've ever been. The campus itself is hidden deep in Kielder Forest, cloaked by powerful magick that keeps it invisible to human eyes. The buildings are a mix of ancient stone structures and more modern facilities."

"And the students?" I ask, curious about who I'll be studying alongside.

"A diverse group," Randall replies. "Vampires, fae, elementals, shifters and other supernatural beings you've probably never even heard of."

I try to imagine a school filled with creatures I've only read about in books or seen in movies. It seems surreal.

"What about the professors?" I ask.

Randall's expression grows serious. "Some of the

most knowledgeable and powerful supernatural beings in the world. Many of them have been teaching at MistHallow for centuries."

Centuries. The word still sends a jolt through me. I'm still struggling to understand the idea of such long lifetimes.

After what feels like hours, Randall turns off the road onto a dirt track that leads into a dense forest. The trees loom over us, their branches creating a canopy that blocks out what little moonlight there was.

"Uhm," I murmur.

"We're nearly there," Randall says softly.

I peer out the window, trying to catch a glimpse of this mysterious University, but all I can see is darkness and trees. Then, suddenly, we are driving through a cloud of shimmering mist, and the forest opens up.

I gasp.

Before us stands an enormous castle, its turrets and spires reaching up into the night sky. It looks ancient, like something out of a fairytale, with ivy climbing up its stone walls and gargoyles perched on its battlements. But there are also modern touches - large glass windows that gleam with warm light and sleek buildings that seem to blend seamlessly with the older structures, all lit up with floodlights that I doubt are powered by electricity.

"Welcome to MistHallow University," Randall says.

I stare in awe as we drive through wrought iron gates that open up on our approach and up a winding driveway. Other cars are parked along the edges, and I can see figures moving about.

As we pull up, Randall turns to me. "Are you ready?"

I take a deep breath, trying to steady my nerves. "As I'll ever be."

"Just remember you belong here, Adelaide."

I nod, taking that ominous-sounding warning and holding onto it. Intimidated doesn't quite cover the sensation that crashes over me as I step out of the car.

"You need to go it alone from here," Randall says, grabbing my holdall and placing it at my feet. "Head to the Housing office as soon as you can."

"And where is that?" I murmur, looking around in awe.

Randall gestures to a large stone building to our right, its windows glowing warmly. "That's the Housing office. They'll get you sorted with your room."

I nod, suddenly feeling very small and alone. "You're not coming with me?"

He shakes his head. "This is your journey now, Adelaide. I can't hold your hand through it. But I'll be around if you need me." He hands me a small black card with a phone number on it.

I take the card, slipping it into my pocket. "Right. Okay then."

Randall gives me a small smile. "You'll be fine. Remember, you belong here."

With that, he gets back into the car and drives away, leaving me standing alone in front of this imposing castle. I take a deep breath, shoulder my backpack, and grip my holdall tighter.

"Here goes nothing," I mutter as I inhale deeply and

try to steady my nerves, which are firing on all cylinders. "Here goes everything."

Chapter 4

Adelaide

But I don't go anywhere. I stand rooted to the spot, my eyes wide as I take in the sprawling magnificence of MistHallow University. More appears before my eyes the longer I stand and stare at it. Almost as if it is revealing itself to me, one bit at a time. It's doing a strip tease, and I wonder what the grand finale is. The central part of the castle looms before me, a colossal structure of ancient stone with modern additions that seem to defy the laws of physics and architecture alike. Turrets and spires reach towards the sky, somehow bypassing the trees as if they don't exist, their silhouettes stark against the inky blackness of night. Ivy crawls up the weathered walls, its tendrils weaving intricate patterns that seem to shift and move in the flickering light of the ornate lanterns that line the pathways.

The campus sprawls out before me, a labyrinth of old and new buildings. Everywhere, there's an air of magick that makes the air around me hum with energy.

I take a tentative step forward, and then I wince, half-expecting someone to materialise out of the shadows and demand to know what I'm doing here. But no one appears, and I continue on, my eyes darting everywhere, trying to take in every detail.

As I walk, I notice how the layout of the campus seems to shift and change. Buildings that I could have sworn were on my left suddenly appear on my right. Paths twist and turn in ways that don't make logical sense. It's as if the entire university exists on some sort of parallel plane, defying the laws of physics and geography.

"Fucking hell," I mutter, my head spinning as I try to make sense of my surroundings. Is this what Randall meant when he said MistHallow was protected by ancient magicks?

I'm so engrossed in my observations that I almost miss the sound of an approaching vehicle. The purr of a powerful engine cuts through the night air, and I turn to see a sleek, black Rolls Royce gliding down the path towards me. The car moves with supernatural grace, its polished surface reflecting the moonlight like a mirror.

I jump out of the way, and it passes me. I catch a glimpse of the driver – a stern-faced man with eyes that seem to glow in the darkness.

The Rolls comes to a stop a few feet ahead of me, and the back door swings open. A man steps out, and my breath catches in my throat.

He's devastatingly handsome in a way that is impossibly inhuman. Tall and lean, he's dressed in a perfectly tailored black suit, black shirt, and a deep purple tie that seems to shimmer in the moonlight. His hair is as black as a raven's wing, styled in a way that looks both effortless and impossibly perfect. Like me, a woman who hates the sun, his skin is pale... and now I know why. Is this impossibly beautiful creature a vampire?

His eyes truly captivate me. They are a shade of purple, with swirls of silver that seem to dance and shift as he moves. There's something both seductive and menacing about him, an aura of power and danger that makes my heart race.

He glances around, his gaze sweeping over the campus with a look of casual ownership. For a moment, I think his stare is going to land on me, and I feel a jolt of anticipation and fear. But I'm left feeling both relieved and oddly disappointed when he doesn't even notice me.

Without a word, he turns and strides away, his movements graceful and predatory. I watch him go, feeling flustered and off-balance. Is he some sort of supernatural royalty?

With a deep breath, I force myself to turn away from the retreating figure and continue on my way to the Housing office. The building Randall pointed out looms before me, its stone facade warm and inviting despite its imposing size.

As I approach the heavy wooden doors, they swing open of their own accord. I hesitate for a moment, then step inside, my eyes widening as I take in the interior.

The entrance hall is a stunning blend of old and new. Ancient tapestries hang on the walls alongside magickal displays that flicker with information. A massive chandelier hangs from the vaulted ceiling, its crystals seeming to float in midair, casting rainbows of light across the polished marble floor.

Behind a curved desk made of what looks like petrified wood, a female creature sits. Her skin has a faint blue tinge, and her hair moves as if it's underwater. She looks up as I approach, her entirely deep blue eyes fixing on me with an intensity that makes me want to squirm.

"Name?" she asks, her voice melodious and slightly echo-y, as if she's speaking from the bottom of a well.

"Adelaide Légère," I stammer, suddenly acutely aware of how out of place I feel.

"Légère. Légère? Are you sure?"

I snort, despite the shot of fear that skitters through my veins. "Completely sure. It's my mother's name and mine since birth."

"I don't have a Légère." She blinks at me. Her stare searches my face. "First name again?"

"Adelaide," I whisper, hoping that this is some sort of misunderstanding, and she is spelling it wrong.

"Adelaide Black," she states with pursed blue lips.

"Erm, no..."

"Yes," she says, turning the screen around so I can see a picture of myself. "Is this you?"

"It looks like me," I murmur.

"Then you are Adelaide Black."

"Dammit, Randall," I mutter as I realise he gave me his surname. Jackass.

The blue lady gives me a weird glare, but I smile and let her do her thing. I guess he needed me to have his surname to get into this institution. But a heads-up would've been nice. But then she gives me an amused and slightly pitying look. "You're quite the rarity, you know. The staff has been abuzz about your arrival for weeks."

Great. So much for flying under the radar.

"Right," I say, trying to sound more confident than I feel. "So, where do I go?"

The woman waves her hand, and a small, glowing orb appears in the air before me. "This will guide you to your room."

Please don't let it be in the basement. "And where is that?"

"Follow the orb." She waves a hand dismissively, and there is nothing else for me to do except move, as a queue is forming behind me.

I reach out hesitantly to touch the orb, half-expecting my hand to pass right through it. Instead, it feels solid and warm, like a smooth stone that's been sitting in the sun.

"Thank you," I say, not sure what else to add.

The woman nods, already turning her attention to the next student.

The orb starts to float away, and I hurry to follow it. As I exit the Housing office, I cast one last glance over my shoulder, half-hoping to catch another glimpse of the mysterious man from the Rolls Royce in the queue, but he is nowhere to be seen.

I'm really here, at a university for supernatural beings, a place where I might finally understand who and what I am. A place where, for the first time in my life, I might truly belong. As unbelievable as this is, I don't regret getting in the car with Randall. The ground beneath me shimmers as I walk. It accepts me, this whole place doesn't think I'm weird. In fact, as I see a woman with snakes for hair saunter past me with a man who has scales for skin, I'm not the wonkiest fruit on this tree. The sense of relief that comes with this knowledge is mind-blowing and makes me lightheaded.

The orb leads me down a short path and through an archway that seems to appear out of nowhere. I pass other students—some who look human, others who decidedly don't—and try not to stare. A group of girls with gossamer wings flutter past, their laughter sounding like wind chimes. A boy with fur and pointed ears gives me a friendly nod as he lopes by on all fours.

I'm not even scared. I'm exhilarated and in awe of every one of these magnificent creatures.

Seconds later, the orb comes to a stop in front of a gothic tower attached to the central part of the castle. Carved gargoyles leer down from above the door, which is a heavy, studded wooden thing that looks like it weighs a ton.

I take a deep breath, squaring my shoulders as I face the imposing wooden door. This is it. My new life starts now.

With a trembling hand, I reach out and grasp the hooped iron door handle. It's cold under my fingers, and for a moment, I hesitate. Am I ready for this? Can I really do this?

But then I think of Wesley in the morgue, of the fear

and confusion I've lived with all my life. I think of Randall's words: 'You belong here, Adelaide.'

Before I can second-guess myself, I lift the handle and turn it. The sound of the door opening echoes through the night, seeming to reverberate through the very stones of the building.

I take a deep breath and step forward, confronted by a set of stone stairs that run up the left side of the tower. Placing my foot on the bottom step, I jump a mile and stifle my scream as a bat comes careening towards my face and narrowly dodges, swooping upwards and out the door before I can gather my wits about me, my heart thundering wildly.

"Fuck," I mutter as I try to calm down enough to take the steep steps while juggling my heavy holdall and backpack, following the impatient orb that is bobbing about like an apple in water at my dawdling. "I'm coming. Hold your horses, orby."

If I didn't know better, I could swear I hear a titter as I take the steps slowly, not wanting to misstep and go arse over tit back the way I came.

Bloody castle towers. Why couldn't they have installed a lift?

Chapter 5

Corvus

Swooping under the eaves of the tower, I perch upside down and wrap my black wings around myself as I contemplate the female who just entered the North Tower. I wasn't expecting anyone to be in here. The North Tower is usually reserved for important guests and visiting faculty members, not students. Yet, everything about her screams 'student'.

But there's something different about this girl. Even in my bat form, I can sense it. There's a power radiating off her, raw and untamed. It calls to the darkness within me, making my fangs ache with need.

Who is she? Why is she here? *What* is she?

Curiosity gets the better of me. I release my grip on the eaves and transform mid-air, landing silently on my feet at the base of the tower. My heightened senses pick up her scent - an intoxicating blend of human and something else. Something familiar yet foreign. I run my hand over my dark hair, straightening it after the shift, my blue eyes narrowed as I stare up at the tower.

From what I saw, she's stunning. Long black hair cascades down her back, her pale skin and dark eyes mesmerising even after only a second of seeing her.

"Who are you, beautiful?" I murmur, debating whether to follow her up the steps.

Deciding not to, I turn and walk away, edging myself with curiosity about this girl. I've never seen her before, and I've never smelt anything even remotely like her. That makes me wary, so sauntering up to her, as I typically would to the hot new girl, is not on the cards, right now as I'm unusually cautious.

Maybe this place is rubbing off on me after all.

I smirk. Not likely. I'm hot-headed and impulsive, and if that's not what a full-blooded vampire is supposed to be, then shoot me. Rounding the corner, I nearly collide with Professor Blackthorn, my Ancient Vampire Studies teacher.

"Mr Sanguine," he says, his tone disapproving as always. "I trust you're not causing trouble on the first night back?"

I plaster on my most charming smile. "Of course not, Professor. Just taking in the night air."

His eyes narrow, clearly not buying it. "Hmm. Well, do try to stay out of mischief. We have some very important new students arriving tonight."

That piques my interest. "Oh? Anyone I should know about?"

Professor Blackthorn's expression becomes guarded. "That's not for me to say. Now, if you'll excuse me."

He brushes past me, his robes swirling dramatically. I watch him go, my mind racing. Important new students? Could that mysterious girl be one of them?

I'm tempted to go back to the North Tower, to satisfy my curiosity about her. But something holds me back. If she's as important as Blackthorn implied, it is definitely wise to tread carefully until I know more.

Instead, I decide to head to the Blood Bar. It's the first night back, after all, and I could use a drink.

When I push open the door, the place is dead. And I don't mean in the vampire sense. It usually bustles with activity as live feedings are strictly forbidden on University property and are subject to an expulsion order, which is worse than it sounds. You are blocked, practically banished from the supernatural community. It's a harsh punishment, but if you are stupid enough to break the most mundane of rules in a place where boundaries are meant to be pushed, then you deserve to be shunted up the arse by a wooden cross in the real world. They say MistHallow is the making of oneself, and they are not wrong. It's an interesting place. Many come here to learn about focus and discipline with their powers and abilities, but some, like me, are here simply because it is a place of containment for those misfits who are more trouble on the outside than they are worth. My parents decided MistHallow was the best place to keep me out of trouble and learn some discipline. Little do they know, I've found plenty of ways to push boundaries here, too. Just more discreetly.

I saunter up to the bar, nodding at the bartender. "The usual, Grim."

Grim, a hulking creature with ashen skin and glowing red eyes, grunts in acknowledgement. He reaches under the counter and pulls out a bottle of crimson liquid.

"First night special," he rumbles, pouring me a generous glass. "O negative, fresh from the source."

I raise an eyebrow. "Oh? And who might the source be?"

Grim's lips curl into what passes for a smile on his skeletal face. "Let's just say we had a very generous donor. But keep that between us, eh?"

"Always," I murmur and take a sip, savouring the rich, coppery taste. It's definitely high-quality, healthy virgin blood. It's a cliché, but clichés are clichés for a reason, right?

As I'm enjoying my drink, the door swings open again. I turn, half-expecting to see the mysterious girl from the North Tower. Instead, it's Lucian and Asher, two of my more aggressive enemies at MistHallow.

"Corvus!" Lucian calls out, his golden eyes gleaming with malice. "Starting early, are we?"

I take another sip of my drink, deliberately slow, before turning to face them fully. "Lucian, Asher. Lovely to see you both. I'd offer to buy you a drink, but I'm not sure they serve hybrid bottom-feeders here."

Asher, the taller of the two vampires, bares his fangs

in a snarl. "Watch it, Sanguine. We're not here for your pathetic attempts at wit."

"No?" I raise an eyebrow, feigning surprise. "Then do enlighten me. What brings two parasites like yourselves to my favourite haunt?"

Lucian steps forward, his movements fluid and predatory. "Just checking in on our loathsome troublemaker," he says, his voice dripping with false sweetness. "Making sure you're not planning anything disruptive for the new year."

I keep my face carefully neutral, even as my mind races. They're fishing for information, but about what? "Is that so? And here I thought you two were too busy kissing the professors' arses to care about little old me."

Asher leans in, his eyes darting around as if checking for eavesdroppers. "We know you're up to something, Corvus. You always are. This time, we're going to catch you in the act and make sure you're booted out of life. Permanently."

I can't hide my amusement at this. "My, my, aren't we paranoid? I hate to disappoint you, boys, but I'm just here enjoying a quiet drink. No nefarious schemes tonight, I'm afraid."

Lucian's eyes narrow suspiciously. "You expect us to believe that? Please. You're always plotting something."

I grin, all teeth and fangs. "Maybe I am, maybe I'm not. That's for me to know and you to, well, never find out."

For a moment, edginess crackles in the air between us. I can see the desire to start a fight burning in their eyes, and part of me welcomes it. It's been too long since I've had a good brawl.

But I'm not about to let these two idiots provoke me into swinging first. Not now, not ever.

"As much as I'd love to continue this delightful conversation," I say, draining the last of my drink, "I have better things to do with my evening than trade insults with you two morons."

Lucian's eyes flash dangerously. "This isn't over, Corvus. We're watching you."

I stand, straightening to my full height of six feet, one inch. Even though both vampires are bulkier than me, not many match my height or my pure-blood strength. It would take two or more weaker hybrids, those who have been turned rather than born of vampires, to take me down, but these two didn't seem to get the memo. Unless they're hiding something, I'm unaware of. "Watch all you want," I say, dropping my voice to a low and dangerous pitch. "But remember, not all shadows hide secrets. Sometimes, they bite back."

With that, I brush past them, ignoring Asher's muttered threats. My mind is racing as I step out into the cool night air. Something's going on, something big enough to have Lucian and Asher on edge and looking to blame me for it. Part of me wonders if it's connected to the girl I saw earlier.

I need to know more—not just out of curiosity now but out of necessity. If trouble is brewing at MistHallow, I need to be prepared. Whether to avoid it or dive head-first into it, I'm not sure yet. That all depends on the players.

I start walking with no particular destination in mind. The campus is quieter now, most students either still settling in or already tucked away in their rooms. But I can feel an excitement in the air, a sense of anticipation. Something big is coming, and I have a hunch that mysterious girl is at the centre of it all.

As I pass by the North Tower again, I pause, looking up at the illuminated windows. Is she up there now? What is she thinking? Does she know the stir she's causing just by being here?

I shake my head, trying to clear my thoughts. I'm getting ahead of myself.

One thing is for certain—wherever this girl goes, I'll be watching. And waiting.

After all, what's university life without a little bit of stalking?

Chapter 6

Adelaide

After much ado and pausing to rest from the heaviness of my holdall, I finally reach the top of the stairs, panting heavily from the climb. The orb hovers in front of a heavy wooden door with an ornate brass knocker shaped like a snarling beast. The orb bobs expectantly as I stare at the door and reach for the handle to turn it, but it's locked.

"Fuck," I hiss. "Blue water lady didn't give me a key!" The thought of going all the way back down, only to join the back of the queue to ask for a key and then come all the way back up these steps, is a bit more than I can take on at the moment. My bandwidth is low, and I needed this to not happen.

The orb bobs agitatedly as I just stand there, staring morosely at the door. Then, it zooms downwards and smacks against my right hand. Annoyed, I glare at it as it bumps the back of my hand repeatedly until I turn it over and it slaps against my palm.

"You're the key?" I murmur and it jumps a couple of times, which I take as a yes.

Scanning the door for orb-shaped keyholes, I don't find any and huff out a breath.

The orb, clearly having had enough of my stupidity in this area, flies out of my hand and bumps up against a smooth panel of wood and holds position until I place my hand over it again. I can practically feel the sigh of relief from the orb that we are finally getting somewhere.

"Sorry," I murmur as the door clicks open a fraction.

The orb flies into the room, and I push the door to stagger in with bags that have decided to moonlight as concrete breeze blocks.

My eyes widen as I drop the bags and take in my new living space. I wasn't sure what I envisaged, but this goes past whatever expectation I was forming. It's a spacious circular room with a high, vaulted ceiling. Moonlight streams through tall, arched windows, illuminating the rich furnishings.

There's a four-poster bed draped in deep purple velvet, a massive oak wardrobe, and a plush armchair by a crackling fireplace that flickers and glows unnaturally. *Magick?* Bookshelves lining one wall are filled with leather-bound tomes.

"Bloody hell," I mutter.

As I explore, I notice little details that confirm the use of magick. The candles in the wall sconces light themselves as I pass. When I glance at the mirror above the ornate vanity, it seems to ripple like water.

I approach the mirror cautiously, mesmerised by its

fluid surface. As I lean in for a closer look, my reflection suddenly shifts and changes. For a moment, I see myself with glowing eyes and elongated fangs. I jerk back with a gasp, blinking rapidly. When I look again, my normal reflection stares back at me, wide-eyed and pale.

"Right," I mutter, running a shaky hand through my hair.

A soft chime draws my attention to the orb hovering over the desk. I notice a thick envelope resting on the polished surface. As I pick it up, the orb settles down on the wood and stops glowing.

I blink at it.

Is that snoring?

Shaking my head, I smile and look back at the envelope in my hand. It's heavy, made of thick parchment with my 'name' - Adelaide Black - written in flowing script across the front. I tear it open, pulling out several sheets of paper.

"Welcome to MistHallow University," I read aloud, skimming the contents. Class schedules, campus rules, a map that seems to shift and change as I look at it. My eyes catch on a particular paragraph:

"As a Vesperidae, you will be required to attend additional sessions to help you understand and control your unique abilities. Your mentor, Professor Blackthorn, will meet with you tomorrow morning to discuss your specialised curriculum."

Sighing, I toss the papers onto the desk and flop onto the bed. It's ridiculously comfortable, like lying on a cloud. I stare up at the canopy, watching as patterns seem to swirl and dance across the fabric.

I should get up and unpack, but after everything that has happened today, I'm exhausted and I only just remember it's my birthday.

"Happy fucking birthday," I mutter as my eyes close, and sleep drags me under.

Chapter 7

Adelaide

An incessant buzzing in my ear wakes me up. Opening my eyes, I realise I'm stiff, still in my clothes and starving. Sitting up on the sumptuous bed, I stretch and see Orby bobbing about, making that infernal racket.

"Shut it," I mumble and climb off the bed to peer out of the floor-to-ceiling windows over the misty canopy of trees. "Well, I can't fault the view," I mutter. "But where is the bathroom and food place?"

Orby, being helpful in all things, zooms across the room to a panel in the wall that I wouldn't have seen had he, yeah, yeah, *he*, not been dancing in front of it. "What's up here then?" I ask, grabbing my toiletry bag in the hopes there is a bathroom... and a lift, seeing as I'm assuming the only place to go is up.

I'm right.

About going up. Not the lift. Sadly, there are only steps, but ones far more civilised than the ones that brought me to my room. Wide and wooden with a railing, I make my ascent, higher still, until I'm in a glorious bathroom nestled under the very top of the tower. "Wow," I murmur as I take it all in. The shower is enormous and has a frosted glass pane that serves as the outer tower wall on the side. It has three shower heads.

But first things first. I'm bursting for a pee, and I need to brush my teeth.

Minutes later, I strip off my clothes and step into the luxurious shower, marvelling at the multiple shower heads, which are all pointing at me, making it feel like I'm standing under a waterfall. The intricate tile work laid out in deep blue and white mosaics is stunning. As the hot water cascades over me, I close my eyes and let out a contented sigh. For a moment, I can almost forget the strangeness of my situation and just enjoy the simple pleasure of a good shower.

Glad of the frosted pane when I see creatures swooping around outside, I giggle and wonder what it must be like to fly.

Washing up quickly, urged on by my growling stomach, I turn off the shower and wrap myself in a fluffy towel. I pad back down to my room, feeling refreshed but ravenous.

"So, where do I go for food?" I ask Orby—now his name—but then I remember the sandwiches my mum made and dig them out of my bag. I sit on the bed with the lunch box and tuck in, the cheese and ham hitting the spot and making things seem a bit less daunting.

Only a bit, though. I can't hide out in this room

forever, although I could quite happily do so. But Professor Blackthorn is expecting me, and I need to go downstairs and figure out how to find him. Perhaps the Blue Water lady can help me.

Finishing my breakfast, I get dressed quickly in a white shirt and black pants. The white makes me look paler than usual, but I think that's what I'm going for. I don't want to look *human* in a university full of non-humans. It makes sense to me, so I shrug and brush out my hair before snatching up my backpack and heading out with Orby next to my ear. I shut the door behind me and hear the lock click. With Orby leading the way, I head down the treacherous steps and out into the early morning, where the entire campus is quiet.

I would say *dead*, but the thought makes me snicker inwardly and is probably wholly inappropriate. Mist swirls around me as I make my way back to the Housing office, where the Blue Water lady helped me yesterday. I really need to find out what her species is called. She'd probably be insulted to know what I call her.

The doors open for me, and I step inside, looking around. There are a few students milling about, who appear to have arrived this morning, but no faculty members are in sight yet.

"Miss Black."

I jump a fucking mile at the smooth voice coming from behind and above me. Turning, I clap eyes on the speaker, a distinguished, tall gentleman who appears to be in his early forties or so. He is dressed in a grey suit and flowing black robe.

"Yes, and you are?" I ask, wincing at how rude that sounds.

"Professor Blackthorn," he states. "You are with me today."

"Yes, I believe so."

"We have much to go over. Have you eaten?"

"Yes, but where do I go for food? I had sandwiches from home."

He blinks. "Do you have the map?"

I blink back. "Oh, the map, right..." I chew my lip. That is upstairs on the desk under the Welcome letter, which I'd forgotten all about.

Professor Blackthorn chuckles and snaps his fingers. A piece of parchment appears in his hand, and he holds it out for me. I take it and stare at it.

"There," he says, pointing to an area on the map that says *Dining*.

"Ah, okay. Jolly good," I say and then roll my eyes at myself. *Jolly good? Who the fuck says that?*

"Come," Professor Blackthorn says and turns on his heel to lead me deeper into the building.

I feel eyes on me as I follow Blackthorn down a darkened corridor lit up intermittently by magickal fire torches. Or I assume they're magickal. They don't give off any heat as I pass them. My skin tingles, and the hair on the back of my neck stands on end as I follow Professor Blackthorn down the winding corridor, trying not to gawk at the ever-changing portraits on the walls.

"So, Professor," I say, breaking the silence, "what

exactly does being a Vesperidae mean? I'm still trying to wrap my head around all this."

He spins back around, his finger on his lips. "Hush, girl. Not so loud."

"Huh?" I mutter, but lower my voice anyway. "Why not?"

"You are a well-kept secret and that is the way we intend to keep it. At least for now."

"Why?"

"Many reasons," he says cryptically. He pushes open a door to an ordinary-looking classroom, ushers me inside, and closes the door.

He bustles about, searching his pockets for something as Orby whizzes around the room before settling on top of my backpack, which I lean up against one of the tables. Finding whatever it is he was after, Blackthorn mumbles some words, and a box appears, bigger than a shoe box, but not by much.

"This is everything we know about your kind."

I press my lips together. That doesn't seem like a lot. "Uhm..."

"Quite," he says wryly. "We believe you only found out about yourself yesterday and arrived here under the gun, as it were. Hunters?"

"Is that what Randall told you?" I venture.

He nods.

"Well, then, yes. My boss at the morgue staked a vampire in front of me and then decided I was next. Whatever protection spells my mother had on me dropped, so he must've been able to sense I wasn't all human." I mean, he seems to know about shit, and I've got nothing to hide. Maybe he can help me make sense of it all.

"Indeed," he murmurs. "Randall did the right thing, bringing you to us right away. You are safe here, but I assume you have many questions."

"Many is putting it mildly," I say, sitting down. "Randall said there weren't many of my kind around."

"Three at the moment. Two who have been around for many years and, well, now, you."

"How many years?"

"Centuries."

"So, they're immortal?"

"Yes."

"But can be killed?"

"Stakes, fire, beheading, the usual suspects."

"So, what makes me so special, then? Do I have powers?"

He smiles. "Powers, no. But abilities... yes. You have enhanced strength, speed, and reflexes, accelerated healing. You can consume blood for a boost, the usual vampiric stuff. But what makes you different from vampires, and this is the crux of your unique situation, Miss Black, you have the ability to amplify others' powers when in physical contact with them."

I stare at Professor Blackthorn, trying to process what he's just told me. "I can amplify others' powers? What does that even mean?"

He nods, his face sober. "It means, Miss Black, that

when you touch someone with supernatural abilities, their powers become stronger. Significantly stronger."

"But I've never noticed anything like that before," I protest.

"Of course not," he says, waving a hand dismissively. "You've never been in prolonged contact with other supernatural beings."

Okay, duh. That makes total sense. I sink further into my chair, my mind reeling. "So what, I'm some kind of supernatural battery?"

Professor Blackthorn chuckles. "That's one way to look at it, I suppose. But you're much more than that. Your kind are incredibly rare and valuable. Which is why we must keep your true nature a secret for now."

"Valuable to whom?" I ask, a shiver running down my spine.

His expression turns grave. "To many, Miss Black. There are those who would seek to use your abilities for their own gain. Some might even try to harm you to prevent others from using you."

"Bloody hell," I mutter, running a hand through my hair. "So what am I supposed to do? Hide in my room forever and not touch anyone?"

"Not at all," he says, shaking his head. "You're here to learn, to understand, and to control your abilities. But we must be cautious. For now, we'll keep your true nature confidential. You'll attend regular classes like any other student, but you'll also have private sessions with me to work on harnessing your unique talents."

I nod, trying to take it all in. "Okay, so do I pretend I'm a vampire, or what?"

"There is no pretence about it, Miss Black. You are a vampire at your core. You need to blend in as much as possible while we work on developing your skills in secret."

"Right," I say, feeling overwhelmed. "But what about... feeding? Do I need to drink blood?"

"You can," he replies. "It will enhance your abilities and healing, but it's not strictly necessary for survival like it is for full vampires. We have synthetic blood available if you wish to try it, or you can stick to human food if you prefer."

I don't grimace at the thought of drinking blood, but I do turn my nose up at the synthetic kind. Let's get real for a second. I've drunk my own blood. Who hasn't, when you've cut yourself, and you put your finger to your lips... or, in my case, sliced into my arms and then licked them, whatever. Same diffs. I have always had a fascination with blood that makes sense to me now and doesn't make me feel weird or gross. I just nod while thinking, what about my fangs?

"You're wondering if you have fangs, aren't you?" he chuckles.

"Obviously," I retort. "Do I? How do I, you know...?" I stick my index fingers out to mimic fangs.

He snorts and snaps his fangs down. "Like that."

"Like how? You didn't show me anything except maybe how to show off."

"Bare your teeth," he says, "and then just..." He blinks, and his fangs snap back.

I stare at Professor Blackthorn, trying to mimic what he just did. I bare my teeth and concentrate, but nothing happens. I feel a bit silly, like I'm just making weird faces at him.

"Don't force it," he says gently. "It's an instinct, like blinking. Try to relax and let it happen naturally."

I nod and decide to forget about the fangs for now. I can practise on my own in my room in front of the mirror for homework. "So, what now?"

Professor Blackthorn clasps his hands together. "Now, we begin your training. But first, let's get you acquainted with the campus and your schedule."

He waves his hand, and a piece of parchment materialises, floating in the air between us. I reach out and grab it, scanning the contents. It's a class schedule, packed with subjects I've never heard of before.

"Elemental Magick Theory? Paranormal Ethics? Advanced Bloodline Studies?" I read aloud, my eyebrows raised.

"All essential courses for someone of your unique background," Blackthorn explains. "You'll also have private sessions with me three times a week to start to work on controlling your amplification abilities."

I nod, still feeling overwhelmed. "Right," I mutter, tucking the schedule into my bag. "So, where to first?"

"Let's start with a tour," he says, moving towards the door. "It's best you get familiar with the logical layout of the campus. MistHallow has a habit of shifting on occasion. Keeps us on our toes!"

Slinging my backpack over my shoulder with Orby bouncing next to me, we step out into the corridor, the feeling of excitement and trepidation hits me in the gut like a punch. This is my new life now - classes on magick, secrets to keep, and abilities I don't fully understand. It's terrifying and exhilarating all at once.

Professor Blackthorn leads me through winding hallways that shift and change as we walk. Portraits on the walls whisper and move, their eyes following us as we pass. We emerge into a sprawling courtyard, where students of all shapes and sizes are milling about.

"This is the main quad," Blackthorn explains. "Most of your classes will be in the buildings surrounding it."

I try not to stare as a group of what look like faeries flutter by, their wings glimmering in the sunlight. A boy with horns growing from his forehead growls as he passes by.

"Remember," Blackthorn says in a low voice, "blend in. Act as if all of this is perfectly normal to you."

I nod, swallowing hard. "Right. Totally normal. Just another day at magical creature university."

He gives me a wry smile. "You'll get used to it faster than you think."

As we continue our tour, I start to relax a bit. The campus is beautiful, and a sense of peace settles over me faster than I thought it would. We pass the library, a massive building that Blackthorn leads me inside. "On the top floor, you will find the section on vampires," he says quietly. "I suggest you start there and learn all you can about that side of you, yes?"

I nod eagerly. I'm quite looking forward to submerging myself into the old texts.

"Your classes start on Monday night. We run a mixed night and day schedule to accommodate all the creatures who attend here."

"Erm, I've just been wandering around in the daylight," I mutter, eyes wide. "If I'm supposed to be a vampire, won't people find that suspicious?"

"No," he says, shaking his head. "Do you see any sunlight out there, Miss Black?"

I peer back outside. It's light but gloomy, shaded by the enormous trees surrounding the campus. "Oh, so it's direct sunlight only that harms."

He nods. "For most. Some are too weak to withstand the daylight as a whole. You are not one of them."

"What do I tell people about me?" I whisper.

"You tell them that you are Randall Black's daughter," he states. "That is all they need to know."

Easy for him to say. He isn't the one who is going to be asked. But okay. I'll try it his way.

For now.

Chapter 8

Adelaide

Professor Blackthorn leaves me alone in the library and I take in the place with wide eyes and an excitement that thrills me. This place is magnificent in every sense of the word. The ceiling soars high above, supported by ornate columns that seem to twist and move when I'm not looking directly at them. Rows upon rows of bookshelves stretch as far as I can see, filled with tomes of all sizes and colours. As I stand in the marble-floored bullpen and look up, I see seven more floors above me. I take a deep breath, inhaling the scent of old books and ancient magick. It's intoxicating. Realising I'm still standing in the middle of the foyer like an idiot, I get a grip and walk towards the stairs. Professor Blackthorn said the vampire section was on the top floor, and in usual MistHallow fashion, there is no lift in sight. Plus side? I guess you'll be able to bounce a fifty-pence coin off my arse by the time this year is out.

As I climb, I marvel at the sheer variety of creatures I see studying at tables or browsing the shelves.

I try not to stare, remembering Blackthorn's advice to act like this is all normal. But it's hard when everything is so fantastical.

Finally, reaching the top floor, it is cooler and darker than the rest of the library. The curtains are pulled closed and lit with candles, magick ones, I hope, with all these books around. The dark wood and plush, deep red carpet fly in the face of the rest of the classical marble, and light wood look down below. I scan the shelves, but I don't really know what I'm looking for. I decide to start with 'V' for vampire, hoping there is a tome tucked away in here that gives me the rundown on these creatures of the night.

I have no idea where to start. I dump my backpack on a table, and Orby goes back to sleep on top of it while I browse through the hundreds upon hundreds of books. Overwhelmed, I huff out a breath and turn on my heel to try a different section when I see a man staring at me from across the table. I hadn't even heard him approach. He smiles, but it isn't friendly. It's sinister and sends my blood spiking in fear, which I realise is a big mistake when he closes his eyes and breathes in deeply, his smile growing wider.

I take advantage and move quickly in an effort to unblock myself from the corner I'm boxed in.

His eyes snap open. "Be still," he murmurs, his shockingly bright blue eyes fixed on mine in an intense way that muddles my brain and roots me to the spot. "Better."

His voice is melodic and quiet. It washes over me and soothes the panic that had reared up at his stealthy approach. He moves in closer until he is standing in front of me. He is tall, and he towers over me as he looks down at me with those hypnotic eyes. His dark brown hair flops over his forehead, but in a stylish way, not unkempt in the least. He is wearing a midnight blue suit and matching tie, loosened slightly at the collar of a crisp white shirt. My gaze is drawn to his neck, where a pulse beats gently.

He smirks when he sees where my gaze lands, showing me the tips of his fangs. So, vampire... check. But a pulse? That's a new one for me. I guess I really do need to do this research.

"Who are—"

"Shh," he murmurs, placing his finger to his lips.

Against my will, I shut my mouth, my eyes widening as it appears he has complete control over my actions. My heart thumps wildly again as the realisation that I'm totally helpless right now surges through me, and my palms start to sweat.

He drops his hand to his side, and he leans in closer, sniffing me like I'm a tasty treat. Who knows? Maybe I am to him. "Pretty," he murmurs.

"Playing with your food again, Corvus?" a low voice murmurs.

I shift my gaze, my eyes seemingly the only thing I can move right now, to the doorway where the impossibly gorgeous man from the Rolls Royce stands, leaning against the frame as his eyes find mine and hold my gaze. I'm unable to lower it as he stares at me, and I swallow, feeling true fear for the first time in my life. If I thought running from Wesley was bad, this is a hundred times worse. I'm a sitting duck.

The vampire named Corvus, chuckles and steps back as he turns his head. "Zephyr. What are you doing this high up?"

"Checking on the new girl," he purrs, his gaze still boring into my eyes. "Word travels fast around here."

"Doesn't it just," Corvus mutters.

Zephyr joins Corvus in front of me and finally moves his gaze from mine, but only to lower it to my cleavage. He licks his lips and reaches out to run the back of his cool finger down my neck and into the collar of my shirt. He tugs gently. "Skin like alabaster," he murmurs. "Just like a porcelain doll... beautiful and breakable."

Revulsion at his touch hits me hard. I hate people touching me. I try to move, but I'm held in place by whatever spell Corvus has dropped over me.

"You do realise that is Randall Black's daughter, don't you?" A third male voice says, almost with amusement, as Zephyr steps back a bit with a slow smile that makes me pant a little. He is fucking gorgeous, but so is Corvus. They are both incredibly strong creatures, but while I know Corvus is a vampire, I don't think Zephyr is, so that begs the question of who and what he is.

Corvus hisses and glares at me as if I'd withheld this information on purpose. "Is this true?"

"Yes," I croak.

"Hmm." He steps back and drops whatever spell he had over me, making me breathe out in relief.

It was like a vice around my soul.

When he moves away, I see the third speaker. A really cute looking guy with pure white hair and white eyes, dressed in black combat pants and a black tee, grins at me and appears way more friendly than these other two aloof and menacing creatures in front of me.

"Hurry along now, boys," he says. "You don't want to get on Randall Black's bad side by messing with his daughter, do you?"

Corvus and Zephyr exchange a look, then move fluidly away from me as if they were made of water or the very air around them. The relief I feel makes me lightheaded.

"My apologies, Miss Black," Corvus says smoothly, though his eyes still gleam with predatory interest. "We were merely welcoming you to MistHallow."

"Some welcome," I mutter, finding my voice at last.

Zephyr chuckles, a low sound that sends a skitter of pure lust through my veins. "We'll be seeing you around, Miss Black," he purrs, before both he and Corvus saunter out of the library.

I let out a shaky breath, my knees feeling weak. The white-haired guy approaches me. "You okay there?" he asks, genuine concern in his voice.

I nod, still a bit shaken. "Yeah, thanks."

"Don't mind those two. Their bark is worse than their bite." He guffaws at his own joke.

"Well," I huff. "Excuse me if I don't believe you."

"Yeah, probably better that you don't. Corvus and Zephyr are both dangerous and ambitious, along with a good old dose of trouble. But then, aren't we all?" His smile turns more malevolent when he says that.

"And you are?" I snap.

"Zaiah. At your service, mi'lady." He bows low, and something about this entire interaction is creeping me the fuck out. He looks up with a wink. "Don't you wish you were stronger so next time you could shake off the compulsion?"

"Compulsion," I murmur. Is that what Corvus was doing to me? Compelling me.

"Hmm. Don't you?"

I frown. "Don't I what?"

"Wish you were stronger?" He blinks at me.

"What are you?" I ask suspiciously.

He grins again, all friendly-like. "Okay, you caught me. I'm a djinn. Dude has to try, you know?"

"No, I don't know. And don't do that again. I don't wish anything, and I never will."

"We'll see," he says with a laugh and snaps his fingers, disappearing in the blink of an eye.

"Fuck," I mutter after this encounter that has left me rattled but more in need of information than ever before. I turn back to the bookshelves, only to find that the stacks have rearranged themselves, and I'm now even more lost than I was. One thing is for sure. I need to get up to speed and with Flash-like abilities before Corvus or Zephyr comes at me again. Next time, I don't think I'll get off so lightly.

Chapter 9

Zephyr

Contemplatively leaning against one of the many trees in this forest, south of the main campus, I narrow my eyes at the top floor of the library, visible from my spot. Corvus is dangling precariously over my head in bat form, but as long as he doesn't shit on me, I don't particularly give a fuck.

"Randall Black's daughter," I murmur, unable to get that out of my head.

"The supernatural world's best kept secret," Zaiah says, blinking in next to me.

I give him a lazy once-over, not startled by his sudden appearance as he would hope. "Yet *you* knew and didn't tell us. Sneaky djinn."

"When will you learn? Sneaky is what I'm made of."

Corvus drops from his perch and shifts in mid-air to land at my feet, fully clothed, thank fuck. "No shit, djinn-lock. You got anything else to share? Like what the fuck she is doing here? How no one knew she existed until right now? And least of all, what the fuck is she?"

"She's a vampire," Zaiah shrugs.

"No," Corvus says with a fangy smile, which makes me roll my eyes. "Not a vampire."

"Totally a vampire," I say, pushing off from the tree, straightening my suit jacket, and brushing off imaginary dirt from my sleeve.

"And how would you know? Dark Fae have zero sense when it comes to not-vampires."

"Who cares, anyway?" I retort, caught out. Corvus is right. Dark Fae are completely useless at sensing other creatures. But I'm not about to admit that to him. "The point is, she's Randall Black's daughter. That makes her off-limits and dangerous."

Corvus snorts. "Since when has off-limits and dangerous ever stopped us? Daddy whip some sense into your arse over the summer, Zeph?"

"Fuck you," I grumble, although he isn't far wrong. Dad is a massive pain in my arse. King of the Dark Fae, although in no way close to retiring, or dying, he is brutal in his discipline, hoping to get me in line before I have to run the Kingdom. The chances of that happening are slim to none, though. I despise rules and will break them every chance I get. However, and there is a giant 'but' to this conversation... she is Randall Black's daughter and that means something around here, whether we admit that to ourselves or not.

"You two are missing the point," Zaiah interjects, his white eyes gleaming with mischief. "Think about it.

Randall Black's daughter, hidden away all this time, suddenly shows up at MistHallow? There's more to this than meets the eye."

I narrow my eyes, considering his words. He's right, of course. Nothing happens by chance in our world, especially not when it involves someone as powerful and influential as Randall Black.

"What do you know?" Corvus demands, taking a menacing step towards Zaiah, but he is all teeth, and Zaiah knows it.

Zaiah holds up his hands, still grinning. "Who said I knew anything? But I'm not blind or stupid, and I will say this—that girl is going to shake things up around here. And personally, I can't wait to see it happen."

I grunt at Zaiah's cryptic bullshit. Typical djinn, always speaking in riddles. But he's right about one thing - Miss Black's presence at MistHallow is going to cause waves. Big ones.

"What's her name?" I murmur.

"Adelaide," Zaiah replies. "In the human world, Adelaide Légère."

"Légère? Light. And yet her name here is Black. Interesting juxtaposition."

Corvus snorts. "Ooh, someone forced into Dark Fae Summer school, these last few weeks?"

I don't dignify that with a response. Despite my natural rebellious attitude, I enjoy learning.

"So, what's the play here?" Corvus asks, interrupting my thoughts, his eyes gleaming with predatory interest.

"Now that I've smelt her, I'm not walking away from that."

"Eww," I mutter. "But we're not. Not a fucking chance. Little Light Dollie is going to turn all the way Black before the first term is out."

"You sense her aura?" Corvus asks, intrigued.

"Naturally," I scoff. "She is pure, not innocent, but she is naïve, delicate. She is terrified of something out there, but more so of us. She is happy to be here, but confused and curious."

"You got all that from a few minutes with her?" Corvus asks, slightly jealous.

I grin, my sharp teeth on display. I may not have fangs, but my canines are wickedly knife-like and will draw blood just as easily. "I did. Blood is your thing, emotions are mine. She will be easy to manipulate for a while."

"Don't be so sure," Zaiah scoffs. "She caught on to me trying to get her to make a wish really fucking quickly. It was…" He breathes hard through his nose. "Irritating."

I raise an eyebrow at Zaiah's admission. It's rare for a djinn to be thwarted, especially him. This Adelaide is proving more interesting by the minute.

"Well, well," I drawl. "Looks like Little Light Dollie has some fire in her, after all."

Corvus chuckles darkly. "All the more reason to get closer. I do love a challenge. And if it's fire we're dealing with, you know who we need."

I chuckle. "Ignatius will be here tomorrow. He had… things to deal with."

"The volcanic eruption in Feeore?" Zaiah asks with a knowing smirk.

"Who am I to say? But back to Miss Black. There's something intoxicating about the idea of corrupting someone so pure."

"Oh, you have no idea how much I'm looking forward to it," Corvus mutters.

My mind drifts back to my summer in the Dark Fae Kingdom. The endless lessons on diplomacy and statecraft, the monotonous ritual ceremonies, the constant pressure to be the perfect prince—it was suffocating. But it also honed my skills and sharpened my powers in ways I hadn't expected. I have levelled up, and that is a secret that I intend to keep for as long as possible.

I flex my fingers, feeling the shadows dance between them. The darkness responds to me now more than ever, a living, breathing entity at my command. I can manipulate emotions with more finesse and weave illusions so real they can fool even the most discerning eye. The nature magick... well, let's just say the forest around Mist-Hallow has never felt more alive to me. My dad's words echo in my head, a mantra drummed into me for the last twenty-one years: *"We are necessary, Zephyr. We bring balance to the light; we remind the world of its shadows. Without us, there is no contrast, no depth to existence."*

"You're plotting," Zaiah observes, pulling me from my incessantly wandering thoughts. "I can practically see the gears turning in that devious mind of yours."

I grin, not bothering to deny it. "Always, my friend. Always."

Corvus leans in, his interest piqued. "Care to share with the class?"

I consider for a moment. These two, along with Ignatius, are my closest allies at MistHallow, as much as I hate to admit it. We've caused our fair share of chaos together, pushed boundaries that should have remained untouched. But this... this feels different. Bigger.

"Not yet," I decide. "Let's see how our Little Light Dollie settles in first. Get a better read on her."

"Fine," he grumbles. "But don't think you can keep me out of this for long. I want a piece of the action."

I nod, acknowledging his claim. "You'll get your chance. We all will. Sharing is caring, after all."

Zaiah claps his hands together, his white eyes gleaming with excitement. "Well, gentlemen, this promises to be an interesting year. I, for one, can't wait to see how it all unfolds."

With that, he blinks out of existence, leaving behind nothing but a faint scent of sandalwood and magick.

Corvus lingers for a moment longer, his eyes searching mine. "Watch yourself, Zeph," he warns. "Randall Black isn't someone to be screwed with."

I give him a feral grin. "Neither am I, Corvus. Neither am I."

He nods, a hint of respect in his gaze, before morphing into his bat form again and taking flight. Do I envy this ability? Sometimes. Fae, unlike faeries, don't have wings, which is fine most days, but today, I'm agitated. Adelaide Black has sunk her claws into my soul and has a grip on it that won't let go.

Alone at last, I let out a long breath, feeling the weight of expectation settle on my shoulders. As the crown prince of the Dark Fae, I'm used to pressure. But this feels different. There's a charge in the air, a sense of impending change that makes my skin prickle with anticipation.

I close my eyes, reaching out with my senses. The forest around me pulses with life, each tree and blade of grass singing its own unique song. I can feel the emotions of the creatures that call this place home—the contentment of a rabbit in its burrow, the hunger of an owl on the hunt, and the nervous excitement of the new students arriving on campus.

And there, just at the edge of my perception, something new—a presence that feels both familiar and utterly foreign—Adelaide. Even from this distance, I can sense the turmoil of her emotions—fear, excitement, curiosity, all swirling together in an intoxicating blend.

I open my eyes, a slow smile spreading across my face. Oh yes, this is going to be fun.

With a thought, I meld into the shadows, allowing the darkness of the dense forest to envelop me. It's a comforting embrace, cool and familiar. I move through the trees unseen, heading back towards the main campus.

As I travel, my mind contrasts MistHallow with my home in the Dark Fae Kingdom. The endless corridors of the obsidian palace, the whispers and plots of the court, the weight of the world on my shoulders. It's a world so different from MistHallow, yet in many ways, the same.

The rules, the discipline, the focus. It's an emotional drain when all I want to do is cause havoc and forget about what I am and just be who I am.

It's a freedom I cherish, even as I know it's temporary.

I emerge from the shadows near the library, my eyes immediately drawn to the window on the top floor again.

For a moment, I'm tempted to use my powers to observe her closely without her knowledge. A simple illusion could make me invisible, allowing me to sit next to her without her knowing. But something holds me back. Maybe it's the lingering influence of my father's lessons on honour and restraint. Or maybe it's just the thrill of the unknown, the anticipation of unravelling her mysteries slowly, piece by tantalising piece.

Instead, I turn away, heading towards my room in the East Wing. As I walk, I can feel the eyes of other students on me. Some filled with fear, others with admiration, still others with poorly disguised hatred. I ignore them all, used to the attention my status brings.

Classes will begin next week, and the games will be in full force. I intend to be at the centre of it all, pulling strings, weaving plots, and seeing just how far I can push before something—or someone—pushes back.

As I reach my room, I pause, my hand on the golden doorknob. Poor little Adelaide thrust into this world of supernatural politics and ancient grudges under the guise of a friendly learning institution. She's going to need allies, friends she can trust in this den of monsters.

With that thought, I enter my room, already planning

my first move in this delicious new game. "Watch out, Little Dollie. Your light is about to meet the darkest shadows MistHallow has to offer."

Chapter 10

Adelaide

Shaking off the lingering unease from my encounter with the three mysterious, otherworldly men, I turn my attention back to the task at hand. The library seems to sense my desperation to know about vampires and how to counteract this creepy ability to make me do whatever they want, simply with an uttered word, as suddenly, a book catches my eye. Its spine glows faintly, as if beckoning me. I reach out and pull it from the shelf, surprised by its weight.

"Vampires: A Comprehensive Guide to the Children of the Night," I read aloud, tracing my fingers over the embossed title. Well, that's certainly on the nose.

I settle into a plush armchair tucked away in a corner, away from prying eyes—not that there is anyone up here to begin with. As I open the book, the pages seem to shimmer, and I'm hit with a waft of something metallic. Blood? I shove back the urge to lick the pages and press on.

The book draws me in quickly. It is fascinating, diving deep into vampire lore and biology. I learn about their enhanced strength and speed, their ability to heal rapidly, and their heightened senses. It explains the compulsion ability that Corvus used on me, a power that allows vampires to control the minds of weaker beings. I shudder, remembering how helpless I felt.

"Weak," I murmur, my fingertips brushing over these words. That is what I am—weak. I don't want to be weak. I don't want these creatures coming after me because they think they can get away with doing whatever they want to me. I've been there and done that at primary school. Bullied into my first self-harming episode, I vowed never to be in that position again. I would be stronger, or failing that, just not care.

I've got apathy down. Most things are of no interest to me, but the last couple of days I have had more emotions running through me than I realistically know what to do with. I'm not equipped to handle this, so I need to figure out a way, fast, to get stronger.

I keep reading, absorbing information about vampire weaknesses, direct sunlight being the worst and most limiting, their need for blood, and their place in the supernatural hierarchy, which is fucking high up the food chain. I suppose I have that going for me, at least in part. I learn about vampires born of two vampires who are strong, whereas turned vampires are much weaker and are subject to more limitations and restrictions. I'm guessing my compeller, Corvus, is a born vampire. There is nothing average or weak about him.

Reading about blood and feeding habits, I find myself getting hungry. Mum's sandwiches are long gone, so I'm going to have to get off my arse and find the dining hall, wondering if I can squirrel away some extras for snacks in my room for later, or even better, enough food so I don't have to come down at all again until tomorrow. I'm extremely wary after being subject to the compulsion and don't want to give these guys a second shot at me.

Not yet, at least.

Reluctantly, I close the book and stand, stretching out the kinks in my back.

I remember my magical map that guides me around campus, so disturbing Orby, I rummage through my backpack until I find the folded piece of parchment.

As I unfold it, it comes to life, ink spreading across its surface to form an intricate map of MistHallow. It's beautiful and slightly dizzying, with buildings that seem to shift and move as I watch.

"Right," I mutter. "How do I use this thing?" As if in response, a glowing dot appears on the map, pulsing gently. That must be me.

"Okay, magical map," I say, feeling only slightly ridiculous talking to a piece of paper. "Where's the dining hall?"

A path lights up on the map, leading from my location in the library down through winding corridors and across a courtyard to a large building.

I shoulder my backpack and set off, following the glowing path, with Orby at my shoulder. The corridors of MistHallow are quiet, which is fine by me.

As I cross the courtyard, the gloomy mid-morning air refreshes me after being cooped up in the library.

I reach the dining hall, pushing open the heavy wooden doors. Inside, the hall is vast, with long tables stretching the length of the room. There are hundreds of students packed inside, which makes me realise it's later than I thought. It's lunchtime, and I couldn't have chosen a worse time to come and find food.

At the far end, I spot the serving area. As I approach, I'm amazed to see the food appears fresh and hot before my eyes.

It all smells heavenly, but my eyes are drawn to the large to-go cups of blood with straws sticking out of them. That must be the synthetic blood Professor Blackthorn mentioned. I reach for one tentatively and then shrug.

"Fuck it, Addy. You might as well give it a shot." Also, it does give me the whole she's-a-vampire vibe that I'm trying to give off.

Finding an empty spot at one of the long tables, I sit down and place my lips over the top of the straw and suck. The coppery taste hits my tongue, and I stifle the groan of pure satisfaction.

A shadow falls over me, making my heart lurch, and I look up to see a girl about my age with vibrant purple hair and eyes that seem to shift colour as I watch.

"Hi," she says, her voice friendly. "You're Adelaide Black, right? I'm Lyra."

I nod, relieved that it isn't Corvus, Zephyr, or Zaiah. "Yeah, that's me. Nice to meet you."

Lyra sits down across from me, her smile wide and

genuine. "Are you settling in okay? I'm happy to show you around and help you get used to the old place if you want?"

Her enthusiasm is a bit overwhelming after the day I've had, but it's nice to encounter someone who doesn't seem to want to eat me or compel me or trick me into making wishes.

"I think I've got a handle on it," I murmur as Orby is rolling around in circles on the table in front of me. Lyra's eyes go to it, and she raises an eyebrow. "You got an orb?"

"Yep. He's quite handy."

"I bet," she mutters, and her friendly attitude drops a notch.

Okay, note to self. Orbs aren't given out to everyone. I hadn't even noticed.

Lyra suddenly stiffens, her eyes fixed on something over my shoulder. "Uh oh," she mutters. "Trouble at six o'clock."

I turn to see what she's looking at, and my heart sinks. Corvus and Zephyr have just entered the dining hall, their eyes scanning the room until they land on me. Slow, predatory smiles spread across their faces.

"Friends of yours?" Lyra asks, her voice low.

I shake my head. "Not exactly. We had a bit of a run-in earlier in the library."

Lyra's expression turns serious. "Be careful with those two, Adelaide. They're bad news."

"Yeah, I got that impression," I mutter.

"Don't let Zaiah fool you into thinking he's the good cop. He is dangerous."

"I know."

She rambles on as if I didn't even speak.

"And the really cute fire elemental that hangs out with them is nice, but watch your back with him as well."

I frown at her. It seems to me she is going overboard in trying to warn me off these guys I have no intention of ever speaking to again if I have my own way. Does she have an ulterior motive, or is she just being helpful?

When she looks down at the orb again and goes stony-faced for a second before adjusting her features, I figure this woman isn't to be trusted. I force a smile and nod at Lyra, but my guard is up now. "Thanks for the heads up," I say, keeping my voice neutral. "I'll keep that in mind."

As Corvus and Zephyr make their way towards us, I feel a surge of panic. I'm not ready to face them again, not after what happened in the library. I need more time to process, to figure out how to protect myself.

"I should go," I say abruptly, standing up and grabbing my backpack as Orby zooms up into the air. "It was nice meeting you, Lyra."

She looks annoyed that I've blown her off. "Sure, whatever. See you around."

I turn to leave, but Corvus and Zephyr are already there, blocking my path. Zephyr's purple and silver eyes dance with amusement, while Corvus's gaze is intense, almost hungry.

"Going somewhere, Adelaide?" Zephyr asks, his voice smooth as silk.

I try to push past them, but Corvus's hand shoots out,

loosely gripping my arm. His touch sends a jolt through me, fear and something else I don't want to name, but it begins with an 'l' and ends with 'ust'.

"Let go," I growl, yanking my arm away. To my surprise, he releases me immediately.

"We just want to talk," Corvus says, his blue eyes boring into mine. "No compulsion, I promise."

I scoff. "Right, because I should totally trust the word of a vampire who's already mind-fucked me once today."

Zephyr chuckles, the sound sending shivers down my spine. "Well, she's got you there."

"Mm, mind-fucking," Corvus murmurs, and I blush for the first time in a really long time. It is mortifying.

I glance around, looking for an escape route, but the dining hall suddenly seems impossibly crowded. Lyra has disappeared, leaving me alone with these two predators.

"Look," I say, trying to keep my voice steady, "I don't know what your game is, but I'm not interested. Just leave me alone."

"No game, Adelaide," Zephyr says, his expression turning serious. "We're here to make amends."

"Amends? For compelling me and touching me against my will," I hiss.

Zephyr's eyes narrow, and he takes a step back, marginally, but he gives me space all the same. His eyes search mine, and he nods imperceptibly, but it's like he gets it. "We apologise, Miss Black."

He grabs Corvus by his upper arm, dragging him away, protesting loudly.

I breathe out in relief, but now I'm more confused

than ever. Grabbing my blood drink, I hurry out of the dining hall as fast as I can without sloshing the crimson liquid all over my white shirt. I forget all about stockpiling food for the next day or so. I just want to get back to my room, where I'm safe, and no one can touch me.

Chapter 12

Zaiah

As the mist thickens around MistHallow University, I hover unseen, smoky and intrigued outside Adelaide Black's North Tower window. She could spot me if she were so inclined to focus and separate the mist from my form, but I doubt she will. This girl is an enigma that tickles my curiosity. I've been watching her since she arrived at MistHallow, intrigued by the waves of change she's already causing in this stagnant pond of supernatural politics.

As a djinn, I'm used to observing from the sidelines. We're not meant to interfere directly, only to grant wishes and let the chaos unfold. But there's something about Adelaide that makes me want to break all the rules. Maybe it's the way she resisted my attempt to trick her into making a wish earlier. Not many can do that, especially someone who I feel isn't as strong as she could be yet. Randall Black has kept her a secret for all this time, but I wonder if her true nature was suppressed somehow. That would mean she isn't all vampire. She is something else mixed in. Human? Witch? Shifter? Something.

I watch as she paced her room, her pet orb agitated by her mood. I glare at the orb as it zings over to the window and hovers, almost as if it sees me. In all fairness, it probably does. Those things are above my pay grade, magickly speaking, and only given to the most 'I' of the VIP students. Clearly, Adelaide Black is one of those. Not that I would expect anything less from the daughter of one of the founding members of MistHallow University. She is about as 'I' as they come.

With a thought, I attune my senses to her wavelength, letting it wash over me. It's a heady rush, like diving into a turbulent sea. Her energy is so raw, so intense. It's refreshing after years of dealing with the muted emotions of long-lived supernatural beings.

Adelaide stops pacing and picks up her blood drink, taking a small sip and appearing to savour the taste of it. "Stupid, arrogant supernatural arseholes," she mutters. "Who do they think they are?"

I chuckle silently. If only she knew the half of it. Corvus and Zephyr think they're hot shit, but they have the necessary power and background to back it up.

She sighs and pulls a book out of her backpack. As Adelaide settles in to read, I draw on her essence, pulling it into every cell in my dissipated form. At twenty-one, I'm barely more than an infant in djinn terms. Most of my kind are ancient beings with centuries or even millennia of experience. But me? I'm an anomaly, a djinn born in the modern age. The only one. That makes me shit hot as well.

My parents, both powerful djinn in their own right, were shocked when I came into existence. Djinn reproduction is rare, happening only once every few centuries. To have a child in this era of technology and scepticism was unheard of.

From the moment I was born, I was different. While other djinn clung to ancient traditions and rigid rules about wish-granting, I embraced the chaos of the modern world. Why stick to lamps and rings when you could hide in smartphones or nest in the cloud?

I flex my magical muscles, feeling the familiar rush of power. As a djinn, I can manipulate reality itself, bending the fabric of existence to my will. But it's more than just granting wishes. It's about understanding the intricate web of cause and effect, seeing the ripples that each action creates in the pool of reality.

With a thought, I create a small pocket dimension within Adelaide's room and move myself into it. To her, nothing has changed. But in this hidden space, I can move freely, experimenting with my powers without fear of detection.

I conjure up a swirling vortex of sand, each grain a potential future, a possible outcome. This is how I see the world - not as a fixed reality, but as an ever-shifting landscape of possibilities. It's what makes wish-granting so tricky, and so fun.

I turn my attention back to Adelaide. She's still reading, oblivious to my presence or the miniature dimension

I've created in her room. I wonder what she would wish for if given the chance. Power? Knowledge? Love?

It's tempting to reveal myself, to offer her three wishes like in the old stories. But that's not how it works, not really. Wishes are tricky things, born from the deepest desires of the heart. But they need to be spoken aloud and granted by a mystical being. They're constantly being made and fulfilled, shaping the world in subtle ways.

My job is to nudge those wishes along. To find the hidden desires and bring them to light, often with unexpected consequences. It's a game of strategy and chaos, and I love every minute of it. That's the beauty of being a djinn. It's not about cosmic power or world-altering magick. It's about the small changes, the butterfly effect that can turn a tiny wish into a hurricane of consequences.

It makes me somewhat of a pariah in our community, which is fine. It's why I'm here at MistHallow in the first place. The institution which takes on misfits, the clueless and the rebels. Quite a mangled mess of creatures ends up here, but that's what makes it even more interesting. You don't know who you are going to come across.

As I focus intently on our girl, I notice she has fallen asleep, the book sliding from her grasp. I'm tempted to use my magick to tuck her in, to ease the furrow of concentration from her brow. But that would be crossing a line I'm not ready to step over yet. Instead, I simply watch as she sleeps fitfully, her dreams no doubt filled with fangs and magick and the strange new world she's found herself in.

I float closer, studying her face. There's power hidden beneath the surface. Power that could rival even the oldest supernatural beings if properly harnessed. It's intoxicating to be near, like standing at the edge of a storm.

Suddenly, the urge to bind us together is poking at me. It's risky, breaking the rules of non-interference that have been drilled into me since birth, but I ignore on a near-daily basis. I want her to be mine as I am hers. I have a longing for her, which makes me ache. It's sudden, dangerous and irrational, but what a djinn wants, a djinn gets.

With a wave of my hand, I send a tendril of magick towards Adelaide's sleeping form. It's subtle, so subtle that even the most powerful beings at MistHallow won't notice until it's too late for her to do anything about it. She is bound to me now, and nothing will change that unless I break it. But I know it's there, a tiny ripple that could grow into a tidal wave.

As I withdraw my magick, I feel a thrill of excitement. This is why I love being a djinn in the modern age. The old ones are content to wait centuries for their meddling to unfold. But I want to see results *now*, to be in the thick of the action as it happens. Instant gratification.

I glance at the clock on Adelaide's bedside table. It's getting late, and my night schedule is all over the place. I should head back to my room and adjust as necessary. But before I go, I decide to leave one more little surprise.

With a snap of my fingers, I create a small, ornate bottle on Adelaide's desk. It's not a traditional djinn lamp but a modern twist on the concept. Inside, swirling mists of possibility await, ready to grant a wish, but only if she figures out how to use it.

It's a risk, leaving such an obvious trace of my presence, especially with that pesky orb floating about, sniffing me out. But something tells me Adelaide is going to need all the help she can get in the coming days. If she's smart enough to resist my first attempt at trickery, maybe she'll be clever enough to use this gift wisely.

As I prepare to leave, I take one last look at the sleeping beauty. Adelaide Black, the girl who could change everything. I may be young for a djinn, but I know enough to recognise a pivotal moment when I see one. Whatever happens next, it's going to be one hell of a ride.

With a grin, I fade from view, my form dissipating into smoke as I close the pocket dimension and travel on the mist back to my room, my mind is already racing with possibilities. How will Adelaide react to my gift? What will she do with the spark of power I've given her? And how can I position myself to be right in the middle of the havoc when it all unfolds?

Back in my room, I materialise fully, stretching out my corporeal form. My room is a mishmash of modern tech and ancient artefacts, a reflection of my unique place in the world of djinn. A state-of-the-art gaming setup sits next to a millennia-old Persian rug... a flying carpet, if you will, protected by magick and unseen forces. My phone—a portal to countless wishes waiting to be manipulated—sits on my desk next to a traditional oil lamp.

I flop onto my bed, my mind still buzzing with the events of the night. Watching Adelaide, binding her to me, leaving the bottle... it's a more direct intervention than I've ever attempted before. My parents would be furious if they knew. But then again, they've never really understood me.

To them, being a djinn is all about maintaining balance and playing the long game. They don't understand why I bother with social media, video games, or any of the trappings of modern life. *We are timeless beings. Why concern yourself with the fleeting fancies of mortals?*

But that's exactly why I love it. The fast pace, the constant change, the endless stream of wishes and desires flitting through the digital ether. It's a playground for me, full of opportunities to cause mischief and mayhem.

I pick up my phone, scrolling through my various social media feeds. Each post, each comment, each like is a tiny wish waiting to be granted or twisted. The girl hoping her crush will notice her latest selfie. The guy wishing his clever tweet will go viral. The influencer desperately wanting to hit that next follower milestone.

With a few taps and a sprinkle of djinn magick, I set a few wheels in motion. The crush will notice the selfie, but only because an embarrassing detail in the background goes viral. The clever tweet will blow up, but spark a controversy the poster wasn't prepared for. The influencer will get a massive influx of followers, but they'll all be bots that destroy their engagement rates.

Small things, but chaos, nonetheless. It's what I live for.

I find my thoughts drifting back to Adelaide. She's different from the usual mortals I deal with. Her wishes and desires are deeper and more complex. She doesn't want fame or fortune or fleeting validation. She wants understanding, control, and a place to belong.

It's refreshing, really. And challenging. How do you grant a wish like that? How do you twist something so pure and focused completely on oneself? It's self-involvement at its finest, but not in a bad way. She is alone, truly alone, so the people and things around her mean nothing.

Yet.

Once my bond has grown in strength, she will have me.

She just doesn't know it.

I lie down with a smile while I continue to flick through my phone.

"Watch out, MistHallow," I murmur. "You have absolutely no idea what's coming."

Chapter 13

Adelaide

I wake with a start, disoriented and groggy. The book I was reading lies open on my chest, and I realise I must have dozed off while studying. Rubbing my eyes, I sit up and glance at the clock. It's late at night now. I must've slept for hours.

When I stretch, something feels off. There's a strange sensation tugging at me, like an invisible thread pulling gently but insistently. I can't quite put my finger on what it is or where it's coming from, but it's there, a constant presence at the edge of my awareness.

"What the hell?" I mutter, shaking my head as if I could dislodge the feeling. But it persists, a subtle pull on my soul. I guess being here at MistHallow is transforming my body in more ways than I'm aware of.

Trying to ignore the sensation, I swing my legs over the side of the bed and stand up. That's when I notice a small, ornate bottle sitting on my desk. I frown, certain it wasn't there before I fell asleep.

Cautiously, I approach the desk. The bottle is beautiful, made of what looks like smoky glass with intricate silver designs etched into its surface. Inside, I can see swirling mists of something. It's hypnotic, and I reach out to touch it before I can stop myself.

As my fingertips brush the cool glass, I feel a jolt of power and magick. I'm not sure, but it makes the strange tugging sensation intensify for a moment before settling back to its previous level.

"Okay, this is officially freaky," I say to Orby, who's hovering nearby as nonchalantly as a magick orb can. "Where did this come from? And what the hell is it?"

Turning it over, there's no label, no instructions, nothing to indicate its purpose or origin. But something about it feels familiar. Like it's meant for me, somehow.

Shaking my head, I set the bottle back down. I've got enough mysteries to deal with right now without adding a mysterious magical artefact into it.

Turning back to my bed, I pick up the library book I was reading before I fell asleep. "Vampires: A Comprehensive Guide to the Children of the Night." Right. Because that's my life now. Studying up on what I am - or at least, half of what I am.

I flip through the pages, trying to focus on the words, but that persistent tugging feeling keeps distracting me. It's like an itch I can't scratch, a thought I can't quite grasp.

Determined to ignore the sensation, I throw myself back into studying. I read about vampire strengths -

enhanced speed, strength, and senses. Not that I've noticed any of that within myself yet.

Then there are the weaknesses that are lesser known. Silver burns on contact. I don't wear jewellery, but I tuck this away anyway, just in case.

I glance at the clock when my stomach growls. It's well past dinner time now, and that blood, while particularly satisfying at the time, did not fill me up. I need human food. I guess I'm going to have to find a balance. Steak pie washed down with a cup of blood. Or maybe a rare steak would be amazing. Slicing into that juicy goodness with blood oozing out all over the plate. My mouth starts to water, and it gets me on my feet and heading towards the door. Unfortunately, there is nothing else for it. I'm going to have to brave the dining hall again. The thought makes me nervous. After my last encounter with Corvus and Zephyr, I'm not exactly eager to put myself in their path again.

But hunger wins out over caution.

Hearing the soft patter of rain on the windows, I grab my coat, remembering the black card tucked away in my pocket, and head for the door. Before I leave, my gaze falls on the mysterious bottle again. Without really thinking about it, I pick it up and slip it into my pocket. Something tells me I shouldn't leave it behind.

The corridors of MistHallow are buzzing with activity, which makes me feel safer, in a way. Finding the dining hall easily this time, I push open the doors, relieved to find it busy but not heaving. A few students are scattered around, some hunched over books, others chatting quietly. There is no sign of Corvus or Zephyr.

I make my way to the serving area, eyeing the selection. Almost as if it knew I were thinking about rare steak, one appears on a plate in front of me with fries and a side of veg. Narrowing my eyes suspiciously, I shrug, eager to get my teeth into it, and carry it over to a table in the corner.

I take my coat off and settle into my seat, keeping my back to the wall so I can see the entire room. As I cut into the steak, the rich aroma makes my mouth water. The first bite is heaven, the meat practically melting on my tongue as the blood fills my mouth. I close my eyes, savouring the deliciousness.

"Enjoying your meal?"

My eyes snap open at the unfamiliar voice with the strange, but light accent. Is that Australian? A guy is standing by my table, a friendly smile on his face. His amber eyes seem to glow slightly in the dim light of the dining hall, and his scarlet hair is artfully tousled.

"Um, yeah," I mutter, caught off guard. "It's good."

He grins wider. "Mind if I join you? I'm Ignatius, by the way."

Before I can respond that no, I'd rather he didn't, he's already sliding into the seat across from me.

"Adelaide," I say curtly, hoping he'll take the hint and leave.

No such luck. Ignatius leans forward, his eyes sparkling with interest. I get over my annoyance a fraction at the sheer cuteness of this guy. He's adorable. "So, Adelaide. You're causing quite a stir around here, you know."

I frown, stabbing a piece of steak with more force than necessary. "I'm not trying to cause anything."

He chuckles. "Sometimes, just existing is enough to shake things up, especially when you're Randall Black's daughter."

I stiffen at the mention of my father's name. How does everyone seem to know who I am? "You know who I am?" I ask anyway, getting pissed off.

Ignatius grins, a mischievous glint in his amber eyes. "Everyone knows who you are, Adelaide. The mysterious daughter of one of MistHallow's founders suddenly appears after being hidden away for years. You're the hottest topic on campus."

Great. Just what I needed - to be the centre of attention. *Wait! What? One of MistHallow's founders? Well, he fucking kept that quiet, didn't he, the fucking arsehole.* I guess that makes sense, though, seeing as how he's managed to get me in here, given me what I think is the best room and this orb thing that Lyra was so envious of.

I take another bite of steak, chewing slowly as I consider my response. "I'm just here to learn," I say finally. "I'm not interested in shaking things up or being a topic of gossip."

"Fair enough," Ignatius says. "But you might not have much choice in the matter. Especially with certain people taking an interest in you."

I narrow my eyes. "Certain people like Corvus and Zephyr, you mean?"

He nods, looking impressed. "You catch on quick. Yeah, those two don't usually pay much attention to new students. But you've got them intrigued."

"Lucky me," I mutter sarcastically. "I guess that makes you the, what was it now? Oh, yeah, 'really cute fire elemental'?"

Ignatius laughs, the sound warm and genuine. "Aww, who told you about me?" As he speaks, I notice the air around him seems to shimmer slightly, like heat waves rising from the pavement on a hot summer's day.

"I was warned about you," I correct him, "and that is none of your business."

"If someone is talking about me, I want to know who it is." His amber eyes bore into mine.

"Do you now? Well, now you know how it feels."

He grins. "Oh, touché, Miss Black. You're a firecracker, aren't you?" He holds out his hand, and sparks dance around his fingertips.

"And you're a bit of a show-off," I state, shovelling the last piece of steak into my mouth before standing up while I'm still chewing. The plate disappears, and I pick up my coat and put it back on, feeling the weight of the bottle in my pocket.

Ignatius stands up, too, his amber eyes glinting with amusement. "Oh, come on, don't run off. We were just starting to have fun."

I roll my eyes. "Your idea of fun and mine are probably very different, firestarter."

He steps closer, lowering his voice. "Prodigy. Great song, but I wouldn't be so sure about that, Adelaide. I think we could have a lot of fun together."

The air around us seems to crackle with energy, and I feel a flush of heat that has nothing to do with his elemental powers. For a moment, I'm tempted to stay, to see where this banter might lead. But the memory of Corvus's compulsion and Zephyr's touch makes me wary.

"Thanks, but no thanks," I say, stepping back. "I've had enough 'fun' with supernatural beings for one day."

Ignatius holds up his hands in mock surrender. "Fair enough. But just remember, not all of us are like Corvus and Zephyr. Some of us actually know how to play nice."

"I'll keep that in mind," I mutter, turning to leave. As I walk away, I can feel his eyes on me, that strange tugging sensation in my chest growing stronger for a moment before fading back down to a soft simmer.

Outside the dining hall, I take a deep breath, trying to clear my head. Between Corvus, Zephyr, Zaiah and now Ignatius, it seems like I can't go anywhere without running into trouble. I just want to focus on my studies and figure out what the hell I am, not get caught up in whatever games these supernatural beings are playing.

"Why aren't you more concerned about all of this?" I mutter to Orby, who is happily floating along next to me. "Do you sense danger? Or are you just a magickal guide, slash companion, slash, key to my room?"

Not unsurprisingly, he doesn't answer me.

As I make my way back to my room, I can't shake the feeling that I'm being watched. The corridors seem darker, the shadows deeper. I quicken my pace, eager to get back to the relative safety of my room.

Chapter 14

Ignatius

Adelaide leaves the dining hall, her long black hair swinging behind her as she strides away. I smile as I savour the lingering heat of our encounter. She's certainly not what I expected - and that's saying something, given the rumours swirling around MistHallow about Randall Black's mysterious daughter.

As I make my way back to my table, I replay our conversation in my mind. Her quick wit, the sharp retorts, the way she didn't back down or simper at my flirtations like so many others do. It's refreshing. Intriguing.

I settle into my chair, absently conjuring a small flame in my palm. The fire dances between my fingers, a reflection of my restless thoughts. Adelaide Black. A force to be reckoned with in her own right, regardless of who her dad is.

The warmth of the flame is an extension of my skin, a

comforting sensation that's been with me since I first discovered my abilities. I'm a fire elemental, but not just any run-of-the-mill pyrokinetic. No, I come from a long line of fire wielders, my bloodline tracing back to the ancient shamans who first learned to harness the raw power of the flame.

I close my fist, extinguishing the visible flame, but the heat remains, coursing through my veins like lava. It's always there, a constant presence that both comforts and drives me. Some days, it feels like my skin can barely contain the inferno in my soul. Those are my more... erratic days. Some might call them destructive.

But it's all down to nature versus nurture.

Growing up in a remote community hidden deep in the Australian Outback, our clan, the Emberkin, has lived there for generations, honing our abilities and keeping our existence secret from the outside world. I remember the first time I called fire to my hands. I was barely five years old and already showed more potential than many adults in our clan.

The elders were thrilled. They saw me as the fulfilment of an ancient prophecy, the one who would lead our people into a new age. But with that excitement came pressure and expectations that sometimes felt like they would crush me beneath their weight.

I flex my fingers, feeling the familiar tingle of heat just beneath the surface of my skin. Even now, thousands of miles away from the sun-baked earth of my homeland, I can still feel the connection to my roots, to the primal force of fire that has shaped my people for millennia.

Adelaide's parting shot - calling me 'firestarter' - brings a wry smile to my face. If only she knew how apt that nickname really is. I'm not just someone who can create and control fire; I am fire incarnate. The flames respond to my will in ways that even other elementals find hard to comprehend.

I glance down at my arms, tracing the intricate patterns of my clan tattoos with my eyes. To the uninitiated, they look like simple tribal designs. But each swirl and line are a conduit for my power, enhancing my control and allowing me to push the boundaries of what should be possible with fire manipulation.

With a thought, I activate one of the tattoos on my forearm. The ink comes alive, glowing with an inner light as warmth spreads through my arm. Suddenly, the air around me shimmers with heat, and I know that if anyone were to touch me right now, they'd recoil from the scorching temperature of my skin.

This is just one of the many abilities I've honed over the years. I can raise my body temperature to near-impossible levels, create and shape fire at will, and even imbue objects with fiery energy. But perhaps most impressively, I can absorb and redirect heat and flame, making me immune to fire-based attacks.

Of course, these abilities come with their own set of challenges. Controlling such raw power requires constant focus and discipline. One slip, one moment of unchecked emotion, and I could easily set the whole campus ablaze. It's a responsibility that weighs heavily on me, a constant reminder of why I need to keep my true potential hidden, and why the clan elders sent me to MistHallow.

I lean back in my chair, letting my gaze wander around the dining hall. The other students, even the other fire users, have no idea of the inferno that rages within me. To them, I'm just Ignatius, the charming, flirtatious fire elemental with a knack for impressive but ultimately harmless flame tricks.

It's a role I play well, a carefully constructed mask that allows me to blend in while still standing out just enough to satisfy my ego. But encounters like the one with Adelaide have unearthed an emotion in me that I didn't think was possible: the need for someone who can see past the act and appreciate the true depth of who I am.

I close my eyes, focusing on my inner fire. With each breath, I can feel it pulsing, growing, spreading through my body until I'm filled with a comfortable, all-encompassing warmth. This is my centre, my true self. The fire that burns eternal, that defines who I am at my very core.

When I open my eyes again, the world seems sharper and more vivid. My enhanced senses, another gift of my elemental nature, kick into overdrive. I can feel the subtle variations in temperature throughout the room and see the faint heat signatures left behind by those who have passed through.

It's in these moments when I allow myself to fully embrace my nature that I feel most alive. The power thrumming through me, the heightened awareness of the world around me—it's intoxicating. But it's also isolating because how can I ever truly connect with others when I have to keep so much of myself hidden away?

With Adelaide's arrival, I can't shake the feeling that things are starting to fall into place. There's something about her, something beyond her quick wit and obvious beauty—a power, perhaps, or a destiny that's intertwined with my own in ways I can't wrap my head around.

But I know it.

I stand up, ready to head back to my room. As I walk, I let a bit of my power seep out, raising the temperature around me just enough to make the air shimmer. It's a small indulgence, a tiny release of the constant pressure of containing my true nature.

Back in my room, I shed my carefully maintained public persona. Here, in the privacy of my own space, I can truly be myself. The walls are lined with fire-resistant materials, a necessary precaution given my tendency to literally ignite when my emotions run high.

I move to the centre of the room and close my eyes, focusing on my breath. In and out, each exhale carrying a wisp of smoke. I feel the fire within me, always burning, always hungry. With a thought, I let it out.

Flames erupt from my skin, engulfing me in a cocoon of fire. But I feel no pain or fear. This is my element, my true form. The fire dances around me, responding to my will and shaping itself into intricate patterns and forms.

I open my eyes, watching the play of light and shadow on the walls. This is the part of myself I can never show to others, the raw, primal power that defines me. It's beautiful and terrifying, a constant reminder of my potential and the responsibility that comes with it.

As the flames recede, sinking back beneath my skin, I move to the window, looking out over the moonlit grounds of MistHallow. Somewhere out there, Adelaide is trying to find her place in this world of magick and mystery. Our paths are destined to cross again, for better or for worse.

I'll keep watching Adelaide and keep trying to unravel the mystery that surrounds her. Not just out of curiosity or attraction, but because I have a feeling that she's going to be key to whatever is coming.

And whatever that something is... it's big.

Chapter 15

Adelaide

"What is with the guys in this place?" I mutter as I use Orby to open my tower bedroom door. "Scratch that, what is with *everyone* in this place?" Lyra wasn't exactly trustworthy either, not that I'm the most trusting person on earth. Quite the opposite, but around here, the only person... creature... I feel I can sort of, maybe trust is Professor Blackthorn. He knows my dad, and he has been kind and helpful. He has not tried to trick me, be envious of me, or try to get in my pants.

Sighing as I close the door and lean against it, I stare out into the night. I feel my energy increase, and everything about my being comes alive. This is my time, and I finally understand why.

Taking off my coat, I place it on a chair near the wardrobe and then pull the vial out to stare at it again. It feels warm to the touch, which I find a bit odd, seeing as it is just a swirling mist inside. Slipping it under my pillow, I strip off my shirt and then wonder how to do my laundry. There must be a place, and the map will show me. I pull it out of my backpack and stare at it. "Laundrette," I murmur.

Smiling when a glowing red dot appears, I nod. Not far from here, fortunately. I didn't relish the fact of parading my dirty clothes halfway across campus. Placing the map back down, I straighten up in just my bra and then my breath hitches. The urge from deep inside rises, the urge that I try to keep at bay so as not to scare my mother or the people around me. But my mother isn't here, and neither is anyone else. Without even thinking about it, I reach for my holdall, which is still half packed, and stick my hand to the very bottom, under the plastic covered insert that keeps the bottom sturdy and pull out the knife that I have hidden there. Glaring at it, I hesitate.

"Wait," I murmur and fling it on the bed, crossing over to the open book on vampires. "Speed healing..."

I've never had that before, just regular old scabs and scars. I've drunk a cup of blood today and eaten that rare steak... could this be something that will kick in now that I'm here and doing things vampires do?

"Only one way to find out, and kill two birds with one stone," I mutter as I go back to the knife and pick it up. A small hunting knife, which is all I could afford, it's nothing special, but it does the job. The blade glints in the moonlight as I hold it up. My heart races with anticipation and a hint of fear. I've done this before, but never with the possibility of rapid healing.

Taking a deep breath, I press the tip of the knife to my forearm. The familiar sting as it breaks the skin sends a rush through me. I drag the blade slowly, watching the blood well up in its wake.

The pain is exquisite, appeasing my ragged edges in a way nothing else can. For a moment, all my worries about this strange new world fade away. There's only this - the sharp bite of the blade, the warmth of my blood.

I wait, watching intently. At first, nothing seems different. The cut bleeds steadily, droplets rolling down my arm. I swallow and then jump a fucking mile when something hits my bedroom with a loud thump, scaring me half to death.

"What the fuck?" I snap, glaring at Orby as if he is meant to know what is going on, as I march over to the door and peer through the peephole. I can't see anything, so I open the door a crack and stare at the giant bat on the floor, which before my very eyes shifts into a well-dressed man with a face that could launch a thousand ships and a wicked smile that gleams when he looks down at me.

"Adelaide," Corvus says. "I smelt blood. Everything okay in there?"

I gulp and make sure the door is covering my arm as much as possible, forgetting for one second that I'm standing in my bra. When that realisation hits me, I freeze like a deer in headlights.

"Adelaide?" Corvus presses, his face falling into a frown.

To his credit, he doesn't stare at my breasts, just my eyes with a laser-like focus that is unnerving, and I get the feeling he is trying to compel me into saying something. Dragging my gaze from his is like trying to push a mountain up a bigger mountain. It makes me pant with the effort, and I feel my knees buckle.

Corvus reaches out and grabs me to steady me before his face goes stony. He lets go of me, hands up, and steps back. But how did he enter my room in the first place? Aren't vampires supposed to get an invite? Now that I think about it, I haven't seen anything that has mentioned this yet and I, clearly, can go wherever I like.

Hmm.

"Thank you," I croak, as he did stop me from hitting the deck, despite laying his hands on me. I stumble back and drop my arm, which is aching now from being sliced into and held at an unnatural angle as I tried to hide it.

Corvus's gaze lands on the gaping wound in my arm, and he freezes like a stunned rabbit.

We are quite the pair tonight.

"I see," he says. "May I?"

He reaches out, holding his hand up slowly so as not to startle me.

"Why?" I whisper. *Does he want to drink from me?*

"I can help heal it," he murmurs, his eyes narrowed in curiosity.

Well, I guess I've blown my cover. No regular vampire girl here. "How?" I murmur.

He raises his hand higher, and I nod once, giving him permission to touch me. It's like my will is stripped away, but I don't think he is compelling me this time. His chilly hand grasps my arm behind my elbow, and he raises it to his lips. He lets out a whimper that I can see by the mortified expression on his face, he didn't mean to let escape.

Lowering his mouth to the cut, I gasp when his tongue flicks out, and he tastes my blood. But then he stops and lifts his head with a slow smile. "Doesn't look like you need me after all," he murmurs.

I glance down and see the cut is healing. Slowly knitting itself back together until my skin is whole with no scar in sight.

"Fuck," I mutter.

"So definitely half vampire," Corvus murmurs. "And your other half is... human, yes? You are a Vesperidae."

It's not a question, but a blunt statement. I don't answer him. I was told that this should be a secret. I don't know Corvus; I sure as shit don't trust him. The big but is though, he is being gentle with me now, like a, what was it that Zephyr called me... a porcelain doll.

I take a deep breath, trying to steady myself. Corvus is still standing there, his intense blue eyes fixed on me. I'm acutely aware that I'm half-naked, but somehow, that seems less important than the fact that he now knows what I am.

"You can't tell anyone," I say, my voice low and urgent. "About... what I am. It's supposed to be a secret."

Corvus raises an eyebrow, a small smile playing at the corners of his mouth. "Your secret's safe with me, Adelaide. But you might want to be more careful in the future. Not everyone here is as... discreet as I am."

I snort at that. "Right. Because you've been the picture of discretion so far."

He gives me that infuriating smirk. "Fair point. But I mean it - I won't tell anyone about your Vesper nature. You have my word."

I eye him sceptically. "And why should I trust your word?"

Corvus steps closer, his eyes boring into mine. "Because, Adelaide, whether you like it or not, we're connected now. Your blood calls to me in a way I've never experienced before, and that makes you very, very interesting to me."

A shiver runs down my spine at his words. I'm not sure if it's fear or something else.

"That doesn't exactly make me feel better," I mutter.

"It wasn't meant to," Corvus says with a wicked grin. "But it's the truth, and in this place, truth is a rare commodity."

I take a step back, suddenly very aware of my half-nakedness and vulnerability. "Right. Well, thanks for the help. I think I'll be fine now."

Corvus's eyes roam over me, lingering on the newly healed skin of my arm before he frowns. "Self-harm isn't the answer, Adelaide, not anymore. There are other ways to deal with the hunger, the intensity of what you're feeling."

I bristle at his presumption. "You don't know anything about me or what I'm feeling."

"Maybe not," he concedes. "But if you ever want to talk about it," he says, "or if you need help figuring out your abilities, you know where to find me."

I snort. "Right. Because you've been so helpful so far."

He chuckles. "What can I say? I'm trying to turn over a new leaf. Give me a chance, Adelaide. You might be surprised."

Before I can respond, he steps back into the hallway. "Sweet dreams, Little Dollie," he murmurs before he turns back into a bat and flies off out of the arrow slit in the tower wall.

"So that's how you got in, creep." I slam the door shut and lean against it, lifting my arm to stare at it in wonder. "Okay, so super speed healing, no, but definitely faster than before." Does that depend on the amount of blood, and what kind? Synthetic versus real? And if so, where do I get real blood around here?

Huffing in frustration, I bet Corvus knows, and I just let him leave. *Way to make friends and influence people, you dick.*

Groaning as I want to call him back and ask these questions, but I have no idea where he went, so I slide down the door and stare at my arm. "You!" I snap at Orby, startling him. "What is your true purpose, hmm? Why are you here?"

Orby bobs in the air, seemingly unfazed by my outburst. Of course, he doesn't answer. He's just a magical orb, after all. Not a sentient being. Right?

Right?

I sigh, running a hand through my hair. "This is ridiculous. I'm talking to a floating ball and expecting answers."

Standing up, I walk over to my bed and flop down on it, staring at the ceiling. The events of the day swirl in my mind - the library encounter, the mysterious bottle, Ignatius in the dining hall, and now Corvus discovering my secret. It's all too much. This day has been shit, and I feel bad that I haven't even tried to contact my mum yet.

"What am I doing here?" I mutter to myself. "I don't belong in this world of magick and monsters."

But even as I say it, I know it's not true. I do belong here, in a way I never belonged in the human world.

I roll onto my side, my gaze landing on the knife lying on the floor where I dropped it when bat-boy thumped into my door. The urge to cut is still there, a constant itch under my skin. But now I know it won't give me the release I'm looking for. The wounds will just heal, leaving me unsatisfied.

I'll have to find other ways to cope with the intensity. It looks like I'm going to have to track Corvus down tomorrow and ask him to show me these other ways. I rest my hand on the back of my elbow where he touched me. I didn't vomit. I didn't run. I didn't find the feel of skin on mine repulsive. Why? Why is that when only my mother has ever been able to touch me, and even then, in short pockets of time? I wasn't always this way. As a child, I was reserved and skittish but not actively icked out by someone touching me. Then I got my period, that day I first saw Randall and things changed.

Blinking, I reach for my phone to check the date. My period. It was due today. Will I still have this now that my truer nature is being revealed? And what does it have to do with anything? Is it all a big coincidence that I started to really feel out of sorts on my thirteenth birthday? Or is there something more insidious at play here?

Exhausted with my thoughts, I dial my mum.

The phone cuts out, and I sigh. Obviously, it doesn't work here. We are in a parallel universe where the mobile network has no coverage. Yet, I've seen creatures with their phones. So, how do I get on their network?

Another thing to find out tomorrow. I just hope Randall told my mum I arrived safe and sound. But right now, I need to keep reading and get myself fully on a night schedule before classes start next week.

Chapter 16

Corvus

As I soar through the night sky in my bat form, the taste of Adelaide's blood still lingers on my tongue. It's intoxicating, unlike anything I've ever experienced before. The moment I caught the scent of her blood, I was drawn to her tower as inevitably as the tide to the shore. I couldn't have stopped myself if I'd tried.

Aiming for my open window, I fly inside my room and transform back into my human form. My mind is racing, trying to process what just happened and that my suspicions were confirmed.

Adelaide Black. A Vesper. Half-vampire, half-human. It explains so much and yet raises even more questions.

Shedding my jacket and loosening my tie, I strip off my shirt. The urge to go back to Adelaide's room, to taste her blood again, is almost overwhelming. But I resist. She will come to me. I know she will. I gave her more than enough to think about, and that was the plan.

The way her blood calls to me, the fierce determination in her eyes, the vulnerability she tries so hard to hide, all forms one allure that I'm finding harder to resist. She's a puzzle I'm desperate to solve.

I pause in front of the ornate mirror hanging on the wall. My reflection stares back at me—a perk of being a pureblood. My blue eyes are bright with an intensity that surprises me. I've always prided myself on my control, on my ability to remain aloof and detached. But Adelaide has shaken that control in a way I never expected. I try to sort through my jumbled thoughts.

The fact that she's a Vesper is significant, of course. Vespers are rare. No wonder Randall Black kept her hidden all these years.

But it's more than that. There's something about Adelaide that draws me in, makes me want to protect her even as I'm tempted to push her to her limits. It's a dangerous combination, one that could lead to trouble if I'm not careful. But then, that's part of the fun.

Turning back to the window, I look out over the moonlit grounds of MistHallow. Adelaide is probably still trying to make sense of her newly discovered healing abilities. I should have stayed and explained more, but the intensity of my reaction to her blood scared me.

My family would be appalled if they knew how badly I've slipped. The Sanguines are one of the oldest and most respected vampire bloodlines. We don't get flustered by pretty girls, no matter how unique their blood might be. We certainly don't make promises to keep secrets or offer help without expecting something in return. *Quid pro quo, always.*

But I've never been one to follow the family playbook too closely. Growing up in the oppressive grandeur of Sanguine Manor in a deserted area of the Lake District, the endless lessons on vampire history and politics, and the constant pressure to be the perfect pureblood heir were suffocating, and I rebelled against them at every turn.

But Adelaide... I don't want her to care about any of that. I want her to look at me and see past the carefully constructed façade, the charming vampire prince act.

I move to my desk, pulling out my leather-bound journal and flip to the page reserved for Adelaide and add:

- *Blood tastes extraordinary*
- *Self-harm tendencies?*
- *Growing stronger with her consumption of synthetic blood (was able to resist compulsion)*
- *Bonds?*

I don't know what that means, but there is a bond—a strange one that you have simply by being of the same species, but also more than that. I can't quite figure it out, which is driving me wild.

There's so much more I want to know. What other abilities does she have? How strong is she compared to a full vampire? And most intriguingly, why has she been hidden away all this time?

I close the journal, sliding it back into its hiding place. The smart thing to do would be to keep my distance, observe Adelaide from afar, and gather information without getting personally involved. That's what my family would expect of me.

But since when have I ever done the smart thing?

A grin spreads across my face as I make my decision. I'm going to help Adelaide figure out her abilities and teach her about the vampire world she's been kept away from for so long, and in the process, maybe I'll figure out why she affects me so strongly.

Crossing over to the bookshelf that takes up one wall of my room, I trail my fingers over the spines of ancient tomes and modern texts. I pull out a dusty volume on vampire lore, flipping through it until I find the very short, very brief section on Vesperidae.

The information is sparse, mainly speculation and myth. Vespers are so rare that few have had the chance to study them in depth. This is my chance to extend that knowledge. The idea that I will have this one upmanship on my family gives me a thrill that is hard to deny, and I smile slowly, knowing things are about to change, not just around here, but back at home as well.

Chapter 17

Zephyr

The mist hangs heavy in the air, a thick blanket of grey that muffles sound and obscures vision. It's early morning, and the forest surrounding MistHallow is eerily quiet, save for the soft patter of rain on leaves and the occasional distant call of a bird.

I move silently through the trees, my Fae nature allowing me to navigate the density with ease. The cold doesn't bother me, neither does the dampness seeping into my clothes, clinging to my skin like a second layer.

As I approach a small clearing, I spot a familiar figure leaning against a massive oak tree. Ignatius, his flame-red hair bright in the grey morning, is staring off into the distance, seemingly lost in thought.

"Bit damp for a fire elemental, isn't it?" I call out.

Ignatius turns, his amber eyes lighting up with amusement. "Zeph. Didn't expect to see anyone else mad enough to be out in this weather."

I shrug, moving to stand beside him under the relative shelter of the oak's branches. "You know me. I live for the drama of it all."

He snorts, a small flame dancing between his fingers as he speaks. "You're a drama queen, no doubt."

"Says the guy who just came back from erupting a volcano," I retort, raising an eyebrow.

Ignatius grins. "Ah, Feeore. That was such a magnificent release of energy. Speaking of magnificent... what do you make of our new arrival?"

I don't have to ask who he's referring to. Adelaide Black has been the talk of MistHallow since she arrived, and she hasn't left my thoughts at all.

"She has me intrigued."

"I had a little chat with her in the dining hall last night. She's got spark, that one."

"Oh? And how did that go?" *Hopefully better than my interactions with her.*

He chuckles. "About as well as you'd expect. Called me a show-off and stormed off."

Despite myself, I laugh. "Sounds about right. She doesn't seem to be one for our usual charms."

"No, she doesn't," Ignatius agrees, his expression thoughtful. "Which makes her all the more puzzling, doesn't it?"

I nod, not trusting myself to speak. Ignatius has always been perceptive, and I don't want to give away too much of my own interest in Adelaide, just yet.

We stand in companionable silence for a while, listening to the rain and watching the mist swirl around us. It's moments like these that I treasure - quiet camaraderie with someone who understands the weight of expectations and destiny.

"You know," Ignatius says suddenly, "I think she might be good for us."

Without looking at him, I ask, "How do you mean?"

"We've been at the top of the food chain here for so long, Zeph. It's easy to forget what it's like to be challenged, to have to work for someone's attention or respect."

I mull over his words, finding a kernel of truth in them. "Can't argue with that."

Before he can respond, a movement at the edge of the clearing catches my eye. A figure emerges from the mist, and I smile.

Adelaide.

She's dressed for the weather in a black raincoat, her dark hair pulled back in a messy bun. She hasn't noticed us yet, her attention focused on something in her hand - a compass, maybe?

Beside me, I feel Ignatius tense slightly. "Well, speak of the devil," he murmurs. "Morning, Adelaide! Bit early for a stroll, isn't it?"

Adelaide's head snaps up, her eyes widening as she spots us. For a moment, she looks like she might bolt. But then her jaw sets in a determined line, and she starts walking towards us.

"I could say the same to you," she replies, her voice carrying clearly despite the dampening effect of the mist. "You look like you're plotting, or skulking."

"Can't it be both?" I ask.

As she gets closer, I can see the wariness in her eyes. It's understandable, given our previous encounters.

Adelaide looks between us, her expression one of suppressed amusement. It's a start. "It could, but that doesn't make it better, only more dangerous."

"And therein lies all the fun."

"Hmm." She turns to go, but Ignatius steps forward.

"Wait," Ignatius says, his voice uncharacteristically soft. "What brings you out here so early, Adelaide?"

She hesitates, glancing between us with suspicion. I can almost see the internal debate playing out behind her eyes. Finally, she sighs. "I'm trying to keep track of the shifts," she admits, holding up what I now see is indeed a compass. "This place is confusing. I keep getting turned around."

I nod, understanding. "It gets bored and moves a lot."

"Bored?" She gives me a quizzical stare.

I nod. "Bored. Once things liven up around here, it will settle."

"And by liven up you mean..." She appears concerned, and so she should.

"He means when the term officially starts," Ignatius pipes up before I could craft a seductive response.

I shoot Ignatius a look, but he just shrugs, a small flame dancing between his fingers. Adelaide's eyes dart between us, her wariness clearly increasing.

"Right," she says, taking a step back. "Well, I should probably get going. Lots to explore before classes start."

I move forward, my movements fluid and predatory.

"Why the rush, Adelaide?" My voice is low, almost a purr. "We've barely had a chance to get acquainted."

She tenses, her hand tightening on the compass. "I think we're acquainted enough, thanks."

"Are we?" I ask, circling her slowly as Ignatius sits back to watch me work. "I don't think you know me at all, Adelaide. Not really."

She turns, keeping me in her sight. Smart girl. "I know enough," she says, her voice steady despite her obvious unease. "You're unpredictable. That means trouble."

I laugh, the sound sharp and cold. "Unpredictable? Is that what they're calling it now?" I lean in close, my breath ghosting over her ear. "I prefer savage. It has such a nice ring to it, don't you think?"

Adelaide jerks away, her eyes wide. "Stay back," she warns, but there's a tremor in her voice now.

Dark energy crackles around me, shadows seeming to deepen despite the early morning light. "Do you even know what I am, Little Dollie?"

"Why do you call me that? And no, I don't, nor do I wish to."

With a flick of my wrist, shadows coalesce around us, leaving us in a bubble of darkness. I can hear her breath coming in short, panicked gasps.

"What are you doing?" she demands, her voice high with fear.

I circle her again, letting magick tendrils trail along her arm. She flinches but doesn't pull away. That tells me a lot about her touch aversion, as I had hoped. "Dark Fae," I murmur.

The shadows pulse around us, taking on monstrous shapes. I can see the terror in Adelaide's eyes as she watches them, unable to look away.

"Fae?" she mutters. "Like faeries?"

"No. We're not your fairy tale creatures," I continue, my voice a seductive whisper. "We're not benevolent spirits or mischievous tricksters. We're the monsters that haunt your darkest nightmares."

Adelaide's breathing is ragged now, her eyes darting around frantically. "Let me go," she pleads.

For a moment, I consider pushing further. The fear rolling off her is intoxicating, awakening the darkest parts of my nature.

But there is time for that later. With a sigh, I release the magick. The shadows dissipate, leaving us back in the misty clearing. Adelaide is staring at me with fear, shaking. Without a word, she turns and runs, disappearing into the mist.

Ignatius chuckles. "Well, that was interesting, but you made her run."

"Good," I say, my voice low. "Let her run. It'll make the chase that much more satisfying."

Ignatius shakes his head, but I can see the amusement in his expression. "You're playing a dangerous game, Zeph."

"Aren't I always?" I reply, flashing him a wicked grin.

"She's stronger than that," Corvus says, joining us from seemingly out of nowhere.

"You lurking?"

"Skulking," he says with a wide grin.

I snort. "Spying."

"Protecting. Adelaide is special."

"Oh, I'm aware," I murmur. This encounter has only accelerated whatever it was I was feeling for her. I'm a creature of shadow and chaos, heir to the Dark Court. I'm not meant for relationships or anything other than a causal fling, but Adelaide has awakened something deep inside me. A beast that is unfurling and stretching its claws, hungry for more. It is clear that Corvus knows something about her we don't. Or thinks he does. Either way, this isn't a competition. Whoever gets to her first, gets her for all of us. We all know that. We don't even need to discuss it. It's an unspoken agreement between us. The thrill of the chase, the challenge of winning her over, is intoxicating.

Chapter 18

Adelaide

I stumble through the misty forest, my heart pounding. The encounter with Zephyr has left me shaken.

Dark Fae.

The monsters that haunt your darkest nightmares.

His words echo in my mind, sending chills down to my soul. I've never heard of Dark Fae before now, but I know I need to do some research. I need to know what his powers are and what he can do to me.

As I burst out of the tree line, I find myself somehow back on the grounds of MistHallow. The imposing gothic structure looms before me, both menacing and comforting in its solidity. I bend over, hands on my knees, trying to catch my breath and slow my racing thoughts.

What the hell just happened? One minute, I was out for an early morning walk, trying to get my bearings in this confusing place, and the next, I was trapped in a bubble of darkness with a guy who claimed to be some kind of nightmare creature.

I find it worrying that there is something undeniably alluring about Zephyr. The way he moves is fluid and predatory. The dark energy crackling around him. Even as I was terrified earlier, a part of me wanted to lean into that darkness, to let it envelop me.

"Fuck," I mutter, running a hand through my damp hair. "What is wrong with me?"

"Miss Black," Professor Blackthorn's voice comes at me out of nowhere. "Everything okay?"

I straighten up. "Yes, Professor. I went for a jog."

He nods slowly, his eyes narrowed, not quite convinced by my lie. "Indeed. There is the House choosing today for those students already here in around an hour or so. It's in the Main Hall."

"Oh? Do I need to bring anything?"

"Just yourself," he says with a friendly smile.

I give a quick nod, trying to keep my composure. "Thank you, Professor. I'll be there."

As Blackthorn walks away, I take a deep breath. The House choosing. What does that mean? It's another step into this strange new world I've found myself in. Part of me is excited, curious to see where I'll end up. But another part is terrified. What if I don't fit in anywhere? What if they take one look at me and realise I don't belong here after all?

I shake my head, trying to push away the negative thoughts. I can't let myself spiral like this.

Heading back to my room, I try to calm myself down.

I have an hour before the choosing. Enough time for a quick shower and a change of clothes. As I step into the hot water, I let it wash away some of the fear from my encounter in the woods.

Clean and dressed in fresh clothes, I take a deep breath and square my shoulders.

"You can do this, Addy," I mutter. "You belong here as much as anyone else."

Making my way to the Main Hall with the help of the map, as Orby is weirdly nowhere in sight, I feel a flutter of nerves in my stomach. The corridors are bustling now with other students heading to this choosing. I catch bits and pieces of excited chatter as I stand off to the side, feeling like a spare part.

Corvus, Zephyr, Zaiah and Ignatius stroll in, thick as thieves, whispering together, which makes me even more nervous.

As I enter the Main Hall, all thoughts of my earlier encounter with Zephyr momentarily fade away. The sheer grandeur of the space takes my breath away.

The ceiling soars high above, a masterpiece of Gothic architecture. Intricate rib vaults stretch across the expanse, meeting at beautifully carved bosses. Stained glass windows line the walls, depicting scenes from various mythologies and supernatural histories. The gloomy sunlight filtering through them casts a kaleidoscope of colours across the polished stone floor.

Massive chandeliers hang from the ceiling, their crystals catching and refracting the light. But these aren't ordinary light fixtures - the flames dancing in them seem to change colour, shifting through the spectrum in a hypnotic display.

At the far end of the hall stands a raised dais, upon which sits a long table. The professors are already seated there, their faces solemn. In the centre, Professor Blackthorn rises, his presence commanding immediate attention.

"Welcome, students of MistHallow," his voice carries effortlessly across the hall. "Today, we gather for the preliminary House choosing ceremony."

A hush falls over the crowd as Blackthorn continues.

"As some of you may know, and for the benefit of our new students, the House you are placed in changes every year. This is to encourage diversity, to challenge you to adapt, and to prevent stagnation."

He gestures to four large banners hanging behind the dais, each bearing a different symbol and colour.

"Our four Houses are Carthage, represented by blue; Athens, in green; Rome, in red; and Troy, in gold. Each House values different qualities, and each will offer you unique opportunities for growth and learning."

I lean forward, intrigued despite my lingering nerves.

"The choosing is not random, nor is it based solely on your own preferences," Blackthorn explains. "It takes into account your inherent qualities, your potential, and what environment will best foster your growth this year."

He pauses, his gaze sweeping across the gathered students. "When I call your name, please step forward. The House emblem that glows will be your home for this academic year."

My heart starts to race as Blackthorn begins calling names. I watch as student after student steps forward, each greeted by a glowing emblem and a round of applause from their new housemates.

"Corvus Sanguine," Blackthorn calls.

I tense, my gaze drawn to the enigmatic vampire.

Corvus saunters forward, looking unusually stiff. For a moment, nothing happens. Then, the blue emblem of Carthage begins to glow.

"Carthage welcomes you, Mr Sanguine," Blackthorn announces.

As Corvus makes his way to the Carthage section, his gaze meets mine briefly but intently.

"Zephyr Nightshade."

"Nightshade," I whisper. "Pretty name for a pretty face."

Zephyr moves with fluid grace, but I can see the tension in his shoulders. The green emblem of Athens lights up, and Zephyr's face remains impassive as he joins his new housemates.

"Ignatius Emberkin."

The firestarter steps forward, a grin on his face. The red emblem of Rome glows brightly, and Ignatius pumps his fist in apparent satisfaction.

"Zaiah Wishmaster."

The djinn practically floats to the front, his expression one of detached amusement. The gold emblem of Troy shimmers to life, and Zaiah gives a theatrical bow before joining the Trojan ranks.

My palms are sweating now. It has to be my turn soon.

"Adelaide Black."

All eyes turn to me, and I freeze for a moment, then force myself to move forward. The hall seems impossibly long, as I'm watched by hundreds of students and Professors as I make my way to the front. I reach the Professor and turn to face the emblems, my heart pounding so loudly I'm sure everyone can hear it.

What if none of them light up? What if I'm an outcast? Houseless? Will they banish me?

Nothing happens for what feels like an eternity. Then, slowly, the blue emblem of Carthage begins to glow.

"Carthage welcomes you, Miss Black," Blackthorn says, a hint of a smile on his face.

Inhaling deeply, I make my way to the Carthage section. As I pass Corvus, he gives me a wink that does things to my soul.

I ignore him and focus intently on Blackthorn as he continues to house everyone.

When there are no students left, Blackthorn turns to us as the other Professors rise and separate into the various Houses.

"To our new Carthaginians," Blackthorn begins, his gaze lingering on me for a moment, "I'm your Housemaster for the year. You have been chosen for your resilience, your adaptability, and your potential for leadership. Carthage values those who can rise from adversity, who can rebuild and reinvent themselves."

His words resonate deep within me, striking chords I didn't even know existed.

"Carthaginians are the phoenixes of our world," Blackthorn's voice rings out, clear and strong. "You rise from the ashes of adversity, stronger and more determined than ever. Your resilience is your greatest strength."

I stand a little straighter, feeling a spark of pride ignite in my chest.

"In Carthage, we value adaptability," he continues. "The world is ever-changing, and those who can bend without breaking will always survive. You are the water that shapes the rock, the wind that redirects the flame."

Memories of all the times I've had to adapt, to change myself to fit in or survive, flash through my mind. For once, I don't feel shame at these memories, but a sense of accomplishment.

"Leadership in Carthage isn't about ruling over others," Blackthorn's eyes seem to meet mine for a moment. "It's about inspiring change, about seeing potential where others see ruin. You are the visionaries, the ones who can build empires from the ground up."

I think of my mother, of how she's always encouraged me to stand up for myself, to forge my own path. Maybe I have more leadership potential than I realised.

"Above all," Blackthorn's voice softens slightly, "Carthage values integrity. In a world of shifting loyalties and hidden agendas, you are the constants. Your word is your bond, your actions speak louder than any proclamation."

A lump forms in my throat. Integrity. It's something I've always strived for, even when it would have been easier to lie.

Maybe this is where I'm meant to be. Maybe here, surrounded by others who value the same things I do, I can finally start to understand who I really am. In Carthage, perhaps I'll find not just a house, but a home.

"Your house colour is blue," Blackthorn continues, "representing the vast ocean that Carthage once ruled. Like the sea, you are expected to be deep, powerful, and capable of great change."

As Blackthorn goes on, I glance around at my new housemates. There's a mix of expressions - excitement, nervousness, pride. Corvus catches my eye and gives me his infuriating smirk.

Great. A whole year of dealing with him up close and personal.

But as I listen to Blackthorn describe the qualities of Carthage, I feel a sense of belonging.

"Now," Blackthorn says with a slow smile. "Let's kick this off with a quest! Who is up for the challenge?"

Corvus raises his hand, his eyes never leaving mine. I raise mine, and I frown for a moment, but I think this is all me. How will I ever know for sure, though?

But this is it. This is a new chapter in my life at Mist-Hallow, and I'd better get used to it fast or be left behind.

Chapter 19

Adelaide

As Blackthorn's eyes sweep over the raised hands, he nods approvingly. "Excellent. Group together now."

My heart races as I move to stand beside Corvus. He leans in slightly as he whispers, "Ready for an adventure, Dollie?"

I suppress a shiver, not entirely sure if it's from unease or excitement. "Born ready," I mutter back, keeping my eyes fixed on Blackthorn as I dig around in my jeans pocket for a hair tie. I find one and scoop my hair up, twirling it around into a tight bun on top of my head with an ease born from years of ballet lessons as a child. I ignore Corvus's eyes on me as I focus on Blackthorn.

The professor's eyes twinkle with something that might be amusement as he addresses us. "Your quest is to retrieve the Chalice of Carthage from the Labyrinth of Shadows."

A collective gasp ripples through the crowd. I have absolutely no clue what that means, but clearly, this is no small task.

"The Labyrinth of Shadows," Blackthorn continues, "is a magical construct that shifts and changes. It's designed to test your physical abilities, your mental fortitude and teamwork as well. The chalice is hidden at its heart."

He pauses, his gaze intensifying. "Be warned: the labyrinth is filled with illusions and traps. Trust your instincts, but more importantly, trust each other. You have until sunset to complete your quest."

With a wave of his hand, a shimmering portal appears to our left. Through it, I can see the entrance to what must be the Labyrinth - a towering arch of dark stone, beyond which lies an impenetrable mist.

"Good luck," Blackthorn says, a hint of a smile playing on his lips. "And remember, in Carthage, we rise to every challenge."

Corvus turns to me, his blue eyes gleaming with excitement. "Shall we, partner?"

I take a deep breath, squaring my shoulders. "Partner? Since when?"

He shrugs. "Might as well buddy up. Haven't you noticed we are the only two vampires in the House this year?"

I glance around but come up empty. I can't tell a vampire from a shifter in human form. "Wonder why that is?" I murmur.

"Oh, I can think of a few good reasons," Corvus

murmurs back. "Shall we?" He bows slightly, letting me pass to step through the portal behind everyone else.

The magick tingles against my skin when we pass under the stone arch, the mist swirling around us, cool and damp. The portal winks out of existence behind us, leaving us alone in the ghostly silence of the Labyrinth.

"Well," Corvus says, his voice unnaturally loud in the stillness, "this is cosy."

I roll my eyes, but I'm grateful for his attempt at humour. The oppressive atmosphere of the place is already starting to get to me.

We move forward, the mist parting reluctantly before us, only to close in again behind. The walls of the Labyrinth loom on either side, made of the same dark stone as the entrance arch. They seem to absorb what little light there is, making it difficult to see more than a few feet ahead.

"Hey!" I say suddenly. "Where is everyone else?"

Corvus looks around, eyes narrowed. "It's separated us."

"And why would it do that?" I snap, my anxiety growing that this idiot Labyrinth has forced me into solitary close proximity with a creature I don't trust one bit.

He shrugs again, unconcerned. "Let's focus on the quest, yeah? This is now a race to find the chalice first."

"So it split us up on purpose? How is that teamwork?"

He doesn't answer me, his eyes scanning our surroundings.

"Any ideas on how to navigate this place?" I ask, trying to keep my voice steady.

"In a normal maze, I'd say we should keep one hand on the wall and follow it. But something tells me this place doesn't play by normal rules."

As if to prove his point, the wall to our right suddenly shifts, melting away to reveal a new passage.

"Okay," I mutter, "that's disconcerting."

"Still got that compass on you, Dollie?"

"Nope."

"Didn't think so. Come on," Corvus says determinedly. "Let's keep moving. Standing still won't get us anywhere."

We press on, taking turns seemingly at random. The Labyrinth is constantly changing around us, passages appearing and disappearing, sometimes even as we're walking through them. It's dizzying and more than a little terrifying.

After what feels like hours of wandering, we turn a corner and find ourselves face-to-face with... ourselves.

I blink, startled. It's like looking into a mirror, except the reflection is moving independently. The other Adelaide and Corvus are staring at us with the same surprised expressions I'm sure we're wearing.

"What the fuck?" I blurt out.

Corvus hisses. "It's an illusion. Don't engage with it."

It?

But as we try to move past, our doppelgangers step into our path.

"Are you sure about that?" the other Corvus says, his

voice identical to the real one. "Maybe we're the real ones, and you're the illusions."

I feel a chill run down my spine. The other Adelaide is looking at me with pity and contempt that feels uncomfortably familiar.

"You don't belong here," she says, echoing my own deepest fears. "You're not special, you're just a mistake. A half-breed freak who doesn't fit in anywhere."

I flinch, the words hitting home harder than I'd like to admit. Beside me, Corvus is staring at me as the other Adelaide's harsh words affect me more than I'd like.

"Don't listen to them," he says.

I reach out on instinct and grab his hand. His skin is cool against mine, but there's a spark of electricity at the contact.

His loose grip on my hand tightens after a hesitation that speaks volumes. "They're just playing on our insecurities. We're real, we're here, and we're going to complete this quest."

I squeeze his hand. "You're right. Nice try other us, but we're not falling for it."

With a sound like shattering glass, the doppelgangers dissolve into mist. The passage ahead is clear.

Grinning at each other, we walk forward, still hand in hand. Neither of us mentions it, but for once in my life, I'm grateful for the contact. It's a reminder that I'm not alone in this strange, shifting world. It feels natural, which is the most unnatural thing in the world to me. I try not to dwell on it and concentrate on what I'm doing.

As we navigate the twisting passages, the Labyrinth

seems determined to test us at every turn. We round a corner, and suddenly, the floor beneath our feet begins to crumble.

"Adelaide, jump!" Corvus shouts, his hand tightening on mine.

I leap forward just as the ground gives way completely, revealing a pit of writhing shadows below. Corvus's vampiric speed allows him to dart forward and catch me mid-air, pulling me to safety on the other side of the chasm.

We stand there for a moment, hearts racing, as we stare at the void where solid ground had been just seconds ago.

"Thanks," I breathe, still clinging to his arm. "Guess my vampire half is slow on the uptake."

Corvus nods, his eyes scanning the path ahead, ignoring my remark. "We need to be more careful. This place is actively trying to take us out."

No sooner have the words left his mouth than we hear a low rumbling sound. The walls on either side of us begin to move, slowly but inexorably closing in.

"Oh, you have got to be kidding me," I mutter, looking around frantically for an escape route.

Corvus grabs my hand again. "This way!" he shouts, pulling me forward at a run.

We sprint down the narrowing corridor, the walls scraping our shoulders as we go. His vampire speed is dragging me along in its wake, and my feet are unable to keep up. I stumble, but he doesn't slow down. Instead, I seem to lift off the ground and hover behind him as he pulls me along. It's the most surreal experience I've ever encountered, and it takes my breath away.

Ahead, I can see the passage ending in a solid wall.

"Corvus, it's a dead end!" I yell, panic rising in my throat.

But he doesn't slow down. Instead, he turns mid-run and wraps one arm around my waist and shouts, "Hold on tight!"

Using his vampire strength, Corvus leaps upward just as we reach the end of the corridor.

"Eeek!" I scream as we go airborne, and I'm being held in place with just an arm.

His fingers catch the top of the wall, and with a grunt of effort, he hauls us both up and over.

We tumble to the ground on the other side, rolling away from the edge just as the walls slam together with a thunderous boom.

For a moment, we just lie there, catching our breath. Then Corvus starts to laugh. No fear, no exhaustion, no panic, only glee.

"Well," he says, sitting up and brushing dust from his clothes, "that was exciting."

"You're fucking nuts!" I retort but join in his laughter, the release of tension feeling almost euphoric. "Is it always like this once the term starts?" I ask.

Corvus grins, helping me to my feet. "Only on the good days."

He releases me and I mourn the loss of his cold skin touching mine. It seems to take the itch away that sits right under the surface.

As we continue on, I become more attuned to the Labyrinth's tricks. When a section of the floor ahead suddenly turns translucent, revealing another pit of shadows, I'm the one who spots it first.

"Wait!" I call out, grabbing the back of Corvus's suit jacket to haul him back. "Look at the floor."

He nods approvingly. "Good catch. But how do we get across?"

I push aside the niggling thought that he let me have that one and look around, noticing a series of protruding stones on the wall beside us.

"Handholds," I say, pointing. "We can climb across."

Corvus raises an eyebrow. "Risky, but it might be our only option. Ladies first?"

"Oh nice, so you can see if I drop to my death first?"

"You're immortal. You'll live," he snickers.

"Fuck off," I grunt and take a deep breath, steeling myself. Then, reaching out, I grasp the first handhold and begin to make my way across the wall. It's slow going, and my arms are soon aching with the effort, but I force myself to keep moving.

Halfway across, my foot slips. For a heart-stopping moment, I'm dangling by my fingertips over the pit of shadows.

"Adelaide!" Corvus calls out, alarm clear in his voice.

But something inside me refuses to give up. With a grunt of effort and a strength I didn't know I had, I swing my body, managing to hook my foot back onto a hold. Gritting my teeth, I continue on, finally reaching the other side.

"Vampire side, activated," Corvus calls out. "Nice work."

As soon as my feet touch solid ground, I turn back to watch Corvus make the crossing. He moves swiftly and gracefully, showcasing his supernatural abilities as he crosses the distance quickly.

He lands beside me, a note of genuine admiration in his voice. "Do you feel it?"

I grin, feeling a surge of pride. "Sort of. Yes, at the time, not so much now."

He nods as if he understands, but how can he when I don't even get it?

As we carry on deeper into the Labyrinth, the challenges become increasingly treacherous. We turn a corner and are immediately confronted by a long corridor lined with ominous-looking holes in the walls.

"I don't like the look of this," I mutter, eyeing the passage warily.

Corvus nods, his body tense. "Stay alert. Something's not right here."

We take a cautious step forward, and suddenly, a jet of flame erupts from one of the holes, nearly singeing my hair.

"Back!" Corvus shouts, pulling me against the wall as more flames shoot out in rapid succession.

The heat is intense, the roar of the fire deafening. I can feel sweat beading on my forehead as we press ourselves against the cool stone.

"We need to time this perfectly," Corvus says, his eyes darting back and forth, studying the pattern of the flames. "There's a split-second gap between bursts. We'll have to run and dodge."

I nod, my heart racing. "Oh-kay, but I'm not as quick as you!"

He grins and holds his hand out. I reach out and take it, mine shaking uncontrollably.

Corvus counts down, "Three... two... one... Now!"

We sprint forward, ducking and weaving as jets of flame erupt around us. The heat is overwhelming, and I can smell singed fabric as a flame catches the edge of my sleeve. But there's no time to stop. We keep running, guided by Corvus's keen vampire senses and my own growing instincts.

Just as we reach the end of the corridor, a final burst of flame shoots out directly in our path. Corvus grabs me and pulls me down into a slide. We skid across the stone floor, the flames passing harmlessly overhead, and tumble into the next chamber, him on top of me, crushing me with his weight.

For a moment, we lie there, panting, staring into each other's eyes. His lips are millimetres from mine, and I let out a little gasp. His gaze drops to my mouth and lingers for a heartbeat. A jolt of electricity runs through me. But then he blinks, and the moment passes. He quickly rolls off me and stands, offering a hand to help me up.

"You okay?" he asks, his voice a bit rougher than usual.

I nod, trying to ignore the lingering coolness where his body had pressed against mine. "Yeah, I'm fine. Just a bit singed." I examine the scorched edge of my sleeve ruefully.

Corvus reaches out and gently touches the burnt fabric, his cool fingers brushing my skin. "That was too close," he murmurs, then seems to catch himself and steps back.

But our reprieve is short-lived. The room around us begins to shift. The floor tilts sharply to one side, then the other. The walls seem to rotate, the ceiling becoming the floor, and vice versa.

"What the hell?" I gasp, struggling to keep my footing as the room spins around us, making me want to vomit from motion sickness.

Corvus grabs onto a protruding stone, anchoring himself. "The gravity's shifting! We need to adapt quickly!"

As he speaks, the 'floor' we're standing on suddenly becomes a wall. I start to fall, but Corvus reaches out, catching my hand. We dangle there for a moment before the room shifts again, and we scramble to find purchase on what was previously the ceiling.

"This is insane!" I shout, my mind struggling to make sense of the constantly changing orientation.

"Don't think about it!" Corvus calls back. "Just react! Trust your instincts! You have a strong vampire in you, Adelaide. Let it take over."

Taking a deep breath, I try to let go of my preconceptions about up and down. I relax and will the vampire inside me to take over. As the room continues to shift, I move with it, leaping from wall to ceiling to floor as gravity realigns itself.

Corvus and I navigate the chamber like a bizarre dance, leaping and twisting, sometimes catching each other, sometimes using the momentum of the shifts to propel ourselves forward. It's dizzying and exhilarating, and by the time we finally reach the exit, I'm not entirely sure which way is up anymore.

We stumble into the next corridor, slumping down as we wait for the world to stop spinning.

"Mind if I vom?" I blurt out, closing my eyes and clutching my head.

"Only if you mind if I do," he retorts.

Before I can respond, the air around us shimmers. Suddenly, we're surrounded by multiple versions of ourselves, each pointing down a different branching path. "Not again," I groan as we get to our feet.

"This way!" they all shout simultaneously, their voices a perfect match for ours.

I freeze, unsure which way to turn. "Corvus?" I whisper, reaching for his hand.

But when I look, there are multiples, each urging me down a different path. Panic starts to rise in my throat. Which one is real? How can I tell?

"Adelaide," they all say, "trust me. This is the right way."

I close my eyes, trying to block out the visual confusion. I think back to what Corvus said earlier about trusting my instincts. Taking a deep breath, I reach out with my senses, trying to feel for the real Corvus.

Near me, I hear a faint pulse, a familiar scent, and a pull in a certain direction. Without opening my eyes, I reach out and grab a hand. "This way," I say firmly, pulling the real Corvus down one of the paths.

As we move, I hear the illusions shattering behind us. When I finally open my eyes, we're alone in a normal corridor for once.

Corvus looks at me with something too soft for my liking. "How did you know?"

I shrug, feeling a bit surprised myself. "I felt it. Something about the others didn't feel right."

He nods slowly, a wicked smile curving up his lips. "You know me, Dollie. I'm touched."

I punch him on the arm as hard as I can, then yelp, shaking my fist out. "You're a douche, you know that?" I snap.

"I've been called worse," he chuckles. "Come. Let's finish this."

I can't help the surge of pride. We're facing these challenges together, yes, but I'm also discovering strengths I never knew I had. For the first time since arriving at MistHallow, I'm starting to see why I'm here.

"These tests seem tailored to vampires," I murmur.

"Definitely. It's why it split us up, to test us with species-built challenges."

"This maze is a dick."

"Don't say that too loudly, we aren't out of the woods yet."

Finally, after what feels like an eternity of tests and traps, we round a corner and find ourselves in a large circular chamber. A gleaming silver chalice sits in the centre on a pedestal of black marble.

"The Chalice of Carthage," Corvus breathes, his eyes wide.

We approach cautiously, alert for any final traps. But nothing happens as we draw near. The chalice sits there, innocently glinting in the dim light.

"Should I...?" I ask, my hand hovering hesitantly.

Corvus nods. "Go for it. You've more than earned it."

"It seems too easy?"

"After what we just went through? You've been watching too many Indiana Jones movies," he jokes.

"Or maybe not enough," I mutter, but I take the leap of faith and reach out.

As my fingers close around the cool metal of the chalice, there's a sudden flash of blue light. The walls of the Labyrinth melt away, and we find ourselves back in the Main Hall of MistHallow.

Blackthorn steps forward, a proud smile on his face. "Congratulations," he says. "You've successfully completed your quest and proven yourselves true Carthaginians."

I look down at the chalice in my hands, then up at Corvus. He's grinning, his usually perfect hair mussed, and his clothes slightly dishevelled from our adventure. I realise I probably look just as worse for wear, but I can't bring myself to care.

"We did it," I say, a slow smile spreading across my face.

Corvus nods, his eyes sparkling with something that

might be admiration. "We make a pretty good team, Dollie."

"Adelaide, Corvus," Blackthorn says, taking the chalice from me. "You've shown exceptional courage, resourcefulness, and teamwork today. These are the qualities we value most in Carthage. But more than that, you've demonstrated the ability to face your fears and overcome them. Adelaide, you placed your trust in Corvus and let him guide you and Corvus, you took on the mantle as a mentor to help Adelaide. You are quite the team. These are the true marks of a Carthaginian. The Chalice of Carthage is more than just a trophy. It's a symbol of the potential within each of you. Just as you two worked together to retrieve it, all of Carthage must work together this year to rise to the challenges that await us."

As Blackthorn finishes his speech, my gaze is drawn to Corvus. He's listening intently, but there's a softness to his expression that I haven't seen before. When he catches me looking, he gives me a small, genuine smile that makes my heart skip a beat.

I quickly look away, feeling a blush creep up my cheeks. What is wrong with me? This is Corvus - arrogant, infuriating Corvus who tried to compel me. I shouldn't be feeling whatever this is. Should I?

But I can't deny that something has shifted between us. Facing the challenges of the Labyrinth together, seeing each other at our most vulnerable has created a bond that I'm not sure how to define.

As Blackthorn dismisses us, Corvus leans in close.

"So, partner. Fancy grabbing a bite to eat? I don't know about you, but near-death experiences always leave me famished."

I laugh despite myself. "Sure, why not? I could eat a horse after all that."

"Well, I can't promise a horse, but I'm sure we can find something to satisfy your appetite," he says with a wink.

As we head towards the dining hall, I find myself stealing glances at Corvus. The way he moves, confident yet relaxed. The way his eyes crinkle slightly at the corners when he smiles. The way he seems to be always aware of where I am, adjusting his pace to match mine.

It's disconcerting but not entirely unpleasant.

We grab our food - a rare steak for me, a cup of synthetic blood for Corvus - and find a quiet corner to sit.

"So," Corvus says as we settle in, "that was quite the adventure, wasn't it?"

I nod, cutting into my steak. "It was intense. I've never experienced anything like that before."

"You handled yourself well," he says, and there's a note of genuine admiration in his voice that makes me look up. "Most people would have crumbled facing their deepest fears like that."

I shrug, trying to brush off the compliment. "I'm sure you've faced worse."

Corvus is quiet for a moment, twirling his cup thoughtfully. "You'd be surprised," he says finally. "We all have our demons, Adelaide. Even those of us who seem to have it all together."

There's a vulnerability in his voice that catches me off guard. For a moment, I see past the cocky exterior to the person underneath - someone who, like me, is trying to find their place in a world that doesn't always make sense.

"Well, I'm glad we faced our demons together."

Corvus looks at me, surprised. Then he smiles, a real, warm smile that transforms his face.

"Me too, Dollie," he says softly. "Me too."

Chapter 20

Adelaide

Swinging by the library on my way back to my room, I search for Dark Fae books in the magick catalogue and find the section on the third floor. Taking the stairs quickly, I find the enormous area in the corner of the floor and start my search for Introduction to Dark Fae Magick. I want to know exactly what powers Zephyr has so I can arm myself next time. Checking out the heavy tome, I make my way downstairs and out into the growing night. For someone who is supposed to be keeping a night schedule, I'm out and about more during the day than ever before. Tomorrow, I plan to rectify this.

Before I can reach the door of the North Tower, I come up short as Zaiah appears in front of me, making me jump.

"Hey, babes," he says. "Heard you won the Carthage Chalice."

"News travels fast," I murmur, staring into his white

eyes. "And no, before you say anything else, I don't wish for anything. I will never wish for anything. Okay?"

He chuckles and holds his hands up. "Okay, keep your pants on. I wasn't going there. Aren't you going to ask me if I won the Trojan Chalice?"

"Well, I wasn't, but I guess you are dying for me to ask, so, Zaiah, did you win the Trojan Chalice?"

"Why, yes, I did. Thanks for asking, Adelaide!" He beams at me, and I giggle like an idiot. This is all so normal that I forget how dangerous genies can be—well, djinn, in his case. We all know that wishes aren't as simple as that. There has to be balance.

"Well, congratulations," I say, trying to step around him. "I really should get back to my room now."

But Zaiah moves with me, blocking my path. His smile is still friendly, but the intensity in his gaze makes me uneasy.

"Everything okay, Adelaide?"

I clutch the book tighter to my chest, feeling my heart rate pick up. "I'm tired," I lie. "It's been a long day."

Zaiah takes a step closer, and I instinctively back up, finding myself pressed against the tower wall. He doesn't touch me, but he's close enough that I can feel the waves of power from his body.

My breath catches in my throat as panic begins to set in. Right now, with Zaiah so close, it feels like my skin is crawling. But he hasn't actually touched me, and a small part of my brain recognises that he's being careful not to. That's when I realise that my skin isn't itching to be away from him, but rather the opposite.

Zaiah places his hands on the wall on either side of my head, boxing me in without making contact. His white eyes bore into mine, and suddenly, I feel that strange tugging in my soul again. It's like an invisible thread is connecting us, pulling me towards him despite my fear.

"What are you doing to me?" I whisper, my voice shaky.

He tilts his head, a curious expression on his face. "Do you feel it?"

It's terrifying and exhilarating, but I feel connected to Zaiah on a fundamental level, as if our souls are recognising each other. The rational part of my brain is screaming at me to run, to push him away, but another part - a part I didn't even know existed - wants to lean in closer, even more so when I see he feels it, too. What does that mean?

My emotions are a whirlwind. Fear, curiosity, attraction, and something more profound, more primal, swirl together until I can't tell where one ends, and another begins. The book in my hands feels like an anchor, the only thing keeping me grounded in reality.

Zaiah's gaze softens, and he leans in slightly. "Adelaide," he breathes, my name sounding like a caress on his lips.

Suddenly, something inside me snaps. Before I can think about what I'm doing, I reach out with my free hand, grab a fistful of Zaiah's shirt, and pull him towards me. Our lips crash together in a deep, passionate, and completely unexpected kiss.

For a moment, Zaiah is frozen in surprise. Then, with a low groan, he responds, his lips moving against mine with a skill that makes my knees weak. It's the best kiss I've ever had. It's like fire and ice, sweet and spicy, soft and hard all at once.

My emotions explode into a kaleidoscope of sensations. The fear is still there, but it's overshadowed by a rush of desire so intense it takes my breath away. My pussy is wet, and I feel powerful and vulnerable, scared and excited. It's overwhelming and intoxicating, and for a moment, I forget everything else.

But then, as suddenly as it began, it's over. Zaiah pulls back abruptly, leaving me stumbling slightly. I open my eyes, confused and a little hurt, only to see him with his arm outstretched, palm facing outward.

My gaze follows Zaiah's arm, and I feel my body freeze in terror when I hear a high-pitched shriek that makes my blood run cold.

Hovering in mid-air, caught in Zaiah's magick, is a creature straight out of a nightmare. It's like an oversized eagle, but with distinctly supernatural elements. Its feathers shimmer with an otherworldly iridescence, and its eyes glow with an unnatural intelligence. But what holds my attention are its talons - razor-sharp and clearly meant for slicing and dicing.

The creature struggles against Zaiah's hold, its shriek rising in pitch until I want to cover my ears. But I can't move. I'm frozen in place, my back still against the tower wall, the book clutched to my chest like a shield.

As I stare at the beast, my mind reeling from the

abrupt shift from a passionate kiss to mortal danger, one thought manages to break through the panic:

What the hell is this thing?

Chapter 21

Zaiah

I felt it seconds before I pulled away from Adelaide. I sensed the danger. It was like a shift in the air, a disturbance in the magical fabric of MistHallow. I reacted purely on instinct, throwing out my hand to catch the creature mid-flight.

The Strix struggles against my magick as Adelaide lets out a scream of panic. Its razor-sharp talons are slashing uselessly in the air. Its shriek pierces the night, and I know we don't have much time before more arrive.

Without hesitation, I wrap an arm around Adelaide's waist, ignoring her startled gasp. "Hold on tight," I mutter, and in a blink, we're no longer in the courtyard but in my bedroom.

I release Adelaide and move swiftly to the windows, shutting them and drawing the heavy curtains. The room plunges into semi-darkness, lit only by the soft glow of enchanted orbs floating near the ceiling.

"Zaiah, what the fuck—" Adelaide starts, her voice shaky.

"Shh," I interrupt, holding up a hand. I close my eyes, focusing my energy. In a low voice, I mutter a call that echoes through the magical frequencies of MistHallow.

"Zephyr, Corvus, Ignatius. Come."

Moments later, when I open my eyes, the air shimmers and Zephyr swirls into the room with Corvus in his tight grip. Ignatius blooms into the room in a flaming tower that dies down to reveal his concerned face. Their expressions shift from confusion to alertness as they take in the scene.

"Strix," I say by way of explanation. "At least one, more on the way."

Corvus's eyes narrow. "Strix? Here? How is that possible?"

"What's a Strix?" Adelaide asks, her voice small and frightened.

I turn to her, taking in her pale face and trembling hands. The book she was carrying is still clutched to her as if it will save her. "It's a supernatural assassin," I explain gently. "And it seems someone has sent them to... well, to put it bluntly, take you out."

Adelaide's eyes widen in shock. "Me? Why not you?"

"I don't have that many enemies."

"Neither do I," she hisses.

"That you know of. You are new to this world, Little Dollie," Corvus murmurs.

"So who..." She trails off, looking even more scared.

"That's the question of the hour, isn't it?" Zephyr

says, his dark energy crackling around him. "The Strix aren't deployed by just anyone. Someone high up."

"What?" Adelaide shakes her head, looking lost. "I don't understand. I don't know anyone who'd want me dead. I've only just arrived here!"

I watch as Corvus moves towards her, his movements slow and non-threatening. He brushes the back of his hand over her cheek. "Hey, it's okay," he says softly. "We're not going to let anything happen to you."

In an instant, I'm next to him, smacking his hand away. "Don't touch her," I snarl.

Corvus's eyes flash red briefly, but he calms instantly and steps back.

Adelaide takes a deep breath, her shoulders relaxing slightly as she looks up at him.

A pang of jealousy shoots through me, surprising in its intensity. Our kiss is still fresh on my lips, our bond now stronger than ever, even if she doesn't know what it is yet.

But seeing her respond to Corvus stirs something primal and possessive within me.

I push the feeling aside, focusing on the matter at hand. "We need to figure out who sent the Strix and why," I say, my voice perhaps a bit sharper than necessary.

Ignatius, who's been unusually quiet, speaks up. "More importantly, we need to keep Adelaide safe until we can sort this out."

A heavy thump against the window makes Adelaide

jump, a small cry escaping her lips. Another thump follows, then another. The Strix are trying to break in.

I cross over to the windows and open the curtains a fraction. The Strix are plastered up against the window, sensing their target's presence in here. They are in a hold for now, but that won't last.

I move instinctively, placing myself between Adelaide and the window. "We need to get her back to her tower," I say. "It's protected."

Adelaide, still standing close to Corvus, shakes her head. "But Corvus could get in," she says. "How is that safe?"

Corvus grins, a wicked glint in his eye. "It's not protected from me, Dollie," he says.

Zephyr steps forward, his expression more curious than anything else. "We'll all go," he says. "To make sure Adelaide is safe."

I nod, even though part of me wants to protest. The bond I share with Adelaide - the one I've been subtly strengthening since she arrived - pulses with a need to protect her. But I know that right now, her safety is more important than my desires.

"But if it's protected, how will we get in?" she asks, her voice trembling.

"I can create pocket dimensions. It will allow us into the room but then you have to be the one to draw us in."

"What? I can't do that!" she says, her pitch going up several notches.

"You can and you will," I say to her. "It is the only

way to get you back to your room without going through them." I wave my hand at the window.

"Fuck," she mutters. "Fuck!"

I place a hand lightly on Adelaide's shoulder. The contact sends a jolt through me, and I see her eyes widen in response. There's no doubt now - she feels the bond too.

With a thought, I transport us all to Adelaide's tower room into a small other world within this world.

"What now?" Adelaide asks, looking around at us all crowded into the pocket dimension.

"Step out," I murmur.

She hesitantly takes a step, and the bubble breaks.

"Now," I say, meeting her gaze, "we figure out who wants you dead and why. We keep you safe until we do."

As I say the words, I make a silent vow. Whoever is behind this, whatever their reasons, they won't succeed. I'll protect Adelaide with everything I have - not just because of the bond, not just because of the kiss, but because I know now that the force that was pulling me towards her wasn't a mere whim or a curious needling. The bond I created between us is real and it's growing every second I'm in her presence as a result.

Zephyr stops pacing as the Strix, clearly visible outside the floor-to-ceiling windows of Adelaide's tower room, circle like vultures. "It doesn't make sense," he says. "Adelaide's only just arrived at MistHallow. Who could she possibly have angered enough to warrant an assassination attempt?"

"Who have you spoken to since you arrived here?" Corvus asks.

"You guys, Blackthorn and some girl named Lyra. Oh, and Blue Water lady at the front desk. Orby!"

"Huh?" I mutter as I turn to look where she has hurried over to. The magickal orb is buzzing about, vibrating intently as she goes to it.

"Where were you earlier?" she asks.

The thing doesn't answer. It can't. It's sentient up to a point, from what I can gather. It understands but can't respond with words. It bounces around the room with such vigour that we all take cover, except Ignatius, who is a bit slow today. The orb careens towards his head and bounces off it, making him groan as we chuckle at his predicament.

"Oww," he grunts. "You little shit."

"Orby, calm down!" Adelaide crosses over to it and snatches it out of the air. It practically drags her over to the window and shakes in her hand. "I know," she murmurs, soothingly patting it. I marvel at how she is scared out of her wits, but is still taking the time to calm the pet orb, which has gone slightly nuts.

"Adelaide," Corvus mutters.

She turns to look at him and shakes her head slightly.

He knows something they aren't sharing.

"Whatever it is, we need to know. Those creatures are bad news, babes. You need to come clean."

"I can't. Professor Blackthorn said it has to remain a secret," she murmurs and flings the heavy book she has been clutching this entire time on the bed.

It catches Zephyr's eyes immediately, and he smirks. "Learning about me, Little Dollie?"

"Stop calling me that," she hisses, "and yes. *You* are bad news. I want to know what I'm up against, and something tells me I'd rather take my chances out there with them." She flings her hand out to indicate the Strix.

Zephyr's smile widens. It's slow and sinister, and I sigh. This just went from a bad situation to much, much worse.

Chapter 22

Zephyr

The strain in Adelaide's tower room has just kicked up a notch. The air is thick with magick and fear. I can taste it on my tongue, sweet and intoxicating. The Strix circling outside the window are a threat, but they're also an opportunity. An opportunity to show Adelaide exactly what I'm capable of.

I walk towards her, my movements smooth and intimidating. She tenses up, her eyes widening as she watches me approach. She's cautious, and rightfully so.

"You want to know what you're up against, Little Dollie?" I purr, my voice low and seductive. Dark energy snaps the air around me, shadows dancing at my feet. "Are you sure you can handle it?"

Adelaide takes a step back. The fear in her eyes is mesmerising, but there's curiosity. Desire, even. It sends a thrill through me.

"I'm not afraid of you," she says, but her voice trembles slightly.

I lean in closer, my lips nearly brushing her ear. "You should be," I whisper.

The others in the room fade into the background as I focus entirely on Adelaide. I can feel her rapid heartbeat and smell the adrenaline coursing through her veins. It's heady.

"We feed on fear and pain and desire. We can shape reality itself," I murmur, shadows swirling around us. "Bend light and darkness to our will. Your mind, your very soul, are playthings to us."

I reach out, trailing a dark shadow along her jawline. She flinches. "Such a delicate little thing," I muse. "So fragile. So, tempting."

"Zephyr," Corvus's voice cuts through. "That's enough."

I ignore him, my focus entirely on Adelaide. "Do you want to see more, little one?" I ask, my voice seductive. "Do you want to know what true power feels like?"

Adelaide swallows hard, conflict clear in her eyes. Fear wars with curiosity, caution with desire. It's a delicious sight.

"I..." she starts, then stops, licking her lips nervously.

I lean in closer, my lips almost brushing hers. "Just say the word," I whisper. "I can show you wonders beyond your wildest dreams. Or horrors that will haunt you for eternity. The choice is yours."

In a fleeting moment, it's just the two of us. Her eyes flutter shut, and there's a magnetic pull between us, my power beckoning to something within her. A small part of her craves to surrender to the darkness. Her longing is mouthwatering.

But then she opens her eyes, and reality rushes back. "No," she states firmly. "I won't be a part of that."

I step back. A slow, wicked smile spreads across my face. "Are you sure about that, little one?" I ask. "Because I think a part of you is very curious."

Adelaide glares at me, her fear morphing into anger. "You're right," she spits. "I am curious. Curious about how to protect myself from manipulative bastards like you."

Her words sting more than I care to admit, but I don't let it show. Instead, I laugh, the sound dark and rich. "Oh, Adelaide. You can try to resist all you want. But we both know the truth. The darkness calls to you. And sooner or later, you'll answer."

"That's enough, Zephyr," Zaiah says, stepping between us. "We have more pressing matters to deal with right now, in case you forgot."

I step back, my eyes never leaving Adelaide's. She's shaken, but there's a fire in her eyes that wasn't there before. It's intriguing.

"Of course," I say smoothly, turning to face the others. "The Strix. Any ideas on how to deal with our little pest problem that doesn't involve me going out there and annihilating them all in a massacre worthy of the darker places than MistHallow?"

"Seems pretty fucking dark here to me," Adelaide mutters, making me smile. Then she raises her voice. "If you can kill them, what are you waiting for?"

"The Strix aren't just any supernatural assassins," I say. My voice is low, but it carries an undercurrent of power that demands attention. "They're ancient creatures, born of shadow and malice. They feed on fear."

"Like you," she hisses.

My eyes fix on Adelaide's. "In many ways, they're not so different from the Dark Fae. We understand each other, you might say."

Adelaide's brow furrows. "You mean you could control them?"

I laugh, the sound rich and dark. "Control? No, little one. The Strix bow to no one except their master."

"I don't want anyone to die, even if they are trying to kill me!"

"And that is where you need to change, Adelaide. Don't you see that it is you or them? There is no negotiation."

Before she can answer, there is a loud bang, and we all turn to the windows. The Strix are being dealt with efficiently by the Order of the Crimson Shadow. "Took them long enough," I murmur.

"No shit," Ignatius agrees. "Excuse me, duty calls." He grins, and with a swipe of his hand, he uses magick to open the window, and then he turns into a firebird, flying for the opening and hurtling to the ground.

"What the hell?" Adelaide screeches as she rushes up to the windows. I reach out and slam the window closed as a Strix spots his opening and dive bombs straight for us.

"Not today, arsehole," I mutter as it slams into the protective glass.

"Ah!" Adelaide screams as it then explodes, flesh and feathers splattering over the glass in all directions. "What is this? What the fuck is this place?"

"This, Adelaide, is the world you've stepped into. Dark, dangerous, and utterly captivating."

Adelaide stumbles back from the window, her face pale. "I didn't sign up for this," she whispers.

"Oh, but you did," Corvus interjects, his voice surprisingly gentle. "The moment you accepted your place here, you became a part of this world. For better or worse."

I watch as Adelaide processes this. The fear in her eyes is slowly being replaced by something else - determination, perhaps. Or resignation. Either way, it's fascinating to witness.

"So, what now?" she asks, her voice stronger than before. "How do we stop these... Strix?"

"We don't," Zaiah says, stepping forward. "The Order will handle them now. Our job is to keep you safe and figure out who sent them."

Adelaide nods slowly, then turns to face me. "And what about you?" she asks, her eyes narrowed. "Are you going to help or just continue to try to scare me?"

I can't help but smile at her boldness. "Oh, Little Dollie. I'm always helping. You just might not like my methods."

She rolls her eyes, but I catch the slight shiver that

runs through her body. She's affected by me, whether she wants to admit it or not.

And that... is progress.

Chapter 23

Ignatius

As I soar through the night air, my form a blazing firebird, I feel a thrill of excitement. The Order of the Crimson Shadow has finally arrived, and it's time to do what we do best - maintain balance in the supernatural world.

I spot my fellow Order members on the ground, already engaged with the Strix. Keira, her silver hair glinting in the moonlight, is wielding a staff crackling with electric energy. Beside her, Roran summons thorny vines that whip through the air, ensnaring Strix left and right. Vex uses tendrils of darkness to whip around him, lashing out at Strix with deadly precision.

Then there's me. Fire personified.

I dive towards them, my fiery form illuminating the night sky. As I approach, I let out a screech that's part battle cry, part greeting.

"About bloody time!" I shout, after shifting back to my human form in a burst of flames.

"Sorry for the delay," Keira grins. "We had some trouble getting here."

Roran grunts as he sends another vine lashing out at a swooping Strix. I launch a fireball at a Strix that's diving towards Vex. It explodes in mid-air, showering us with ash and feathers.

"Questions later," Vex calls out, his voice calm despite the chaos around us. "But this is need to know."

He's right. It is. We need to know who fucking sent these arseholes. But right now, I concentrate on the battle, letting the familiar rush of adrenaline take over. Fire dances at my fingertips, responding to my will as easily as breathing.

The Strix are formidable opponents. Their razor-sharp talons and beaks are a constant threat, and their ability to move through shadows makes them slippery targets. But we're not exactly pushovers ourselves.

I send a wave of fire sweeping across the courtyard, herding a group of Strix towards Keira. She grins fiercely, her staff spinning in a blur of motion. Lightning arcs from its tip, striking the Strix with pinpoint accuracy.

Roran has created a veritable forest of thorny vines, trapping several Strix. I send jets of flame through the vines. The Strix explode, alive no more.

"Vex, your three o'clock!" I call out, spotting a Strix diving towards his blind spot.

He reacts instantly, a wall of shadow rising to meet the creature. The Strix slams into it, disoriented, and Vex's tendrils of darkness wrap around it, crushing it into nothingness.

"Appreciated," he nods, already moving to engage his next opponent.

A particularly large Strix suddenly breaks away from the main group, heading straight for Adelaide's tower. I curse under my breath. "Cover me!" I shout to the others, already shifting back into my firebird form.

I streak towards the tower, pushing myself to fly faster than I ever have before. I can see the Strix approaching the window, its talons extended, ready to shatter the glass or die trying.

I collide with the Strix in mid-air, my fiery form engulfing it. We tumble through the air, a ball of flame and shadow. I can hear its shrieks of pain and fury in my soul, feel its talons raking against my flaming skin.

The ground is rushing up to meet us. At the last second, I disengage from the Strix, spreading my wings to catch an updraft. The Strix, disoriented and badly burned, isn't so lucky. It slams into the ground with a sickening crunch.

I land nearby, shifting back to human form. The Strix twitches weakly, then dissolves into shadow, leaving nothing but a scorch mark on the grass.

"Ignatius!" Vex calls out, jogging over to me. "Status report?"

I nod, panting slightly. "Operational. Slightly singed around the edges." I joke ruefully. "Current situation?"

He glances around, his dark eyes taking in the battlefield. "I believe that was the last of them. Keira and Roran are conducting a final sweep to confirm."

As we walk back to Keira and Roran, I wonder who

sent them. The appearance of the Strix is troubling, to say the least. Someone powerful wants Adelaide dead or captured, and they're not afraid to make a bold move.

But at the same time, I can't deny the thrill of it all. This is why I joined the Order in the first place - to be on the front lines, protecting the balance of our world.

Vex's expression is serious. "This level of aggression is unprecedented. Someone's making a statement. Do we even know who the target is?"

"Adelaide Black," I murmur, looking up at the tower.

That catches everyone's attention. "Randall's daughter?"

"The one and only... that we know of," I retort. "The question is, what are we going to do about it?"

Keira twirls her staff, electricity crackling along its length. "Whatever it takes, Fire-boy."

Vex nods in agreement. "We'll maintain surveillance, but from a distance for now. Our priority should be tracing these Strix back to their source. Our presence here is disruptive."

"The Strix's presence is more disruptive," I murmur, but Vex is right. The Order of the Crimson Shadow is a force of elite warriors that operates in the shadows, and our presence at MistHallow could raise uncomfortable questions.

"Anything special about Adelaide Black that we should know?" Vex asks.

I shake my head. "Nothing we know of. She has a powerful father who is over a millennium old. I'm sure I don't need to say that it's likely he has more enemies than he has friends."

Vex snorts. "Very likely, indeed. Now, we had better go and see Ellis. He is going to have questions."

"Good luck with that," I mutter and watch them disappear to speak to the Headmaster of MistHallow. I'm exempt from such a debrief unless called in. As a student, it's my job to be here if the Order need me on campus. I'm fairly sure they will get to the bottom of this. After all, that's what the Order does best. We find the truth, no matter how deeply it's buried.

Something tells me that the truth about Adelaide Black and who wants her dead is going to be one hell of a revelation.

Chapter 24

Adelaide

A siren blares throughout the MistHallow campus, and a loudspeaker crackles.

"Everyone back to their assigned room. We are on a temporary lockdown while we secure the campus."

The adrenaline from the Strix attack is starting to wear off, leaving me feeling drained and more than a little overwhelmed.

"Well, that was exciting," Zaiah says, his tone far too cheerful for my liking. "Nothing like a near-death experience to spice up your first week at school, eh?"

I shoot him a glare. "Is this normal for MistHallow? Because if it is, I think I might need to reconsider my educational choices."

Corvus chuckles. "Trust me, Dollie, this isn't normal. Even for us."

"Quite right," Zephyr adds, his purple eyes scanning the room as if searching for hidden threats. "Someone's gone to a lot of trouble to get to you, Adelaide. The question is, why?"

I sink onto my bed, suddenly feeling very small and very alone. "I don't know," I mutter.

Zaiah snorts. "Oh, come on. You're the daughter of Randall Black. That alone makes you a target."

"Not helping, Zaiah," Corvus mutters.

I look up at them. "So, what do I do now?"

"For now, you stay put," Zephyr says. "The lockdown will give the Order time to sweep the campus and make sure there aren't any more nasty surprises lurking about."

As if on cue, a voice crackles over the intercom system as if it is speaking specifically to us. *"Attention all students and faculty. MistHallow is under temporary lockdown. Please go back to your assigned rooms until further notice. This is not a drill."*

Zaiah stretches, his movements languid and cat-like. "Well, as much as I'd love to stay and chat, we're being unduly kicked out."

He moves towards me, and for a moment, I think he's going to try to touch me, kiss me even. But he stops just short, giving me a wink instead. "Stay safe, babes. Try not to miss me too much."

With that, he disappears in a puff of smoke, leaving behind the faintest scent of exotic spices and a pang in my heart at his absence.

Corvus rolls his eyes. "Show-off," he mutters. Then he turns to me, his expression softening. "You going to be okay, Dollie?"

I nod, trying to project more confidence than I feel. "Yeah, I'll be fine. You'd better go."

He hesitates for a moment, then nods. "If you need anything..."

"I know where to find you," I finish for him, even though that's not strictly true.

He nods and turns to the door. He opens it and transforms into a bat to fly off through the arrow slit.

That leaves just Zephyr. He's been unnervingly quiet, his dark energy swirling around him like a cloak.

"I suppose you should also go," I say, not sure if I want him to stay or leave.

Zephyr smiles, and it's not a comforting expression. He takes a step closer, and I have to force myself not to back away. "What a shame," he murmurs. "You fascinate me, Adelaide Black. I like to protect what fascinates me."

"So, what does that mean, exactly?"

"It means you're mine, Little Dollie." His eyes are now completely black, and with that, he melts into the darkness, leaving no trace behind.

I'm left alone in my room, my heart pounding. The silence, after all the chaos, is almost deafening.

"Fuck's sake," I mutter. "This is ridiculous. Randall Black, you have a lot to answer for."

I spot the book on Dark Fae magick that I'd thrown on the bed earlier. Well, at least the lockdown gives me a chance to catch up on some reading, and to get on a proper night schedule, finally.

As darkness falls outside my window, I settle in with the book. The words swim before my eyes at first, my mind still reeling from the day's events. But gradually, I start to focus.

The book, "Introduction to Dark Fae Magick," is far more comprehensive than I'd initially thought. It's not just a dry textbook; it's a window into a world I never knew existed. The pages are filled with intricate illustrations of Dark Fae in various forms, from hauntingly beautiful to terrifyingly grotesque. I can see both in Zephyr. As much as I hate to admit it, he fascinates me as well, and the thought of being *his* isn't as unpleasant as it should be.

The first chapter delves into the origins of Dark Fae, tracing their lineage back to the primordial darkness that existed before light. It's a poetic, almost mythological account, but the author insists it's based on factual evidence.

As I read on, I find myself drawn into the complex hierarchy of Dark Fae society. There are courts and kingdoms, alliances and feuds that have lasted millennia with stakes higher than I can imagine. There is a coloured portrait of the Dark Fae King, who has been in power for centuries. He is regal and savage. I can tell from the cruel sneer on his face. I trace my finger over it lightly and see a familiarity that piques my interest.

"What are you hiding, Zephyr of the Dark Fae?"

The section on Dark Fae abilities is particularly fascinating. It talks about their power over shadows and darkness, their ability to manipulate emotions and dreams. Some Dark Fae, the book claims, can even bend reality itself to their will. I have seen Zephyr do that, so that raises even more questions about who he really is.

There's a whole chapter dedicated to Dark Fae and their relationships with other supernatural beings. Vampires, werewolves, witches - each has their own complex history with the Dark Fae. I can't help but wonder where Vesperidae like me fit into this intricate web.

As I delve deeper into the book, I find myself both terrified and oddly excited. This world of darkness and shadow, of power and ancient magick, is all so new, but it feels familiar somehow. Like a part of me has always known this existed, has always been waiting to discover it.

I'm so engrossed in my reading that when a knock sounds at my door, I nearly jump out of my skin.

Heart racing, I approach the door cautiously.

Peering through the peephole, I'm surprised to see Professor Blackthorn standing there, looking as calm and collected as ever.

"Professor?" I call out, not opening the door yet. "How did you get in here? I thought the tower was protected."

I hear a chuckle from the other side of the door. "Ah, Miss Black. Always asking the right questions. I set the wards on this tower myself, my dear. They recognise me."

Okay, well, that's not suspect at all.

I hesitate, eyes narrowed, not convinced. "How do I know you're really Professor Blackthorn?"

"Well," comes the amused reply, "we did have quite

an interesting conversation yesterday about your unique heritage. I left you in the library to do research."

Knowing all of that is true, I'm still cautious, but I unlock the door and open it, stepping back to let him in.

Professor Blackthorn enters, his eyes quickly scanning the room before settling on me. "I trust you're unharmed, Miss Black?"

I nod, closing the door behind him. "Yes. What were those things?" Might as well hear it from the Prof while he's here.

"Strix. Supernatural assassins sent by only the strongest of masters."

"And that would be...?"

"What we need to find out." He stares at me for a moment, making me uncomfortable. "You seem to have quite the protective circle forming around you already."

"If only I knew why," I sigh.

"Well, Corvus, I understand... he can teach you, guide you... but be aware that these men are trouble, Miss Black. Do not go into an alliance blindly."

"Alliance?"

He nods. "We need to work on building up your abilities." He snaps his fingers, and a tray appears on the dresser with a silver-domed plater and a large silver flask. "In the flask, you will find human blood," he murmurs. "This is not something we allow on campus, so do keep that to yourself for now, if you don't mind. But I believe this is the key to activating your dormant abilities."

"Oh?"

"Take small sips often. Do not try to drink the

entire thing all at once, no matter how tempting it might be. We need a slow build, not a sudden, overwhelming rush. Tomorrow night, we will meet and see if your abilities have manifested at all. I had hoped being in the Labyrinth under pressurised circumstances with Corvus would have sparked something, but I fear it didn't."

"You set me up? It was fucking dangerous in there!" I snap, angry that he could've got me killed.

"Corvus wouldn't have let that happen," he says dismissively. "And all students have to go through it at the start of every year. Had we held you back, more questions would've been asked."

I growl softly, but I don't argue. He's not wrong, after all. "Do you have any idea why the Strix were after me?" I ask.

He gives me a slow smile that does nothing to comfort me. "Who said they were after you, Miss Black?"

Our gaze holds for a few seconds before he vanishes from sight in a way that makes me think he wasn't really here at all.

"Who said they were after you? Good fucking point. The guys said so. Zaiah, in particular, was adamant it wasn't him."

I sink back onto my bed, suddenly feeling very tired. "I don't understand any of this. My head hurts."

Orby sidles over and nuzzles me, offering me some comfort in this storm I've descended into the middle of.

"Thanks, Orby. I wish you could talk."

My mind whirls with questions and possibilities. I

look down at the book on Dark Fae magick, still open on the bed next to me.

Well, they say knowledge is power, so I've got a lot of reading to do. Whatever's coming for me, or not; whatever I'm destined to become, or not; I'm determined to get on with it. I've gone twenty-one years not knowing who I really was in my skin. I know now, and I need to step up. These dormant abilities need to rise to the surface, and I need to show everyone at MistHallow that the new girl isn't a pushover.

Most especially these guys who have taken such a keen interest in me. As seductive as they are, as gorgeous as they are, as much as they make me feel alive and not like some dried-up old crone waiting to wither and die, I *have* to be wary of them. They are the most dangerous of them all.

Groaning, I flop back to the bed and then curl up on my side, propping the book up to keep reading. Vampires, I've pretty much got down. The truth isn't that far from the myth in most cases, but the rest? I don't have a fucking clue. The library and me are going to become real close in the next few days while I learn about these creatures who have set their sights on me.

Chapter 25

Adelaide

The moon is disappearing, bringing with it the growing dawn. It's been a hell of a few days at MistHallow but I'm getting the feeling that's nothing new. My brain is screaming for rest from all these thoughts that won't leave me alone about the guys, the Strix, *me*.

I push the book aside as mist swirls outside, the gloomy light barely a flicker.

I'm out almost instantly, diving straight into the deep end of oblivion.

My eyes flutter open, and I'm wide awake in my tower room—except it's different. It's charged with an energy that buzzes against my skin. The air is thick with a dark, sweet scent that wraps around me like a blanket.

My heart races. Shadows cling to the corners, watching, waiting. It feels like the room is alive and hungry, and it matches the desire building inside me.

I moan as desire floods over me. I'm alone, but it doesn't feel that way. There's a presence here, familiar and calling to the supernatural part of me that's been stirring under my skin all my life and more so since I learned what I am.

"Who's there," *I mumble, challenging the shadows, sensing another presence.*

The expectation grows, thick and irresistible. I can almost taste it, and it tastes like power, like secrets shared in the dead of night. It's intoxicating.

Zaiah appears with those trouble-promising eyes. "Knew it was you," *I mutter, but before I can say more, his presence surrounds me, drawing me in like a magnet.*

His voice is a caress that sets my nerves on edge. "Good things come to those who wait, Adelaide."

"Screw waiting."

He grins, sharp and quick. "As you wish."

"Not a wish," *I murmur as he steps closer, close enough that I feel his heat. It's unnatural, this pull between us, but it's real as the ground beneath me. His fingers trail up my arm, light but searing.*

"Fuck," *I breathe, my skin coming alive under his touch.*

"Is that an invitation?" *Zaiah teases, but his eyes hold a hunger that tells me he's serious.*

"Maybe," *I shoot back, trying to keep my voice steady. I can feel the Vesper inside me responding to his djinn magick, rising to the surface. It's there, I know it.*

His hand hovers near my cheek, and my body reacts, arching towards him. My breath hitches, a moan escaping me. "Let me touch you, Adelaide. I can make you feel things you have never experienced before."

"Please," I pant, wondering in the back of my mind why I'm allowing this. "Zaiah—" I don't finish because his touch wipes every thought from my mind as he cups my cheek, and I gasp.

"Shh," he says, close now. "Just feel, Adelaide. No more words."

The room shifts, turning into a lush garden under a moonlit sky. It's like some dark Eden, filled with the scent of jasmine that wraps around us, thick and intoxicating.

"Where are we?" I whisper, turning in a circle to gaze at the wonder around me.

"Somewhere perfect," Zaiah murmurs.

The sight takes my breath away. He is like some naked dark god, with powerful lines and stunning beauty. My fingers itch to touch him, to confirm he's real.

I reach out, trailing my hands over his chest. His warmth sears me. I can feel his heartbeat, the ripple of muscle. I look down as the breeze caresses my sensitive skin, and I notice I'm naked, too.

How did that happen?

"Keep touching me, Adelaide. It feels so good."

Every touch sends shockwaves of desire through me that have been unknown to me before now. I've had sex. Twice. Kissed a few guys here and there. Being touch aversive makes it hard to want to be with someone in this way, but Zaiah is smashing those walls down without even really doing anything except standing there, naked, hot, *with a cock the size of... I gulp. I can't even compare it to anything.*

His arms go around me, pulling me flush against him. The contact is electric as my breasts squash up against his chest.

"Zaiah," I murmur, but it sounds more like a plea than anything else. "What are you doing to me?"

"Only what you want," he whispers in my ear. "Only what you've always wanted."

"Zaiah," I breathe out, my voice trembling. He grins, that wicked curve of his lips promising trouble.

"My Adelaide," he murmurs, and then his mouth is on mine. The kiss isn't just a meeting of lips; it's a clash of who we are—Vesper and djinn, bound by night whispers and unspoken secrets. His lips are crushing mine, drawing out a response from me that's both primal and new.

I don't know how to navigate this, to let go without losing myself. But as our mouths move in sync, I realise I don't need to know. It's about trusting him, about drowning in the moment.

His fingers trail fire down my spine, each touch a spark. The garden fades, the jasmine scent just an echo behind the storm he's stirring within me.

"Fuck," I gasp against his mouth, and he chuckles, the sound vibrating through me. His hands roam possessively, fanning the flames higher.

"Let it burn, Addy," Zaiah breathes, his voice laced with sin. "Let it consume you."

When he guides us to down, I'm back on my bed, the cool sheets welcome against the heat of Zaiah's skin as he presses down on me. His hips grind against mine, drawing out ragged moans from deep in my soul.

"Fuck, Zaiah," I pant. "Don't stop."

"Never," he growls, his voice raw.

He plunges his cock inside my pussy with one swift stroke, and I cry out, arching my back and bucking my hips. It's hard and fast, then achingly slow, teasing me to the edge. Each thrust stokes the fire in my blood, the Vesper part of me alive and clawing at the surface.

"Addy," Zaiah whispers, his lips brushing my ear. "You feel so fucking good."

His words are a caress as I roll us over, needing to take control. His hands explore every inch of me, cupping my breasts and pinching my nipples. The room is a blur as I circle my hips, driving us both wild.

"That's it, Addy. Make me come like a good boy."

My eyes snap open at these murmured words that have lit a whole new fire in me. "Fuck," I gasp.

"More," he begs shamelessly. "Give me more."

I respond by capturing his mouth in another kiss, silencing his pleas as I pick up the pace, riding him hard and fast.

"Christ, you're tight," he mutters. His fingers find my clit, circling slowly, which has me teetering on the edge.

But I don't want it yet. I want this to last.

"Ride me with your vampire speed," he pants. "Give me everything."

I hesitate. I don't have vampire speed.

But even as I think it, I know it's not true. I can feel it bubbling up. I can feel my hips moving faster.

My focus sharpens, and an ache in my teeth has me gasping in pain. Running my tongue over my top teeth, I hiss when I slice my tongue open. "Fuck," *I mutter. My nails have sharpened to claws, and I dig them into his chest.*

He groans, his cock jerking wildly inside me as I turn him on. "That's it, Mistress. Hurt me, make me bleed for you."

"Zaiah..." *His name is a mantra, a prayer, as I lose myself in the sensation. There's no room for thought, only feeling—the rod of his cock buried deep inside me, the pressure of his fingers, the relentless build of pleasure.*

"Come for me, Addy," *Zaiah urges, his voice desperate for my release.* "I need to feel you."

My response is a muffled cry, my body tightens as I convulse, my pussy clutching his cock as I come apart. Zaiah's groans mix with my moans, raw and unfiltered.

"Fuck, yes," *I gasp, riding out the waves of my climax.*

Zaiah grips my hips and, with a quick motion, slams me back to the bed, pounding into me so hard I think I might break.

His movements become erratic, giving way to something primal. I wrap my legs around his waist, pulling him deeper, and with one final thrust, he stiffens above me as he unloads into me, filling my pussy with so much cum, I can feel it sliding back out.

Panting, I cling to Zaiah, our sweat-slicked bodies pressed against each other as we both reach that shattering brink. His cock pulses inside me, each thrust sending shockwaves through my core.

"Addy," he growls, and the sound of my name on his lips is like a spark to tinder.

"Zaiah, I—" Words fail me; they're useless when every part of me is focused on this crescendo of pleasure. But it's not just the orgasm. It's the touch. The intimacy of the moment, the connection of our souls. Tears fill my eyes as the thought of him leaving me is agonising.

For a moment, time stills. We're frozen in time, chests heaving, the only sound our ragged breaths syncing in the silence.

But then what I know is reality, seeps back in. The dream's grip loosens, but the intensity of what we've shared lingers, tethering me to Zaiah with an invisible thread.

"Fuck, I don't want this to end," I whisper, feeling the dreamworld slip away as I hold on tight to his strong arms to keep him with me.

Zaiah's fingers trace my jawline, a quiet promise in the gesture. "I'm never far away, Addy."

And then it's just darkness, the memory of his touch burning on my skin. I'm left gasping for air, aching for more, knowing that when I open my eyes, the room will be empty—but the connection, that fierce and fiery bond that I now know is the tugging in my soul, will remain.

* * *

"No!"

My shout jars me. My eyes snap open, I'm met with the cold emptiness of my tower room. My skin prickles with lingering heat, Zaiah's touch is etched into every nerve ending. The sheets underneath me are damp, and I'm naked and aching.

"Fuck," I mutter, my heart still racing. The sensation of Zaiah's lips on mine clings stubbornly, refusing to fade with the rest of the dream.

But it wasn't a dream. I know it wasn't.

My body rebels against the loneliness that descends. The craving is clawing at my insides. The need to be with Zaiah, to have his arms around me, his lips on mine, his cock inside me. The logical part of my brain wants to believe it was just a dream, but the raw, primal part whispers that it was something more—a connection, a bond that spans beyond the physical realm.

My hands tremble as I rake my fingers through my hair, and I run my tongue over my regular teeth with crushing disappointment. "What have you done to me?"

I swing my legs out of bed and take the stairs to the bathroom to clean up.

Seeing the blood as I wipe, I groan. "Perfect fucking timing, as always," I mutter and reach for the tampons as a large black figure smacks against the window of the tower, somehow clinging to the sheer glass pane, the shape of his wings showing me it's a bat.

"Corvus," I mutter and glance down. "Oh, for fuck's sake! Are you kidding me?"

Chapter 26

Zaiah

The first rays of dawn are creeping through my window as I materialise back in my room, my body tingling with residual energy from the encounter with Adelaide. The dream-like connection we shared feels more real than the physical world around me, and for a moment, I have to steady myself against the wall.

"Shit," I mutter, running a hand through my hair. The scent of jasmine still clings to me, a phantom reminder of the garden we created in that shared dreamscape. It's so vivid, so tangible, that for a moment, I wonder if I've brought a piece of that world back with me.

I make my way to the window, looking out over the MistHallow grounds. The early morning mist is just beginning to lift ever so slightly, revealing the ancient trees and sprawling lawns that have been home to countless supernatural beings over the centuries. Everything seems so ordinary, so mundane compared to what just happened. But I know better. Nothing will ever be ordinary again, not after connecting with Adelaide on such a profound level.

The bond between us, the one I've been nurturing since she arrived, has grown exponentially stronger. I can feel it pulsing in what exists as my soul, a live wire connecting our essences. It's exhilarating and terrifying. When I first created this bond, I never imagined it could become something so intense. It was meant to be a way to toy with her, to make her want me. I never expected it to grow into something that consumes me.

Does she feel the same?

I've always prided myself on my control, on keeping my emotions in check. It's a necessity when you're as powerful as I am. One slip, one moment of unchecked emotion, and the consequences could be catastrophic. But Adelaide has shattered that control with a single touch, a single kiss.

My mind races, replaying every moment of our encounter. The way she responded to my touch, the fire in her eyes, the raw need in her voice. It was more than just physical attraction. It was a meeting of souls, a recognition of something more profound. Something ancient and powerful, something that goes beyond the bond I created.

It's fate.

"Fuck," I groan, leaning my forehead against the cool glass. I'm in way over my head, and I know it. I have never felt this way about anyone or anything before. I have never needed anyone in this way. It hurts to be without her. What started out as mischief has backfired in a way that has taken me by storm.

I turn away from the window, pacing the length of my room. The energy coursing through me refuses to settle. It's like my very essence is reaching out and seeking Adelaide's presence. I can feel her confusion, her desire, her strength, even from this distance. It's maddening and exhilarating.

What I feel for Adelaide goes beyond simple attraction or curiosity. It's a pull so strong, so all-encompassing, that it frightens me. And that, more than anything, is what's truly terrifying. Her strength, her vulnerability, and the way she's embracing her supernatural self is powerful. There is something about the power she holds. It's enough to make my head spin. I can sense it, just beneath the surface, waiting to be unleashed. The potential is staggering. But I don't know why. What else is there about her that could cause this?

I'm falling for her, and there isn't a damn thing I can or want to do about it.

The thought hangs in the air, heavy with implications. This is dangerous territory. A djinn and a vampire? It's unheard of. There are rules and boundaries that shouldn't be crossed. The very fabric of reality could be at stake if we were to fully combine our powers.

But since when have I ever cared about rules?

The bond between us thrums with potential. I can feel it growing stronger with each passing moment, bridging the gap between us even now. What started as my creation has become something real, something alive. It's no longer just a magickal construct; it's a living, breathing connection between our souls.

I sink onto my bed. As I close my eyes, I reach out through our bond. Even from this distance, I can sense her - her confusion, her desire, her strength. I can feel her grappling with what happened between us, trying to understand the depth of our connection.

For a moment, I consider going to her. I want to hold her, feel her warmth against me, lose myself in her eyes, explain everything, and help her understand what's happening between us.

But no. Not yet. She needs time to process what happened between us and to come to terms with the intensity of our bond. I need to get my head on straight. I need to figure out how to navigate this new reality we've created.

The world seems brighter and more vibrant. The colours are more intense, and the sounds are clearer. It's as if Adelaide has awakened something in me that has lain dormant all my life.

I try to calm my racing thoughts, but all I can see is Adelaide—her flushed skin, her parted lips, the way she writhed against me. The memory of her touch sends electricity coursing through my body.

"Fuck," I mutter, opening my eyes. This is getting out of hand. I need to regain some semblance of control.

I stand up abruptly, needing to move, to do something. My powers are swirling just beneath the surface, begging to be used. I could grant a thousand wishes right now and reshape reality on a whim. But the only wish I want to grant is my own - to be with Adelaide again.

But that's the irony here. I can't wish for anything. I'm forced to see others get their whims seen to, to create unbalance while I do it, but for me, a wish is as far away as the stars.

Chapter 27

Corvus

I cling to the window, trying desperately not to slide down the glass and hit the deck several hundred feet below. Trying to get a better look inside, I see Adelaide approach, wrapping a towel tightly around herself. Her scent hits me again, stronger now, and I have to fight to keep my composure. The smell of her blood is spellbinding, stirring something primal in my vampire soul.

She cracks the window open, her expression annoyed. "Corvus, what the hell are you doing?" she hisses. "Isn't this place supposed to be on lockdown?"

I can't respond in this form, but I flap my wings and duck inside, making her squeak with surprise. Once inside, I transform back into my human form, landing softly on the bathroom floor.

"Sorry for the dramatic entrance," I say, trying to keep my voice steady despite the overwhelming scent of her blood. "It was lifted a few minutes ago, and then I smelt your blood."

"Again? You are seriously creeping me out with that!" she snaps.

"I can't help it. You're like a drug to me," I murmur, scanning her body up and down but not seeing any harm done.

Adelaide's eyes widen slightly, and she pulls the towel tighter around herself. "I'm fine," she grits out.

It takes a moment to read between the lines, and when I do, I feel like a complete idiot. "Oh," I say eloquently. "Right. Sorry, I didn't mean to... intrude."

Adelaide rolls her eyes, but there's a hint of amusement in her expression now. "It's fine. Though maybe next time, try knocking instead of face-planting into my window?"

I chuckle, grateful for the break in tension. "Noted. Though in my defence, bats aren't known for their graceful landings."

She smiles, amusement dancing in those black depths. "Do you think I can change into a bat?"

Grinning back, I shrug. "Maybe a half-bat. Ooh, maybe like a human head but with a bat's body! Or—"

"Oh, shut up," she laughs, throwing her bath sponge at me. "Blackthorn says you're meant to be my mentor, not some goof who makes fun of me."

I catch the sponge with ease, my vampire reflexes kicking in. "I can be both," I say with a wink. "A mentor with a sense of humour. It's a package deal."

Adelaide shakes her head, but I can see the smile tugging at her lips. "Lucky me," she says dryly.

The air between us shifts, becoming charged with something more than just playful banter. I'm acutely aware of her state of undress, the thin towel barely concealing her curves. The scent of her blood is still strong, mixing with the lingering smell of her arousal. It's intoxicating.

"Corvus," she says softly, her voice taking on a husky quality that sends a shot of lust straight to my cock. "You should probably go."

I know she's right. I should leave, give her privacy, maintain some semblance of propriety in this time of humanity for her. But every instinct in my body is screaming at me to stay, to close the distance between us, to taste her.

"I know," I murmur, taking a step closer instead of backing away. "But I don't want to."

Adelaide's breath hitches, her pulse quickening. I can hear it, the rushing of her blood in her veins, her thumping heartbeat.

"This is a bad idea," she whispers, but she doesn't move away. If anything, she leans in slightly, her body betraying her words.

Adelaide's words hang in the air between us, but neither of us moves. I can hear her heartbeat quicken, see the flush creeping up her neck.

"Probably," I agree, my voice low. "But when has that ever stopped me?"

Her eyes flick to my lips, then back up to meet my

gaze. "Corvus," she breathes, and it's both a warning and an invitation.

I step closer, drawn in by her scent, her warmth. We're barely inches apart now. "Tell me to leave," I murmur. "Tell me you don't want this, and I'll go."

Adelaide swallows hard. Her fingers grip the edge of the towel tightly. "I... I can't," she admits.

That's all the permission I need. In one fluid motion, I close the distance between us, capturing her lips with mine. She gasps into the kiss, her body melting against me. Her lips are soft, but there's an underlying hunger that drives even more arousal to my cock.

My hands find her waist, pulling her flush against me. The thin towel does little to hide the heat of her body. Adelaide's arms wind around my neck, her fingers tangling in my hair.

I deepen the kiss, my tongue seeking entrance. She opens for me willingly, a soft moan escaping her. Her taste is intoxicating, better than I could have imagined.

But there is something else that is distinctly not her.

Zaiah.

The djinn has been with her recently. His scent is all over her. I growl, but not out of jealousy. No, it's out of a longing to have seen them wrapped around each other...

I break the kiss, panting slightly. Adelaide's eyes flutter open, confusion and desire warring in their depths.

"What's wrong?" she asks, her voice husky.

I run my thumb over her bottom lip, savouring the softness. "Zaiah's been here, hasn't he?"

Adelaide's eyes widen, a blush creeping up her cheeks. "I... how did you know?"

"I can smell him on you," I explain, my voice low. "His scent is all over you."

She looks away, guilt flashing across her face. "It was just a dream," she whispers. "At least, I think it was."

I cup her chin, gently turning her face back to me. "Not a dream, Dollie. A bend in reality. He is a little shit. Did you want it?"

"Yes," she says instantly, and that's all I need to know. "But I want you as well... what does that say about me?"

"It says that you have room for more than one in your heart, Dollie. Your vampire is stretching its muscles."

"It's a vampire thing?" she asks with a frown, and I can tell exactly what she's thinking.

I chuckle. "It is, and if you're wondering if I have more than you in my life, the answer is no."

"I wasn't thinking that! And even if you did, this between us is..."

"Is what?"

"I don't know." She sighs.

My hands rest lightly on her hips again, and I tighten the hold, pulling her closer. "Let me taste you," I murmur.

"I'm not ready for that. Biting is... I'm not ready for that."

"Who said anything about biting?" I murmur and pull her towel away.

She gasps as she gathers my meaning and shakes her head, "No."

"Yes," I murmur.

"Corvus, no." She holds her hands up, but I grasp them lightly and drop to my knees. "Fuck. No. That's gross. It's... no!"

Smiling at her, I pull a small compulsion over her. Not enough so she can still be able to tell me to go to hell, but also enough to take the edge off her inhibition.

"Corvus," her voice shakes as her knees tremble.

I let go of her hands and place my hands on her hips again, lowering my mouth to her pussy.

She moans in mortification as I flick my tongue out and taste her.

"Fuck," I groan. "Adelaide."

"Jesus," she mutters, hands over her face. "This is..." She throws her head back as my tongue presses down on her clit.

Her hands go into my hair, and I feast on her hungrily, lapping up the blood pooling in her pussy, glad I caught her before she staunched the flow with the tampon that lies uselessly on the floor next to us.

Adelaide gasps as my tongue delves deeper, exploring every inch of her perfect pussy. Her fingers tighten in my hair, holding me against her as her hips begin to rock. The taste of her blood mixed with her arousal is irresistible, driving me wild with need.

"Corvus," she moans, her voice breathy and desperate. "Oh god..."

I growl against her, the vibrations making her shudder. My hands grip her arse, pulling her closer as I devour her. Her scent surrounds me, filling my senses until there's nothing but Adelaide.

Her legs start to tremble as I focus on her clit, circling it with my tongue before sucking gently. Adelaide cries out, her back arching as she grinds against my face.

"Don't stop," she pants. "Please don't stop."

I have no intention of stopping. Not when she tastes this divine, not when her pleasure is building so beautifully.

Adelaide's moans grow louder, more desperate. Her hips move erratically as she begs for her climax. I can feel how close she is, taste it in the flood of wetness coating my tongue.

"Corvus!" she cries out as she comes, her body shaking. I hold her steady, lapping up every drop as waves of pleasure crash over her.

When her trembling subsides, I stand up. Adelaide's eyes are hazy with pleasure, her cheeks flushed. She jumps into action immediately, handing me the sponge she threw at me earlier.

Snorting, I take it from her and clean up. "Thanks," I chuckle.

Adelaide blinks. "That was intense," she breathes.

"Just wait until I can really taste you," I say, running my tongue over my fangs.

She shivers and says nothing, but there's heat in her gaze that tells me it will happen. Soon.

"See you tonight," I murmur, knowing it's time to leave now before I drag her to her bed and nail her to it with my cock whether she wants it or not.

"See you later," she murmurs and waits as I transform back into my bat form. I take one last look at Adelaide and take flight through the open window, still tasting her blood on my tongue. That was the single most erotic thing I've ever been involved in, and that's saying a lot.

Lost in thought, I almost don't notice the two figures lurking in the shadows near the base of Adelaide's tower, but they are kind of hard to miss with their very conspicuous presence here.

I bank sharply, transforming mid-air and landing gracefully on the ground. "Lucian. Asher," I growl in warning. "Bit far from your rooms, aren't we?"

Lucian steps forward, that vicious sneer making his face even uglier. "Corvus," he drawls. "Fancy meeting you here. Checking up on the new girl, are we?"

Asher chuckles, a nasty sound that sets my teeth on edge. "Yeah, real noble of you, Corvus. I'm sure the faculty would love to hear about your late-night visits to a student's room."

"Go ahead. Blackthorn knows I'm here. But you two... yeah, not so much."

Lucian shrugs, feigning innocence. "We're just taking in the night air and keeping an eye on things. You know how it is, Corvus. Gotta make sure everyone's following the rules."

The threat in his words is clear. They're looking for dirt, for any excuse to get me in trouble. But they're barking up the wrong tree. I didn't lie. Blackthorn *does* know I'm here.

"Listen carefully," I say, my voice dropping to a

dangerous whisper as I bare my fangs and hiss. "Adelaide Black is under my protection. If I so much as suspect you're planning to hurt her, or use her to get to me, I'll make you scream with so much agony, you will wish you could die. Are we clear?"

Asher takes a step forward, his fangs glinting in the moonlight. "Is that a threat, Corvus?"

I meet his gaze steadily. "It's a promise. No one fucks with her. Spread the word."

For a tense moment, we stand there, the air thick with unspoken challenges.

"Sweet dreams, Corvus," Lucian calls as he and Asher back away. "Do give our regards to the lovely Miss Black next time you see her."

I wait until I'm sure they're gone before I take to the sky again, heading back to my room. Adelaide is protected in that tower. Only Blackthorn and I can get in without an invitation. Or a pocket dimension to another world... asshat djinn.

I land gracefully in my room and transform back to human form. The encounter with Lucian and Asher has left me on edge. Their presence near Adelaide's tower was no coincidence, and their thinly veiled threats make my anger issues have anger issues.

I try to calm the rage building inside me because that will lead to no good, and more than likely, it will end up kicking my own arse. Something tells me she won't be amenable to being locked up in her tower, so she is safe from idiots like Lucian and Asher, not to mention the Strix and, more importantly, the master of those assassins.

The taste of Adelaide still lingers on my tongue, a bittersweet reminder of what just transpired between us. But now, that moment of bliss is overshadowed by the looming threat and the increasing urge to keep this Vesper safe, not just because of what she is, but who she is becoming to me.

Chapter 28

Adelaide

I stand there in shock for several moments after Corvus leaves, my body still tingling from his touch. What the actual fuck just happened?

First that insanely vivid dream, or not-dream with Zaiah, and now this with Corvus? My head is spinning. I feel like I'm losing control, like I'm being pulled in multiple directions at once. And the scariest part is that I kind of like it.

I catch sight of myself in the mirror and barely recognise the woman staring back at me. My cheeks are flushed, my lips swollen, my eyes bright with a hunger I've never seen before. Is this what embracing my vampire side looks like? Because if so, then I definitely need to do more exploring.

But first I need to sort out the human side of me. I bend to pick up the tampon still in its packet and get to work.

After a quick shower, my legs are still a bit wobbly as

I pull on a fresh pair of pjs. These two otherworldly men have made me feel things today that I have never experienced before, and I want more.

Peering into the mist of the early morning, my stomach grumbles and I turn away from the window to the dresser where the flask of human blood awaits. I haven't tried it yet. I chickened out several times during the night, but I need to do this because Professor Blackthorn is expecting me to have drunk this entire flask and he said in small and frequent doses.

With a shaking hand, I pick it up and unscrew the lid. The scent hits me and I growl quietly. My fangs drop, slicing into my tongue and lips. It's an automatic thing. I have no control over them.

I take a deep breath, steeling myself. The scent of blood is overwhelming, making my head spin. But I need to do this. I need to embrace who I am.

Slowly, I raise the flask to my lips. The first taste is indescribable. Rich, metallic, potent. My body hums with energy as I swallow, feeling the blood slide down my throat.

"Fuck," I whisper, licking my lips.

I take another sip, larger this time. The effect is instant. My senses sharpen, colours become more vivid. I can hear the rustling of leaves outside my window with crystal clarity.

My fangs ache, wanting more. It takes all my willpower not to down the entire flask in one go. But I remember Blackthorn's words about pacing myself.

Reluctantly, I screw the cap back on and set the flask down.

My reflection catches my eye again. There's a wildness in my appearance, a predatory gleam that terrifies me. Is this who I truly am?

I shake my head, trying to clear it of the savage thoughts that descend. I want to hunt, to feed, to feel my fangs slice into a warm vein...

"Fuck it," I mutter and grab the flask again and open it. I take another sip, as slowly as I can, which turns into a gulp and another. With a gasp, I drag my mouth away from the top and force myself to recap it. Slamming it back to the dresser, I cross over to the other side of the room, needing to get away from it.

"Did you know this would happen?" I murmur, glaring at the flask. "Did you know I'd want to lose control?"

My trust in Blackthorn drops a notch or two. He must've known.

Shoving my hands into my hair, I crawl back into bed and pick up the book on Dark Fae to carry on reading about Zephyr. Next time we meet, I will have a better handle on what he is capable of. Not that I can do much about it, but at least I won't be caught off guard.

I try to focus on the words in front of me, but my mind keeps drifting back to Zaiah and Corvus. The intensity of those encounters has left me reeling. Part of me wants to chalk it up to some weird vampire mating instinct, but I know it's more than that. There's a connection forming between us, something I can't quite explain but is very real and very intense.

The book falls from my hands as another wave of hunger washes over me. My gaze darts to the flask on the dresser. Just one more sip...

No. I clench my fists, fighting the urge. I need to stay in control.

I get off the bed and take my pillow and book to the window where I curl up in the small patch of weak sunlight fighting to get through the misty morning. Instantly, I feel the lethargy hit me. It's like pulling a pair of curtains closed. I yawn and settle down to keep reading.

But the longer I sit there, the worse the tiredness becomes. Yawning again, I feel my eyes close.

* * *

I jolt awake, disoriented. The book has fallen to the floor and sunlight has moved away from the window, but it is still light outside. I must have dozed off for a while.

Groaning, I stretch and check the time. I've slept most of the day away, which I suppose is what I need to be doing to get on a full night schedule. The flask of blood catches my eye. Without thinking, I get up and grab it and take another long swig before I can talk myself out of it. The effect is immediate - a rush of energy and heightened senses.

"Fuck," I mutter, recapping the flask. I need to be

more careful with this stuff. It's far too easy to lose control.

I set the flask down, trying to ignore the lingering taste of blood on my tongue. My mind is clearer now, the fog of sleep lifting. I need to get ready for my meeting with Professor Blackthorn. As I get dressed in jeans and a tee and gather my things, I can't help but think about Zaiah and Corvus. The intensity of those encounters still lingers, making my skin tingle at the memory.

But there's no time to dwell on that now. I have responsibilities, classes to attend, a whole new world of the supernatural to learn about. I can't let myself get distracted, no matter how tempting it might be. I need to stay focused. I have a lot to learn, and I'm determined to make the most of my time at MistHallow now that I'm here.

Orby appears by my side. He seems to be flitting in and out at the moment and I find that I miss him when he isn't there. "Come on then," I say to him. "Let's get this party started."

I grab the flask and shove it in my backpack, but then think better of it and take it out. Blackthorn said human blood wasn't allowed on campus. The vampires will be able to smell it a mile away.

As I descend the tower stairs, I steel myself for whatever the night might bring when I push open the tower door.

Startled, I come face to face with a burly creature, who I would say is a vampire, but I could be way off base. "Hey," I say as I close the door behind me.

He is not lurking as such, but he isn't exactly passing by either. "Hey, Adelaide, right? I'm Lucian."

"Hi, Lucian and yeah, Adelaide."

He grins, but there's something predatory in his gaze that sets me on edge. "Pleasure to finally meet you. We've all been so curious about the new third-year vampire on campus."

I force a smile, trying to keep my tone light. "Well, here I am. Nothing too exciting, I'm afraid."

Lucian takes a step closer, invading my personal space. "Oh, I wouldn't say that. A vampire coming in so late is pretty fascinating if you ask me."

My instincts are screaming at me to get away from him, but I stand my ground. "I guess. Look, I'm meeting Professor Blackthorn, I need to go."

"Of course," he says smoothly, but he doesn't move. "I just wanted to introduce myself. Maybe we could grab a drink sometime? I'd love to hear more about how you didn't know you were a vampire until recently."

"Who says I didn't?" I ask suspiciously.

That smile widens. "Word around campus."

"Well, thanks for the offer, but I'm pretty busy getting settled in," I reply, trying to sidestep him.

Lucian's hand shoots out, gripping my arm. It's not painful, but it's firm enough to stop me in my tracks and to give me the biggest ick of my entire life. My skin wants to shrivel up and crumble from his touch through my jacket. "Come on, don't be like that. We're all friends here at MistHallow."

I narrow my eyes, feeling a surge of anger. "Let go of me," I snap.

For a moment, Lucian looks like he is going to argue but then a blur of black and purple zooms past me and slams Lucian into the tower wall, ripping him away from me and making me stumble.

"Zephyr," I mutter as I see the Dark Fae snarling at the vampire he has in his grip.

"Don't *ever* touch her," Zephyr states, all coolness and calm while my heart is beating like a wild bird trying to escape my rib cage.

"We were just getting acquainted," Lucian snaps back.

"No," Zephyr says and flicks his fingers towards Lucian.

The Dark Fae magick, a black shadow of pure malevolence wraps around Lucian's throat, choking him. His eyes widen in panic as he claws at the invisible force.

Zephyr turns to me, his eyes glowing with an otherworldly light. For a moment, I see the true power of the Dark Fae, and it's disturbing. "Are you okay?"

Unable to speak, I simply nod, even though my arm feels bruised from the touch.

Zephyr turns back to Lucian, still choking away on the magick. "You dared to touch her," he growls, his tone like ice. "You need to learn your place, vampire."

Lucian's face is turning purple, his struggles growing weaker.

"Zephyr," I murmur but it's not to stop him. My

vampire side is revelling in this darkness and it's an encouragement.

Zephyr ignores me though, his focus entirely on Lucian. "You think you can touch what's mine?" he states, waving his hand gently and sending gashes across Lucian's face that make him squeal with pain.

I'm captivated. There's a dark seduction to Zephyr's savagery, and a primal part of me responds to his brutality.

Lucian's eyes roll back, his body going limp. Zephyr releases him, letting him crumple to the ground. He turns to me, his eyes still glowing with that haunting light. "No one touches you," he states coldly.

There's a part of me that wants to rail against his possessiveness, to assert my independence. But there's another part, a darker part, that is aroused by his words.

Our gazes lock and the rest of the world fades around me.

Zephyr's eyes search mine, the glow fading slightly. "You're not afraid," he murmurs.

I shake my head. "No, I'm not."

He takes a step closer, his hand reaching out to cup my cheek. His touch is gentle. "You allow me to touch you. That makes you mine to protect," he murmurs, his thumb brushing against my skin.

Before I can respond, he leans in, his lips brushing against mine in a soft, fleeting kiss. It's over before I can react, leaving me stunned and breathless.

Zephyr pulls back, his gaze boring into mine. "Mine,"

he says, and then he's gone, disappearing into the shadows as quickly as he appeared.

I stand there for a moment, my fingers touching my lips where he kissed me. My mind is a whirlwind of thoughts and emotions, trying to process what just happened.

A groan from Lucian brings me back to reality. I look down at him, still crumpled on the ground. He looks pathetic, all his earlier bravado gone.

"Get out of here," I snap, nudging him with my foot. "And if you ever come near me again, I'll let Zephyr finish what he started, *after* I'm done with you."

Lucian scrambles to his feet, giving me a wide berth as he stumbles away. I watch him go, a sense of satisfaction washing over me. I've never stood up for myself like that before, never had the power to back up my words. It feels good. I giggle and feel a weight lifting from my shoulders that I didn't know was crushing me.

Acceptance for who I really am.

I take a deep breath, as I walk towards Blackthorn's office. Zephyr is a contradiction, a puzzle I want to solve. His savagery, his possessiveness, his unexpected gentleness. And that kiss... fuck, it was barely anything, but it left me craving more.

I shake my head, trying to clear it. I need to focus. I have this meeting with Blackthorn, and I need to be on my game. But as Orby leads me to the room where Blackthorn and I met before, I can't shake the feeling that my world has just shifted, that I've taken a step down a dark path from which there's no turning back.

But I don't want to.

Blackthorn opens the door, his eyes scanning me from head to toe. "Miss Black," he greets, stepping aside to let me in. "You look different."

I raise an eyebrow as I enter his office. "Different how?"

He closes the door behind me, his gaze lingering on my face. "More alive," he says finally. "More you."

I smile, taking a seat in front of his desk. "I feel more me," I admit. "Like I'm finally waking up after a long sleep."

Blackthorn nods, taking his own seat. "Good. That means you're embracing your true nature. Now, tell me about your progress with the blood."

I shift in my seat. "It's intense," I say, choosing my words carefully. "I can feel the power in it, the energy. It is a craving, one I'm finding hard to resist." I lay it out there to see if I can tell if he knew this would happen to me.

Blackthorn leans forward, his eyes intense as he ignores my question. "And how does it make you feel? Physically, emotionally?"

I think back to the rush of energy, the heightened senses, the wild hunger. "Strong. Like I can do anything."

A slow smile spreads across Blackthorn's face. "Excellent. That's exactly how it should feel. These cravings, are you resisting them?"

I nod. "Yes, but it's hard. I want more, always. But I'm controlling it, not letting it control me."

"Good," Blackthorn says, leaning back in his chair.

"Very good. Finish the flask and then switch to synthetic blood. You can drink as much of that as you like."

"Good to know," I murmur, already planning to swing by the dining hall to grab some after this.

Inside I'm a swirling mass of dark desires and newfound power.

"Now, Miss Black, it's time we discuss your unique abilities. As a Vesper, you possess powers that go beyond those of an ordinary vampire. One of these, as I mentioned before, is the ability to enhance the powers of others."

"How does that work exactly?"

"That's what we're here to find out," Blackthorn says, standing up. He moves to a cabinet and retrieves a small, ornate box. "This contains a magical artefact. On its own, it has a limited range of influence. I want you to hold it and focus on enhancing its power."

He places the box in front of me. It's made of dark wood, intricate carvings adorning its surface. I reach out hesitantly, my fingers brushing against the cool wood.

"Go on," Blackthorn encourages. "Pick it up and concentrate. Imagine its power growing, expanding."

I take a deep breath and lift the box. It's surprisingly light. I close my eyes, trying to sense the magick. At first, there's nothing. Then, slowly, I become aware of a faint pulsing, like a heartbeat.

"I can feel something," I murmur, my eyes still closed. "It's pulsing."

"Good," Blackthorn's voice comes from somewhere to

my left. "Now, focus on that pulse. Will it to grow stronger, to expand."

I furrow my brow, concentrating hard. In my mind, I picture the pulse growing, spreading out from the box in waves. Suddenly, I feel a surge of energy. My eyes fly open.

The box in my hands is glowing, a soft blue light emanating from the carvings. Blackthorn is standing a few feet away, his eyes wide with excitement.

"Remarkable," he breathes. "The artefact's range has doubled."

I stare at the glowing box, awe and trepidation washing over me. "Is this normal?"

Blackthorn shakes his head. "No, Miss Black. This is extraordinary. Your ability to enhance is far more potent than I anticipated. With practice, who knows what you might be capable of?"

I set the box down carefully, watching as the glow fades. "What else can I do?"

Blackthorn's eyes gleam with excitement. "Let's find out, shall we? I have a few more tests prepared." He retrieves a small, iridescent stone from his desk drawer. "This is a basic protection charm," he explains, placing it in my palm. "Normally, it can shield the wearer from minor hexes within a radius of about three feet. Let's see if you can expand its range."

I close my eyes, focusing on the smooth surface of the stone. I imagine its power as a shimmering bubble, beating gently. Concentrating hard, I will the bubble to grow, to stretch outward. A tingling sensation spreads from my hand up my arm.

"Remarkable," Blackthorn murmurs. I open my eyes to see him pacing the edges of the room, waving a wand that emits sparks. "The charm is now protecting the entire office. You've increased its power tenfold."

Next, he produces a vial of swirling green liquid. "A simple healing potion," he says. "Typically, it can cure minor cuts and bruises. I want you to enhance its potency."

I cradle the vial in both hands, picturing the potion inside becoming brighter, more vibrant. The liquid begins to glow, its colour deepening to a rich emerald.

Blackthorn takes the vial, examining it closely. "Fascinating. This could now heal broken bones, possibly even severe internal injuries. The implications for magical medicine are staggering."

For the final test, Blackthorn stands before me, his expression serious. "I'm going to cast a simple illumination spell," he says. "I want you to try to enhance my magical output."

"Wait," I say. "You have magick? I thought you were a vampire?"

He smiles but doesn't answer my question which makes me even more wary about this creature now, but he is definitely helping me realise my potential. So, I push it aside and try to focus on the good.

As he begins to mutter the incantation, I imagine his power as a bright flame. I mentally stoke that flame, willing it to burn brighter and hotter.

Suddenly, the room is flooded with blinding light. I shield my eyes, spots dancing in my vision. When the glare fades, I see Blackthorn staring at his hands in awe.

"In all my years," he whispers, "I've never produced such powerful magick."

I'm drenched in sweat, my body trembling with exertion. The rush of power is intoxicating, but it's taken a toll. I collapse into my chair, breathing heavily.

"You've exceeded all expectations, Miss Black," Blackthorn says, looking both impressed and slightly concerned. "But remember, with great power comes great responsibility, and great risk."

I nod weakly, too drained to speak. Despite the exhaustion, there's a deep sense of satisfaction settling in my bones. For the first time, I feel like I'm touching the surface of my true potential. It's exhilarating but at the same time, it's scaring me beyond anything I've encountered here at MistHallow so far. "Thanks, I think. So, what happens now?"

Blackthorn sits back down behind his desk, his expression turning serious. "Now, we begin your real training. You need to learn to control these abilities, to use them effectively, and more importantly, you need to learn when not to use them."

I nod, understanding the gravity of his words. "I'm ready," I say, and I mean it. Despite the exhaustion, I feel more alive than ever before.

Blackthorn gives me a small smile. "I believe you are, but be careful. Power like yours... it can be intoxicating. Don't let it consume you."

As I leave Blackthorn's office, my mind is reeling. The extent of my abilities, the potential I possess, make me feel like I'm standing on the edge of something massive, something that could change everything.

But as I make my way to the dining hall, Orby bouncing along next to me, I touch my lips, remembering Zephyr's kiss, the dark thrill I felt watching him torture Lucian. I think about the rush of the blood, the power I felt enhancing those magical objects.

I'm walking a fine line, between control and chaos, between light and dark. Légère and Black.

I'm convinced that means something more than just two random names. I simply need to find out what.

Chapter 29

Ignatius

The dining hall is bustling with activity as I enter, the cacophony of voices and clattering dishes washing over me. My eyes scan the room, a habit born from years of being hyper-aware of my surroundings. That's when I see her standing near the synthetic blood dispenser, a look of concentration on her face as she fills a large tumbler.

My heart does that stupid little skip it seems to do whenever I catch sight of her. It's ridiculous. I'm a powerful fire elemental, for crying out loud. I shouldn't be getting flustered like some lovesick teenager.

But Adelaide is different. Special.

Whatever it is about her that makes her unique is pressing at my senses, urging me to find out as much as I can about her. Coryus already knows, but he is not talking. So that means I need to do the digging myself.

I make my way towards her, trying to appear casual.

"Hi," I say, reaching for a glass of water. "How are you after the Strix business?"

I cringe inwardly. What a fucking thing to ask her.

She turns to me with a soft giggle, and I'm struck again by how beautiful she is. Her dark hair falls straight down her back, and her eyes seem to glow with an inner fire that wasn't there before. She's changing, coming into her power, and it's a sight to behold.

"Well, hey there, Australian firestarter of the mysterious Order," she says, her eyes lighting up. "I'm doing alright, I think."

I nod, understanding that confusion all too well. "It's a lot to take in, I'm sure. Especially for someone who didn't grow up in this world." That's a testing comment, but it's as clear as the nose on my face that she didn't.

Adelaide takes a wary sip of her blood. I notice the way her eyes close briefly, savouring the taste. When she opens them again, there's a hint of embarrassment in her expression. "Yeah, that seems to be the news of the day. Everyone is talking about it, about me."

I chuckle, remembering my early days at MistHallow. "The first few weeks are always the hardest. But you seem to be adapting well."

We move to a nearby table, sitting across from each other. I'm hyper-aware of her presence, the way she moves, the subtle changes in her expression. It's like my senses are dialled up to the max around her.

"I've been meaning to ask you something. About your powers, actually."

I raise an eyebrow, intrigued. "Oh? What would you like to know?"

She hesitates for a moment as if gathering her thoughts. "Well, I know you're a fire elemental. But what exactly does that mean? What can you do?" She lowers her voice to ask, "And what is that Order thing?"

I consider her questions. It's not often that I discuss my abilities, but with Adelaide, I find myself wanting to open up.

"Well," I begin, "I can't say anything about the Order, but as a fire elemental, I have a deep connection to the element of fire. I can create and control flames, manipulate heat, and even sense thermal energy around me."

To demonstrate, I hold out my hand, palm up. With a thought, a small flame dances to life above my skin. Adelaide leans in, fascinated.

"That's amazing," she breathes. "Does it hurt?"

I shake my head, smiling. "Not at all. Fire is a part of me. It's as natural as breathing."

With a flick of my wrist, I extinguish the flame. "But it's not just about creating fire," I continue. "I can also absorb heat and flames, making me virtually fireproof. And in extreme situations, I can even transform my body into a living flame."

Adelaide's eyes widen. "Wow. That sounds incredibly powerful."

I nod, my expression turning serious. "It is. But the fire is volatile. It can warm and nurture, but it can also destroy if not properly controlled."

She nods, a flicker of understanding in her eyes. "I'm

starting to realise that myself, and it's overwhelming sometimes."

I feel a pang of sympathy, remembering my struggles with control as a small child, where I would burst into flame involuntarily. "It will get easier," I assure her. "You just need time and practice."

We fall into a comfortable silence, Adelaide sipping her blood while I take a drink of water. I study her, noticing the subtle changes in her posture, the way she holds herself with more confidence now.

"Can I ask *you* something now?"

She blinks and nods. "Fair's fair."

"What are you? Really?"

"Tell me about your Order, and I'll tell you what I really am," she counters with such ease that I choke on my laugh.

"Well, fuck, You drive a hard bargain, don't you?"

Adelaide grins at me, a mischievous glint in her eye. "I'm learning to play the game."

"Touché. Okay, how about this—I'll tell you one thing about the Order, and you tell me one thing about yourself. It's an exchange of secrets, if you will."

She considers this for a moment, then nods. "Deal. You first, seeing as I asked first."

I lean in closer, lowering my voice. "The Order of the Crimson Shadow is ancient, older than most of the supernatural races. We're tasked with maintaining balance in the magickal world."

Adelaide nods slowly, and I can see the wheels turning. "Interesting. It's my turn, I suppose." She takes a deep breath and lowers her voice to a whisper. "I'm a Vesper—half-vampire, half-human."

Now it's my turn to be surprised.

Shocked, actually.

Vespers are incredibly rare, almost mythical. "That's... wow, okay. This is definitely not what I expected you to say..." I frown at her. "That is one doozy of a secret, girl."

"Yeah, I know. But I get the feeling from what you *didn't* say that yours is as well, so we're even, right?"

I study her for a moment. "Clever girl," I murmur, impressed she read between the lines, but also slightly worried. I didn't expect that either. In fact, this woman is full of surprises. "Yeah, we're even."

"You've got a cute accent, you know," she says, standing up and taking her cup with her. "It makes me want to know more."

"Then where are you going?"

"I've got shit to learn. Catch you around, firestarter."

"Later, smartarse."

She lets out a loud laugh and wiggles her fingers at me.

I watch her walk away, a number of emotions swirling inside me. Intrigue, attraction, and a hint of unease. A Vesper. I've only ever read about them in ancient texts. They're supposed to be incredibly powerful, with abilities that surpass many supernatural creatures when fully tapped.

As I sit there, mulling over our conversation. Her secret is safe with me. It will come out eventually. It has to. It's too big to keep safe, but no fucker will hear it from me.

I finish my water and stand up, my mind racing. I need to talk to Corvus and find out if this is what he knows. If so, we can discuss it and be prepared for whatever that might mean.

Flaming out of the dining hall, I land outside Corvus's room and knock loudly. He opens the door, his eyes narrowing as he sees me. "Iggy. What's up?"

I place a hand lightly on his shirt to push him out of my way so I can enter his room, not waiting for an invitation. "We need to talk about Adelaide."

Corvus closes the door behind me. "What about her?"

I turn to face him. "Do you know what she is?"

He blinks. "Do you?"

Good. He hasn't just blurted it out. That's good. That means he will protect her. Even from me.

"Yes, she just told me."

He sneers. "Don't believe that for one second."

"Why? She told you, if you're telling the truth about knowing."

"Actually, I figured it out." He gives me a superior glare.

"Well, good for you," I murmur. "So if you know, you know we have to make sure this secret remains locked away for as long as possible."

"No shit."

"I don't believe you know," I challenge him.

"Well, I don't believe *you* know either," he retorts.

I shrug. "Look, you know something, I know something. I don't want to say in case you don't have all the facts."

"Same."

We stare at each other.

"On three?" I suggest as a trick.

"Oh, please. You expect me to fall for that."

"Nah, not really. Okay, look, I know she's rare."

"Very."

"How are we going to get past this?"

"Get her here and ask her."

I consider Corvus's suggestion for a moment. Getting Adelaide here to confirm what we know could work, but it also feels like a violation of her trust. She shared that information with me in confidence.

"No," I say finally. "We can't do that to her. She's already dealing with enough, trying to adjust to all of this. We shouldn't put her on the spot like that."

Corvus raises an eyebrow. "Since when are you so concerned about her feelings?"

I feel a flare of irritation at his tone. "Since the day I first spoke to her."

He studies me for a long moment, his dark eyes unreadable. Finally, he says, "You care about her." It's not a question.

I don't deny it. There's no point. "And you don't?"

A flicker of emotion crosses his face. "I do. A lot. But what I feel is irrelevant. What matters is keeping her safe."

I nod, relieved we're on the same page about that, at least. "Agreed. So, what do we do?"

Corvus paces the room, thinking. "We watch her. Protect her when we can. And we keep what we know to ourselves, even from each other."

"Deal," I say, and we shake on it because shit just got serious, and I can see this escalating quickly once the secret is spilt. It always does.

Chapter 30

Adelaide

After my informative chat with Ignatius, I know I have some major research to do, like I didn't have enough already. It's catching up on twenty-one years of missed supernatural study. My mind buzzes with thoughts of fire and the warmth of Ignatius's smile. Of the four men I've come to be acquainted with, well, five if you include Lucian, he is the least threatening. He is sweet and smart and super cute. I feel a friendship brewing, and I like it.

The stone walls seem to absorb the flickering light from the torches as I walk through the courtyard towards the library. The air is cool and slightly damp, carrying the scent of the forest and something else, something distinctly magickal that smells like ozone.

I nearly collide with Professor Blackthorn as he marches across the courtyard, lost in his thoughts. His tall, imposing figure looms suddenly before me, and I have to stifle a gasp of surprise.

"Miss Black," he says.

"Professor," I mutter, but then a thought strikes me, pushing past my embarrassment. "Actually, I'm glad I ran into you. I meant to ask you earlier. I was wondering... is there any way to get a magickal signal on my phone? I'd really like to call my mum. I've seen students on their phones, so there is a way, right?"

Blackthorn smiles. "Of course. Your phone?"

I pull it out of my backpack and hold it up. He places his hand over it, and, with a *zing,* it goes warm but then settles again quickly.

"There you are," he says. "You should have a signal now. You can contact your mother on the outside, but she can't contact you. Okay?"

I nod, clutching the phone to my chest like a lifeline. "Thank you, Professor. I understand."

As Blackthorn walks away, his robes swishing softly against the ground, I sink down onto a low bench near the edge of the courtyard, my fingers trembling slightly as I dial my mum's number.

It rings a few times, and then my mum answers. "Hello?"

"Mum, it's me."

"Adelaide," My mum's voice fills me with a rush of homesickness so intense it's almost painful. "Oh, sweetheart, is that really you?"

"Yes, Mum," I say, my voice thick with emotion. I have to clear my throat before I can continue. "Yeah, it's me. How are you?"

"I'm fine, love. But forget about me. Are you okay? Is everything good there?"

I can hear the worry in her voice, and it makes my chest ache. "I'm okay, Mum. It's different here, but I'm adjusting. But I really need to know that *you* are okay. No weirdness or strangers turning up?"

She giggles, and I frown. "No, no weirdness or strangers. Your father is making sure I'm quite safe."

My mouth drops open in, well, not surprise exactly, but a bit of eww, I think. The way she said that was... not good for my ears.

There's a rustling, and then Randall comes on the line, "Adelaide. You got a signal. Good. How are things?"

"Fine," I mutter. "Is Mum really okay?"

There's a pause, and I can almost see my parents exchanging glances, probably deciding how much to tell me. The silence stretches for a moment too long, and I feel anxiety building in my chest.

"Yes, she's perfectly fine," Randall says. "Are you? Has Luke started your training yet?"

"Luke?" I croak.

"Blackthorn."

"Oh, well, yeah, *Luke* and I have met a couple of times for training."

"Excellent." He breathes out what sounds like a sigh of relief and hands the phone back to Mum.

"Addy, we'll speak to you again soon."

We? Since when did they become a 'we'?

"Okay, Mum. I'll ring again soon."

"Bye, love."

"Bye, Mum."

We hang up just as Lyra crosses the courtyard, aiming straight for me. "Hey, Adelaide," she says, her tone friendly but cautious.

I smile, trying to keep my expression neutral as I rise. "Hey, Lyra." After our last conversation, I'm wary of Lyra, but I remind myself that I need allies here at Mist-Hallow. Maybe I judged her too harshly the other day.

"So," I say, forcing a smile and searching for a neutral topic, "how are things?"

"Good," she says. "Did you hear that they're naming House Captain tonight? All the students are here, so it's happening."

"Oh? No, I didn't, but that's nice. Which House did you end up in?"

"Troy," she says with a beam. "I was hoping for that this year. I need to stretch my leadership wings."

"Good, good."

"Yeah, I want House Captain," she says. "It's been a guy for the last five years running. I want to show them that girls can captain, too."

"Oh, fuck, yeah," I say with a grin as she laughs and holds her hand up for me to high-five. "Totally with you!" As our hands connect, I get a warm sense of, not camaraderie as such, but something, *girl power*, maybe. I dunno. Something positive, anyway. Maybe this can be turned around, and we could end up friends.

Lyra starts chatting about her class schedule as we make our way to the Hall. The massive doors stand open, spilling warm light and the buzz of excited voices into the corridor. As we enter, I'm struck again by the sheer grandeur of the room. The ceiling seems to stretch impossibly high, enchanted to reflect the night sky outside. Stars twinkle above us, occasionally punctuated by the streak of a comet or the soft glow of a nebula.

The room is buzzing with excitement and speculation as we stand around while the Hall fills up. I spot Corvus across the room, deep in conversation with a group of other vampires. He catches my eye and gives me a quick nod, which I return with a small smile.

Headmaster Ellis, I presume, seeing as I've never seen him before, stands at the podium, and claps his hands. The enchanted candles floating above us seem to dim slightly, focusing all attention on him.

"Good evening, students," he begins, his voice resonating through the Hall with a power that seems to vibrate in my very bones. "Tonight, we are searching for our new House Captains. In the spirit of inter-House cooperation, we will be conducting a series of cross-House activities."

A murmur ripples through the crowd. I catch sight of Ignatius across the room, and he gives me a small smile and a wave that sends warmth flooding through me. I wave back with a grin and then refocus on Ellis.

"For our first activity," Ellis continues, his eyes sweeping across the gathered students, "you will be paired with a student from another House for a magickal scavenger hunt. The pairs have been randomly selected to ensure fairness."

My stomach churns with excitement, but also anxiety

as Ellis begins reading out the pairs. The names wash over me, meaningless, until I hear a familiar one.

"Adelaide Black from Carthage," Ellis calls out, and I hold my breath. "You will be paired with Zephyr Nightshade from Athens House."

My breath catches in my throat. The protection from Lucian and that kiss swim into my mind as Zephyr sidles up to me with a cunning smile. "Adelaide."

"Zephyr," I murmur as a faculty member I recognise as the Blue Water Lady hands us an envelope with our task inside.

When I look up, the familiar tug in my soul tightens, and I glance around. My eyes lock with Zaiah's. He's standing next to a golden-haired girl, but his gaze is fixed solely on me. He smiles, and I feel that inexplicable pull towards him. It's like a physical force, drawing me in.

Without thinking, I take a step in his direction, drawn to him by whatever this is growing between us. But before I can move any further, a strong, cool hand clamps around my throat, halting me in my tracks.

"Not so fast, princess," Zephyr's low voice murmurs in my ear.

I freeze, my body tensing at his touch. Zephyr's grip isn't painful, but it's firm enough to remind me of the power he holds. I can feel the inhuman strength in his fingers, the barely contained magick vibrating through him.

"Listen carefully, Little Dollie. I want to be Athens House Captain, and seeing as you are my partner, you're going to help me get there."

I turn my head, my face neutral of all expression as my gaze bores into his. He loosens his hold on me a fraction. "Yeah, well, I want to be Carthage House Captain, and I will hold you personally responsible if I don't get it."

He chuckles, but it's dark and deadly. "Then you'd better be good at scavenger hunts."

He releases me, and I resist the urge to rub my throat. I can still feel the phantom pressure of his fingers, a reminder of the danger he represents. "I guess we'll find out," I mutter, turning to face him.

Chapter 31

Zephyr

The night air is crisp against my skin as Adelaide and I make our way across the moonlit grounds of MistHallow. The scent of magick hangs heavy in the air, tinged with the earthy aroma of the surrounding forest. I can feel the power pulsing through me, eager to be unleashed. It's a familiar sensation, this restless energy, but tonight it feels different. More intense. I wonder if it has anything to do with the woman walking beside me.

I cast a sidelong glance at Adelaide. She's trying to hide it, but I can see the nervous energy radiating off her in waves. Her eyes dart around, taking in the shadows and the strange, ethereal glow that seems to permeate MistHallow at night. It's almost endearing.

"Right then, princess," I say, breaking the silence. My voice cuts through the night air like a knife. "Let's see what we're dealing with."

I pull out the envelope containing our task list,

relishing the way Adelaide bristles at the nickname. Her eyes flash with annoyance, a spark of defiance that sends a thrill through me. It's an attractive look on her, I have to admit.

"Don't call me that, and while we're at it, don't call me Dollie either," she snaps, snatching the envelope from my hand. Her fingers brush against mine for a moment, and I feel a jolt of something. Static electricity, perhaps. Or something more.

I chuckle, low and dark. "I don't take orders from you, *princess*. Besides, there is shit you don't know about yourself yet." I lean in close. "You might be a vampire plus extras, but you're still new to this world. You'd do well to remember that."

She glares at me. "And what don't I know about myself yet? That I'm capable of kicking your arse?"

I snort, caught off guard by the sass. "Do you know who I am?"

Her eyes narrow. "A Dark Fae dickhead."

The urge to laugh and kiss her passionately war with each other. "That's Prince Dickhead, to you."

She squints harder and clicks her fingers loudly in my face. "I knew it," she hisses. "You look just like your father."

I raise an eyebrow. "Oh? Since when have you met him?"

"He's in the book I'm reading about your kind. So, Prince Dickhead, where do we start?"

"We start with me calling you princess and don't think that's just some endearment, Little Dollie," I snap, but not out of anger or frustration. I want her to know exactly what I mean.

She glowers at me but says nothing, instead focusing on the list of items we need to find. I watch as her eyes widen slightly, taking in the near-impossible task before us. The moonlight catches in her eyes, making them shine with an otherworldly light. For a moment, I'm captivated.

"A feather from a phoenix's tail," she reads aloud. "A vial of mermaid tears. A book that writes itself. A mirror that shows the future. A key that opens any lock. A flower that blooms only in moonlight. A stone that whispers secrets. A cup that never empties." She looks up at me, a mix of disbelief and excitement in her eyes. "How are we supposed to find all this in one night?"

I grin, feeling the familiar rush of adrenaline that comes with a challenge. This is what I live for - the thrill of the impossible, the chance to prove my power and cunning. "That, princess, is where the fun begins. Now, let's start with something easy, shall we? The flower that blooms only in moonlight."

Without waiting for her response, I set off towards the edge of the campus, where stone wall meets towering tree. The grass is slick with dew beneath my feet, but I move with the grace of a predator, sure-footed and silent. I can hear Adelaide hurrying to keep up, her footsteps quick and light on the ground. She doesn't move like a vampire. Not stealthy and smooth. This thing about her is needling me. How did she not know she was a vampire? How is that even possible for all this time?

What is that *extra* that makes her not a vampire but something more?

Come on, Zeph, Figure it out. This isn't like you to be so oblivious to the facts.

"And how exactly is that easy?" she asks, interrupting my thoughts, slightly out of breath. I can hear the frustration in her voice.

I stop abruptly, turning to face her. She nearly crashes into me, and I have to resist the urge to steady her. Instead, I lean in close, my voice dropping to a whisper. The proximity allows me to catch her scent that draws me in, and that I haven't been able to get out of my nasal passages since I first met her. Jasmine and blood. It's a heady combination that fires up the lust in me like nothing else ever has.

"Because, princess," I murmur, my lips nearly brushing her ear, "I happen to know exactly where to find one."

I can see the curiosity warring with caution in her eyes. It's delicious, and I want to push her further, to see just how far she'll go. There's something about Adelaide that draws me in, despite my better judgement. She's a puzzle I'm itching to solve.

"Follow me," I say, plunging into the darkness of the forest.

The trees loom overhead, their branches reaching out like gnarled fingers. Shadows dance around us, taking on strange, almost sentient forms as I pass by. I navigate the twisting paths with ease, my Dark Fae nature at home in this realm of shadow and secrets. Adelaide stumbles behind me, cursing under her breath as she trips over roots and gets caught on thorny bushes.

"You're not very graceful, are you?" I say, not bothering to hide my amusement.

"Fuck you," she grits out, but I can hear the determination in her voice. It's impressive, I have to admit. Most would be cowering in fear by now, as we enter what can only be described as a dark realm of nature, but Adelaide pushes on, her chin set in a stubborn line.

We reach a small clearing, bathed in silvery moonlight. In the centre, a single flower stands tall, its petals closed tight. The air here feels different, charged with an ancient magick that seeps into my soul.

"There," I say, pointing. "The Lunar Lily. It only blooms at the stroke of midnight."

Adelaide checks her watch, her brow furrowing. "That's in two minutes. How did you know it would be here?"

I shrug, a smirk playing on my lips. "It's part of my charm." I don't tell her about the hours I've spent exploring these woods, learning their secrets. Knowledge is power, after all, and I'm not about to give away my advantages.

As we wait, I can feel the magick in the air intensifying. The forest seems to hold its breath, anticipating the moment. Even the usual nighttime sounds - the hoot of owls, the rustle of small creatures in the underbrush - have fallen silent.

Suddenly, a beam of moonlight pierces through the canopy, landing directly on the flower. As if in slow motion, the petals begin to unfurl, revealing a blossom of such exquisite beauty that even I am momentarily stunned. The petals are a shimmering silver, edged with the faintest hint of blue. They seem to glow from within, pulsing gently in time with some unheard rhythm.

Adelaide gasps beside me, her eyes wide with wonder. "It's beautiful," she whispers, her voice filled with awe.

I nod, reaching out to pluck the flower. As my fingers brush the stem, I feel a sharp sting. Blood, so dark a red it's almost black, wells up from a small cut, and I curse under my breath. The Lunar Lily's thorns are as deadly as they are beautiful, it seems.

Adelaide hisses, and when I turn to her, her fangs are gleaming in the moonlight. *Definitely a vampire then, but still, there's that 'more' to figure out.*

In a flash of grace and speed that I have expected of her this entire time, she grabs my hand and lifts my finger to her lips. She suckles it in a move so fucking erotic my cock bounces to attention, stiff as a rod of steel.

"Fuck," I mutter as I watch her drinking my blood. I have absolutely no idea what this will do to her. Make her drunk probably. My blood is where my power lies, like most supernatural creatures. She is about to get a massive kick off this, but the crash and burn will be... interesting.

"Well," I say, breaking the tension. My voice sounds strained even to my ears. "That's new."

She lifts her head and drops my hand immediately, a look of utter horror on her face. "Fuck!" she cries out.

"I'm sorry, that was such a violation! I'm sorry, Zephyr, I don't know what came over me—"

"Hey," I say, moving into her frantic space and cupping her face so she will stop and look at me. "It's fine. You can have my blood whenever you want, princess. But I think small doses. Do you feel the rush?"

She gulps. "I did that without your consent," she murmurs. "I, of all people, should know better than that. Can you forgive me?"

"Nothing to forgive, princess," I murmur, but she still looks so forlorn, it breaks my cold, dead heart. What. The. Fuck? "Yes," I amend, tighten my grip on her. "I forgive you."

She smiles sadly. "Thank you. I won't do it again, you have my word. It's no excuse, but I'm having control issues."

"Perfectly fine excuse if you ask me."

Her smile falls away. "You're being too kind to me."

"And you are being too hard on yourself." I tuck the Lunar Lily safely into my pocket, ready to move on from this and take her hand. "Shall we?"

She nods, and we make our way back out of the forest, the air between us charged with unspoken questions and simmering tension. I can feel Adelaide's gaze on me, curious and wary. She's reassessing me. Just as I'm reassessing her.

"Next on the list," I say, consulting the paper. The writing seems to shimmer in the moonlight, the letters rearranging themselves as if alive. "A vial of mermaid tears. This should be interesting."

Adelaide raises an eyebrow, a hint of excitement creeping into her voice. "How are we going to get this?"

I grin, a plan already forming in my mind. The thrill of the hunt is coursing through my veins, made all the more potent by the unexpected developments of the night. "In the Black Lake. And I know just how to get what we need. We need to speed this up now, princess. Are you over your pity party for one?"

She gasps, her eyes wide, but then she laughs. "Only if you truly forgive me."

"Truly, madly, deeply."

"Fuck off," she mutters but relaxes again and hurries along next to me as I lead her towards the vast, dark lake.

We approach the shore. The surface is like glass, reflecting the starry sky above. It's beautiful, in a haunting sort of way. But I know the dangers that lurk beneath that placid surface.

I drop her hand and close my eyes, reaching out with my powers. The world around me fades away, replaced by a landscape of energy and life. I can feel the creatures beneath the water, their magickal forces pulsing like beacons in the depths. The merfolk are down there, their energies bright and complex. And something else... something ancient and powerful, slumbering in the deepest part of the lake.

"Watch and learn, princess," I murmur, opening my eyes. I can feel the dark power swirling around me, responding to my call.

I raise my hands, magick swirling around my fingers like living smoke. With a swift motion, I plunge my power into the lake. The water begins to churn, frothing and bubbling as if boiling. The placid surface erupts into waves, the peaceful night shattered by the roar of disturbed waters.

Suddenly, a mermaid bursts from the surface, her scales glittering in the moonlight. She's beautiful in an otherworldly way, with iridescent scales and long, flowing hair that seems to move of its own accord. But her face is contorted with anger, her eyes flashing dangerously.

"Dark Fae," she hisses, her voice like broken glass. It echoes across the water, filled with ancient power and barely contained rage. "How dare you disturb our waters!"

I smile, cold and cruel. This is a dance I know well, a game of power and intimidation. "Now, now. Is that any way to greet an ally?"

The mermaid's eyes narrow, and she bares her sharp teeth. They glint in the moonlight, razor-sharp and deadly. "We are not allies, Zephyr Nightshade. State your business and be gone."

I can feel Adelaide tensing beside me, ready for a fight. Her hand brushes against mine, and I feel a jolt of energy which does something to send my magick into a state of frantic chaos. It's distracting, but I can't afford to lose focus now. I want that Captainship. Nothing else matters.

"We need a vial of mermaid tears," I say, my voice smooth as silk. I infuse it with a hint of my power, a subtle compulsion that most creatures find hard to resist. "Surely that's not too much to ask?"

The mermaid laughs, a harsh, grating sound that sends ripples across the water's surface. "And why would we give you our tears, dark one? They are precious, not to be wasted on the whims of land-dwellers."

I smile, letting a hint of my true nature show through. The air around me darkens, shadows writhing at my feet like living things. The temperature drops, frost forming on the grass at the water's edge. "Because if you don't," I say, my voice low and deadly, "I'll freeze this lake solid and every creature in it."

The mermaid's eyes widen in fear, and I can see the moment she realises I'm not bluffing. She glances at Adelaide, perhaps hoping for some intervention, but my precious Little Dollie remains silent, watching the exchange with horrified fascination.

"Very well," the mermaid says, her voice trembling slightly. She raises a webbed hand to her eye, and a single, pearlescent tear falls into the vial I hold out. It glows faintly, containing magick beyond measure.

"A pleasure doing business with you," I say, tucking the vial away. The mermaid disappears beneath the waves without another word, leaving only ripples in her wake.

As we walk away from the lake, I can feel Adelaide's eyes boring into me. The weight of her gaze is almost physical, filled with unasked questions and conflicting emotions. I turn to face her, expecting disgust or fear. Instead, I see inquisitiveness and admiration and a growing understanding of the power dynamics at play in this world she's thrust into.

"That was interesting," she says, her voice low. There's a slight tremor in it, but whether from fear or excitement, I can't tell.

I shrug, trying to appear nonchalant. "Sometimes you have to be cruel to be kind, princess. Or, in this case, cruel to win." I pause, studying her face.

She nods slowly, and I can see the wheels turning in her head. She's learning, adapting to this world faster than I'd given her credit for. It's both impressive and slightly concerning.

"What's next?" she asks, a new determination in her voice.

I grin, feeling a surge of something that might be pride. "Now, we go hunting for a phoenix."

As we set off towards the aviary, I feel a growing respect for Adelaide. She's tougher than she looks, this Little Dollie of mine, and as this night grows, so does my interest in her.

We approach the towering structure of the aviary, its spires reaching towards the starry sky. The building is a marvel of magickal architecture, designed to house creatures of flight from the mundane to the mythical. I can hear the rustling of feathers and the soft coos of sleeping birds as we draw near.

"So, how exactly are we going to do this?"

"A simple case of pluck and run," I grin, brimming with the thrill of how dangerous this is. But I want to test her.

"Pluck and run?" she repeats in disbelief. "Jesus. I have a bad feeling about this."

"Jesus won't help you here, princess. Ready?"

"Ready?"

I grab her hand, and we run into the aviary, laughter bubbling up as we aim straight for the sleeping phoenix. I snatch a feather from its tail, earning ourselves a loud squawk as we dash away, whooping with delight that we are three items down and making excellent time as well.

Chapter 32

Adelaide

My heart is still racing from our encounter with the phoenix as Zephyr and I make our way across the moonlit grounds of MistHallow. The feather in my pocket feels warm, almost alive, and I marvel at the events of the night so far. The cool night air carries the scent of magick and possibility, and I'm excited by what might come next, with both the hunt and Zephyr.

"What's next on the list?" I ask, trying to keep my voice steady despite the adrenaline coursing through me. My vampire senses have kicked in on a massive scale from drinking Zephyr's blood. I can pick up the rustle of all the leaves, every shift in the shadows, every shuffle from the woodland creatures... every beat of Zephyr's heart. It's slow. Almost as if it is too cold to pump faster. It makes sense. His blood was cool to drink, not warm like the synthetic blood or the human blood from the flask. It has given me a kick that I know is going to be hard to resist seeking out again.

Zephyr pulls out the list, his remarkable eyes gleaming in the moonlight. The way the silvery light catches his features makes him even more cruelly beautiful. "A book that writes itself," he reads, his voice low and melodious. "Now that's an interesting challenge."

I furrow my brow, thinking. The logical part of my brain, the part that still clings to the normalcy of my old life, wants to dismiss the idea as impossible. But after everything I've seen since I arrived, I'm starting to believe that anything is possible in this new world. "Surely that's not going to be hard to find in this place?"

"You'd be surprised. That is next level magick."

"Next level?" I murmur. "As in faculty type level?" My voice cracks at the end, and it draws Zephyr's attention away from the list.

His eyes narrow, but the smile curving up his lips is wicked. "What do you know, princess?"

"The library," I murmur, remembering something I saw while looking for the book on the Dark Fae.

Zephyr nods, taking me seriously, which surprises me. I thought he would dismiss me and my ideas. There is a lot more to this creature than his savage exterior, but I would be a fool to forget those things I've seen him do.

As we make our way to the library, I study Zephyr out of the corner of my eye. I'm drawn to him in ways that, before coming here, I would say were impossible. But feeling the way I do about a certain djinn and a certain vampire, I can't really say that this is wrong, or irrational. It *feels* right. Perhaps even more so with him than the others, if that's possible. The way he manipulates the shadows, the casual display of power... it's arousing both my body and my mind. I can't explain it, and I don't want to resist it.

I move in a bit closer, marginally so he won't notice and brush my hand against the back of his. There is a spark of electricity, like a mini lightning bolt. I hiss and draw my hand back as he frowns down at his. Without looking at me, he reaches out and grips my fingers tightly. I suppress the groan of undeniable lust that shoots through me at his touch.

The library looms before us, a massive structure of stone and magick. Its spires reach towards the star-studded sky, and as we approach, I can see the faint, luminous script running along the walls, ancient words in languages long forgotten. The doors swing open silently, welcoming us. Inside, the air is thick with the scent of old books and ancient magick.

I love it. It's my new favourite place.

"So, how do we find a book that writes itself in this labyrinth?" he whispers.

I'm awed by the endless rows of shelves stretching into the darkness. The sheer scale of knowledge contained here is overwhelming, and I feel a sudden, intense desire to explore every corner, to absorb every bit of magickal lore I can.

"This way," I say, leading him deeper into the library.

We wind our way through the stacks, the shadows seeming to part before Zephyr. Books rustle on their shelves as we pass, whispering secrets to each other. I reach out to touch the spines, feeling the magick contained within each tome. It's mesmerising, and I find myself wanting more.

Finally, we reach a small alcove where a single book rests on a pedestal. Its pages are flipping on their own, words appearing and disappearing in a dizzying dance. The air around it shimmers with magick, and I can feel the power radiating from it.

"This was written by Ellis," I whisper. "I saw it the other day, but it vanished before I could get a proper look at it. Something about it... I don't know. What do you think?"

"I think you're right," Zephyr murmurs, his gaze turning to mine with a look of admiration. "Now, we just need to convince it to come with us."

I step forward, drawn by an instinct I don't quite understand. As I reach out to touch the book, this time, it lets me, and I feel a surge of power rise up. It's like nothing I've ever experienced before, a warmth that starts in my core and spreads to my fingertips. "May we borrow you for our quest?" I ask softly.

To my amazement, the book's pages flutter in what almost seems like agreement. It floats gently into my waiting hands, its weight both substantial and ethereal. I can feel the magick pulsing from it, responding to my touch.

Zephyr's eyebrows shoot up, genuine surprise etched on his features. "Well, well. Looks like you've got a way with words, princess. And more power than you realise."

I grin at him, feeling a sense of accomplishment and a growing confidence in my abilities. "Four down, four to go," I say. "What's next?"

"A mirror that shows the future," Zephyr reads, his eyes scanning the parchment. "That one might be tricky. Divination magick is notoriously unpredictable."

As we leave the library, I notice Zephyr watching me with a growing lust in his eyes.

I can relate.

I'm this close to forgetting the hunt and taking him back to my room to ravage him. The only thing that stops me is the knowledge that I have my period. Something tells me he won't be as turned on by that as Corvus was. Or let's just say, I'm not willing to find out.

"You're stronger than you give yourself credit for, Adelaide."

The use of my actual name, rather than one of his nicknames, catches me off guard. I look up at him, searching his face for any hint of mockery, but find only sincerity. It's a side of Zephyr I haven't seen before, and it makes my soul ache for his touch. All this time, pushing people away, not wanting their hands on me, suddenly has a reason. I was waiting for these four idiots. It's as clear to me as nothing ever has been before.

But I don't understand it fully. Why these four in particular and no one else?

We reach a small courtyard, where an ornate fountain stands silent in the moonlight. The water's surface is perfectly still, reflecting the stars above like a mirror. The entire area shimmers with an unearthly energy.

"Here," Zephyr says, his voice low and intense. "This fountain is said to show visions of the future on certain nights. Maybe we can convince it to work for us."

I step closer to the fountain, feeling the magick humming in the air around it. It's different from the magick of the library or the Lunar Lily - older, wilder, less predictable. Without thinking, I reach out to touch Zephyr's arm. As our skin makes contact, I feel a surge of power flow between us.

He rasps softly, gaze on mine. Zephyr's Dark Fae magick is cold and potent, mingling with my growing Vesper abilities. The combination is potent, filling me with a sense of limitless potential.

The water in the fountain begins to swirl, images forming and reforming on its surface. I see flashes of possible futures - some bright and hopeful, others dark and foreboding, and in many of them, I see Zephyr and myself, side by side. Fighting together against unseen enemies. Laughing in moments of joy. Standing before a crowd, leaders of some great change.

As the visions fade, I look up to find Zephyr staring at me with an intensity that takes my breath away. His eyes are glowing faintly, and I can feel the mystical energy still crackling between us.

"What did you see?" he asks.

I gulp, still processing the images. "Lots of things," I reply, my voice shaky. "Some good, some bad. But in a lot of them, we were together. Fighting, leading, changing things. It was intense."

Zephyr's expression is unreadable, but I feel his hand

tighten around mine. "Now, do you see why I call you princess?" he murmurs.

I blink, unable to answer that loaded question.

The moment is broken by a distant bell tolling, giving us the halfway mark. Zephyr shakes his head, as if clearing away cobwebs, and consults the list again. "Grab a vial of that, will you, and we'll move on. A key that opens any lock," he reads as I take the vial he conjured up that is floating in midair near my face and do as he asks. "Now that's going to be a challenge."

"Aren't they all?" I drawl, making him snicker.

We make our way towards the centre of the campus, laden down with our items, where the administrative buildings stand. The architecture here is more imposing, with sharp angles and gleaming surfaces. I can feel the protective magick humming in the air, warning away those who don't belong.

"The key we're looking for is kept in the Headmaster's office," Zephyr explains as we approach the main building. "It's one of the most heavily guarded artefacts in MistHallow. Getting to it won't be easy."

I eye the building warily. "How are we supposed to get past all the magickal security?"

Zephyr grins, a mischievous glint in his eye. "With a little bit of Dark Fae trickery and a whole lot of whatever you've got going on there. Are you ready to push your limits, princess?"

I take a deep breath, steeling myself. "And what would those limits be, exactly?"

"You enhance my magick," he murmurs, reaching up

to brush a stray lock of hair away from my face. "I felt it at the lake, and again before. I know what you are, princess."

"What am I?"

He gives me that wicked smile. "I'm not saying it out loud. There is a reason you and the faculty are keeping it a secret."

"I trust you," I blurt out.

His gaze softens, and that sinister smile turns genuine for the first time ever. "That means everything, Little Dollie."

"You had to go and ruin it, didn't you," I murmur.

He chuckles. "Have to remind you who you belong to."

"I don't need the reminder."

The words hang there; the unspoken ones screaming louder.

Zephyr clears his throat. "To be continued... right now, we need to focus on this. I'm going to use my powers to create a distraction and slip us past the outer defences. But once we're inside, we'll need your ability to boost my powers enough to break through the final barriers. It's risky, but it's our best shot."

I nod, fear and excitement coursing through me. "Let's do it."

Zephyr closes his eyes, concentrating. The shadows around us deepen, coalescing into shapes that look like living creatures. With a gesture, he sends them scurrying towards the building, creating a chaotic dance of darkness that draws the attention of the magickal wards and makes me gasp in wonder.

"Now," he whispers, grabbing my hand. We dash towards the entrance, slipping through the momentarily distracted defences.

Inside, the air is thick with protective magick. I can feel it pressing against us, trying to push us out. Zephyr leads us through winding corridors, always staying just ahead of the building's awakening awareness of our presence.

Finally, we reach the Headmaster's office. The door is sealed with layers upon layers of magickal locks, each more complex than the last.

"This is it," Zephyr says, his voice strained with effort. "I need you to enhance my powers, Adelaide. Focus on the connection between us, on amplifying my magick. Can you do that?"

I nod, placing my hand on the back of his. He hisses as sparks fly, and the space between us heats up. I close my eyes, concentrating on the flow of energy between us as I did with Blackthorn. Zephyr's magick is cold and powerful, the complete opposite of Blackthorn's, and I focus on making it stronger, pushing my own energy into it.

The effect is immediate and overwhelming. Zephyr grunts. His eyes are glowing brightly now, filled with power that should scare the shit out of me, but all it does is make me pant with need for him. He raises his hands, mine still pressed against his, and the shadows around us come alive, attacking the magickal locks with a preciseness that is beautiful to watch.

One by one, the barriers fall. The building shudders under the assault of our combined power. But just when I think we can't possibly succeed, the final lock breaks with a sound like shattering glass.

We stumble into the office, breathing hard. In the centre of the room, in an open box, sits a small, unassuming key. It looks ordinary but is anything but. It's waiting for us.

Zephyr snatches it up, grinning triumphantly. "We did it, princess. You were magnificent."

Before I can respond, we hear footsteps approaching. "Time to go," Zephyr says, grabbing my hand again.

We race through the corridors, my enhanced speed that has sprung up, allowing us to stay just ahead of our pursuers. As we burst out of the building, Zephyr pulls me close, wrapping us both in shadows. For a moment, the world disappears, replaced by a cold, dark void. Then we're back on the grounds, far from the administrative buildings.

"Shadow walking," Zephyr explains, seeing my confused expression. "Handy for quick getaways."

I nod, still catching my breath. The adrenaline is wearing off, leaving me feeling drained but exhilarated. "That was wild."

Zephyr laughs, a sound of pure joy that I've never heard from him before. "You were amazing in there, Adelaide. Your ability is staggering. Be very, very careful who you give that to."

"Including you?"

His face turns deadly serious as he moves in closer and cups my face, brushing his thumb over my bottom lip. "Especially me."

I lower my gaze and bite my lip in an effort not to suck his thumb into my mouth and slice his skin with my fangs so I can drink from him again. "We make a good team," I say softly instead.

"I'm not surprised, princess."

We stand there for a moment, the night air cool on my flushed skin, the weight of what we've just accomplished settling over us. I'm acutely aware of how close we are, of the electricity still fizzing between us.

Finally, Zephyr clears his throat, breaking the spell. "We should keep moving," he says, his voice slightly husky. "We still have two items left to find."

I nod, trying to ignore the way my heart is racing. "What's next?"

"A stone that whispers secrets," Zephyr reads from the list. "And after that, a cup that never empties."

As we set off in search of our next target, I can't help but feel that something has fundamentally changed between us. The connection we formed in the Headmaster's office, the way our powers intertwined... it was incredible. Powerful, addicting.

I steal a glance at Zephyr as we walk, clutching the book to me that has become a part of my soul since I picked it up. He's back to his arrogant self, but there's a new warmth in the way he looks at me, a respect that wasn't there before.

The temperature has grown colder as Zephyr, and I make our way towards the ancient stone circle near the edge of the MistHallow grounds. The mist is descending again, and our breath forms small clouds in front of us. I can feel the weight of our collected items, and I shuffle uncomfortably. We're so close to finishing the hunt, but it's not over yet.

"A stone that whispers secrets," I mutter, repeating the next item on our list. "Any ideas where we might find that?"

Zephyr's eyes gleam in the moonlight as he points towards a cluster of standing stones in the distance. "There. The Whispering Stones. They're ancient, older than MistHallow itself. If any stone can whisper secrets, it'll be one of those."

"How do you know all of this?" I ask as we approach the stone circle. I feel a chill run down my spine that has nothing to do with the cold. The air here feels different, charged with an energy that makes the hair on the back of my neck stand up. The stones loom over us, their surfaces etched with symbols I can't decipher.

"Be careful," Zephyr warns, his voice low. "These stones are powerful. They don't give up their secrets easily. It's all nature. It's all been heavily explored by myself and those who came before me. My father has maps of maps relating to this place. There are very few nooks and crannies left that haven't been chartered already."

I purse my lips. "So, you knew about the book."

He grins. "Of course I did. But you were excited to contribute."

"Contribute? How dare you? You couldn't have gotten this far without me. We are a team, remember!"

"I don't need reminding." His casual tone is infuriating, but that's the point. He is doing this on purpose.

Resisting the urge to growl at him, I nod swiftly, moving carefully between the towering monoliths. As I pass each one, I hear faint whispers, like voices just on the edge of hearing. Some sound enticing, others threatening. I try to focus, to find the one we need.

Suddenly, I feel drawn to a smaller stone near the centre of the circle. Unlike the others, its surface is smooth, unmarked. As I approach, the whispers grow louder, more distinct.

"This one," I say to Zephyr, reaching out to touch the stone.

As my fingers brush its surface, I'm hit with a flood of images and sensations. Secrets of the past, present, and future swirl through my mind. "Ahh!" I cry as it overwhelms me and becomes too much. I am dangerously close to losing my grip on reality when Zephyr's hand closes over mine, anchoring me.

"Focus, Adelaide," he says, his voice cutting through the chaos in my mind. "We need a stone that whispers secrets, not the secrets themselves."

With effort, I pull myself back, concentrating on the task. I feel the stone beneath my palm start to shift, and when I pull my hand away, a small, polished stone rests in my palm. I can still hear faint whispers coming from it, but they're contained now, manageable.

"Empathetic abilities?" Zephyr murmurs, staring at me as if I just crawled out of the rocks surrounding us.

I don't even know what he means, so I ignore him, tucking the stone safely away with our other items. "One more to go. The cup that never empties. Let's end this."

We make our way back towards the main buildings of MistHallow, both of us scanning our surroundings for anything that might lead us to our final item. As we pass by the dining hall, a thought strikes me.

"Wait," I say, grabbing Zephyr's arm. "What if it's in there? A cup that never empties would be pretty useful in a dining hall, right?"

Zephyr considers this for a moment, then grins. "Princess, I think you might be onto something. Let's check it out."

We slip into the dining hall and look around. "The refill station," I murmur and make a beeline for it with Zephyr hot on my heels.

I thrust the book at him, and he grabs it as I peer around the back of the drinks dispenser and laugh. "Gotcha. You, my friend, are out of order for a while." I snatch it up, just as Lyra and Corvus rush into the dining hall, scanning the area for whatever it is they were after. Apparently, it is the same item I'm currently waving about in triumph.

"Time to bounce," Zephyr murmurs as Corvus and Lyra charge us.

"Hey!" I yell as Zephyr grabs my arm and moves us

through time and space to the main Hall, where we shimmer into view, making me feel nauseous.

Everyone in the room turns to us. Professor Ellis stands at the front, a look of surprise on his face as we approach with our collection of magical items.

"Well," he says, his voice carrying across the hushed hall. "It seems we have our winners. Congratulations to Mr Nightshade and Miss Black."

There's a smattering of applause, some genuine, some grudging. I can see Lyra and Corvus arrive. He is pissed off but not at me. He shoots me a grin, and I smile back, hoping things are okay between us.

"And now," Ellis continues, as the rest of the groups arrive behind us, "it's time to announce our new House Captains."

My heart starts to race. This is it, the moment we've been working towards. I didn't even know there was a House Captain until Lyra mentioned it and I didn't even want it until Zephyr threatened me. But I know, and I want it so badly, I can taste it.

"For Athens House," Ellis says, "the new Captain is Zephyr Nightshade."

I turn to Zephyr, grinning. He accepts the title with a regal nod, but I can see the pride shining in his eyes.

"And for Carthage House," Ellis continues, and I hold my breath, "the new Captain is Corvus Sanguine."

For a moment, I'm sure I've misheard. But as I see Corvus step forward, accepting the title with a gracious smile, the reality sinks in. I wasn't chosen. Despite everything I've done, everything I've accomplished tonight, it wasn't enough.

I feel a hand on my shoulder and turn to see Zephyr, concern etched on his features. "Adelaide," he starts, but I shake my head.

"It's fine," I say, forcing a smile. "Congratulations on your captaincy."

"Lyra Scott, for Troy Captain."

The crowd cheers as I clap half-heartedly.

"And our Rome Captain is Asher Stanton."

Corvus growls loudly, but I ignore him and turn away, defeated and embarrassed. Why did Zephyr get it and not me? We both worked hard for this hunt, and we won. Together. It makes no sense.

As the crowd begins to disperse, I slip away, needing to be alone. The night that had started with such promise now feels hollow. I've proven myself in so many ways tonight, pushed my abilities further than I ever thought possible. But in the end, it wasn't enough. Alone in the cold dead of night, as I make my way back to my room, I wonder if it will ever be enough.

Chapter 33

Zaiah

Making my way across the MistHallow grounds, my feet barely touching the earth, I shiver. Something is coming. Something dark, something powerful and something that sets off my senses like nothing else.

The scavenger hunt has just ended, and I feel the excitement and disappointment coming from the students returning to their rooms. But there's one emotion that cuts through all the others, sharp and painful: Adelaide's disappointment.

Our bond, still new and not fully formed, pulses with her anguish. It's a sensation I'm still getting used to, this constant awareness of her emotions. Her pain calls to me, drawing me towards her, impossible to ignore.

As I approach her room, I pause, considering my options. I can't get in unless she invites me in through normal channels, however, I'm anything but normal. Instead, I close my eyes, focusing on the pocket dimension I created in her room a few days ago. With a thought, I slip into the space between realities, observing Adelaide unseen.

She's sitting on her bed, still in her clothes from the hunt, her hair dishevelled and her eyes red-rimmed. In her hands, she's toying with the small, ornate bottle I left for her. My breath catches in my throat as I watch her fingers trace the intricate designs on its surface.

Will she open it? The question hangs in the air, charged with possibility. I've been waiting for this moment, wondering if she would take this step, if she were ready for what it might mean.

Adelaide turns the bottle over in her hands, her expression full of curiosity and trepidation. I can see the battle raging in her. The caution that's kept her safe, warring with the thirst for knowledge and power that's brought her this far.

Finally, with a deep breath that visibly steadies her, she uncorks the bottle.

The effect is immediate and breathtaking. A soft, golden light emanates from the bottle, enveloping Adelaide in its warm glow. I watch, fascinated, as the light seeps into her skin, her eyes flashing with power.

The change in her is subtle but profound. Her posture straightens, and her eyes become sharper, more aware. I can feel her abilities expanding, growing in ways she probably doesn't even realise yet. It's a heady sight, one that fills me with cautious pride.

I've seen what power can do to people, how it can

corrupt and twist. But with Adelaide, there is a strength in her that goes beyond mere magickal ability.

As the golden light fades, Adelaide looks around her room, her gaze seeming to penetrate the fabric of reality. For a moment, I think she might have sensed my presence in the pocket dimension. But then her eyes move on, and I relax.

It's time, I decide. I can't keep watching from the shadows. She deserves more than that.

"Adelaide," I call softly, my voice resonating in the space between dimensions. "Can I come in?"

She starts, her eyes widening as she searches for the source of my voice. "Zaiah?" she asks, confused. "Where are you?"

"Yes," I confirm. "I'm in the pocket dimension connected to your room that I created the other day. I can enter if you give me permission."

There's a moment of hesitation, and I hold my breath, waiting for her decision. "Yes," she says. "You can come in. Were you lurking?" Her accusation comes with crossed arms and a really cute, annoyed expression.

With a thought, I step out of the pocket dimension and into her room. The air shimmers around me as I materialise, and I see Adelaide's eyes widen at the display of magick.

"Who, me?" I ask with a smile meant to disarm. "I never lurk, babes."

"Humph," she mutters but drops her defensive stance.

"Hi," I say softly, suddenly feeling awkward now that

I'm face-to-face with her. "I felt that you were upset. I wanted to check on you."

Adelaide's expression softens, a small smile tugging at the corners of her mouth. "You felt it? Through our... bond? Is that the right word for it?"

I nod slowly, moving closer to her. "Yes. It's getting stronger. I can sense your emotions more clearly now, especially when they're intense."

She looks down at the bottle in her hands, then back up at me. "Did you see...?"

"Yes," I admit. "I saw you open the bottle. How do you feel?"

Adelaide takes a deep breath, considering the question. "Different," she says finally. "Stronger, somehow. More aware. Was this from you? What was in it, Zaiah?"

I sit down next to her on the bed, close enough to feel the warmth from her body that has dimmed a bit since the last time I was close to her. She is becoming more of a vampire and less of a... I want to say human, but that can't be right, can it? A Vesperidae in our midst is unexpected. There again, so is a djinn, so I guess we were meant for each other. "It's called Essence of Awakening," I explain. "It's a very rare and powerful elixir that enhances latent magickal abilities. It only works on those who it deems worthy."

"And you think I'm worthy?" Adelaide asks, her voice small and uncertain.

"Not me," I say, touching the bottle. "Although I wouldn't disagree with the elixir's assessment."

I take her hands in mine. The contact sends a jolt of

electricity through me, our bond humming with energy. "Adelaide," I say, my voice sincere, "you are more than worthy. You're extraordinary. Your potential is like nothing I've ever seen before."

She blushes, looking down at our joined hands. "I don't feel extraordinary," she mumbles. "I couldn't even become House Captain."

Ah, so that's what upset her. I squeeze her hands gently. "Adelaide, look at me," I say, waiting until she meets my gaze. "Being passed over for House Captain doesn't define your worth or your abilities. You've accomplished so much in such a short time. You completed the scavenger hunt, didn't you?"

She nods, a flicker of pride crossing her face. "Yeah, Zephyr and I found all the items. *He* got Captain, and I didn't."

"But who did in your place?"

She purses her lips and sighs in annoyance. "Corvus."

"And you don't think he deserves it?"

"No, it's not that! But we won, me and Zephyr, and he got it, and I didn't." She blinks and then growls. "I realise I sound like a petulant child. Obviously, Corvus deserves it. He has been here longer, he has more experience, Christ, he has been a vampire his whole life!"

"So have you."

"No," she says, shaking her head. "No, I haven't. Not really. And I'm not even a real vampire. Only half a one."

"But a powerful half. The other side of you makes it so."

Her gaze flies up to meet mine. "You know?"

"I think so."

She leans into me slightly, and I wrap an arm around her shoulders, pulling her close. We sit like that for a while, the silence comfortable and charged with unspoken feelings.

"Zaiah," Adelaide says finally, her voice muffled against my chest. "What's happening to me? With these powers, with us?"

I take a deep breath, considering how to answer. "Your Vesperidae nature is awakening," I whisper. "The Essence of Awakening is accelerating the process, bringing your latent abilities to the surface. As for us..." I trail off, unsure how to put into words the complex tangle of emotions and mystical connections between us.

Adelaide pulls back slightly, looking up at me with those piercing eyes. "I feel drawn to you," she admits. "To you, to Corvus, Ignatius, and Zephyr. It's like there are threads connecting us, pulling us together. Is that normal?"

I chuckle softly. "Normal? No. But then again, nothing about you is normal, Adelaide. You're special. Unique. The connection you feel is real. It's a magical bond, one that's incredibly rare."

"But why?" she asks, frustration creeping into her voice. "Why me? Why us?"

I reach up, gently tucking a strand of hair behind her ear. The simple touch sends a shiver through both of us. "I don't have all the answers," I admit. "But I believe it's because you're meant for great things, Adelaide. And we - Corvus, Ignatius, Zephyr, and I -

we're meant to help you, to support you on your journey."

She's quiet for a moment, processing this. "It's a lot," she says finally. "Sometimes I feel like I'm drowning in all of this - the magick, the expectations, these feelings."

I pull her close again, resting my chin on top of her head. "I know," I murmur. "But you're not alone, Adelaide. I'm here for you."

We stay like that for a long time, the warmth of our embrace keeping the chill of the night at bay. I can feel Adelaide relaxing against me, her earlier distress fading into a calm contentment that resonates through our bond.

"Zaiah," she says after a while, her voice soft and sleepy. "Will you stay?"

"Of course," I say, shifting us so we're lying down on her bed, Adelaide curled against my side. "I'll stay as long as you need me."

Adelaide drifts off to sleep as dawn breaks. I lie awake, marvelling at the turn my life has taken. I've never allowed myself to form any deep connections. But now, with Adelaide, I feel anchored. As if I've finally found a place - a being - who will look after my carefully guarded essence.

Adelaide's growing powers will bring challenges and dangers I can't yet foresee. The bond between us - between all of us - will be tested in ways we can't imagine. But as I lie here, holding this remarkable creature in my arms, I'm filled with a sense of hope and purpose I haven't felt before.

As Adelaide sleeps peacefully beside me, I gaze out

the window at the lightening sky. The first rays of dawn are starting to peek over the horizon, painting the clouds in soft pinks and golds. It's a beautiful sight, but my mind is elsewhere.

Her powers are growing rapidly. The Essence of Awakening has accelerated her development, which is what I wanted, but that was before I knew who she really was. But I can sense that thing looming. Danger.

I don't know how, when or in what form, but I know I will protect Adelaide with my last breath if I have to. This bond is growing more intense the longer I lie with her here, and I know soon, I won't be able to be without her nearby.

Chapter 34

Adelaide

My senses gradually come alive as I drift out of a deep sleep filled with the most magnificent dreams. The first thing I notice is warmth - a solid, comforting presence beside me that I instinctively curl into. As I open my eyes, blinking against the soft, late afternoon light filtering through my curtains, I'm met with the sight of Zaiah's sleeping face.

For a moment, I'm struck by how peaceful he looks. The usual intensity that marks his features is softened in sleep, and I'm reminded of just how mystically beautiful he is. I resist the urge to trace the line of his jaw with my finger. My heart swells with emotion. Affection, desire, and something deeper, more profound.

Our bond, still new and not fully understood, pulses gently between us, a living thing. I can feel his presence not just physically but on a spiritual level, as if our souls are intertwined. It's a sensation that should frighten me with its intensity, but instead, I find it comforting. Like finding a piece of myself that I knew was missing all this time.

As I lie there, watching Zaiah sleep, I ponder the strange turns my life has taken. Just a few weeks ago, I was a somewhat normal twenty-year-old, apathetic towards most things in life, and now I'm a half-vampire with growing magickal abilities. The sheer absurdity of it all hits me, and I have to stifle a laugh to avoid waking Zaiah.

Is this fate? Some grand design that I'm only beginning to see and experience? The idea is wild but also comforting. I've never been one to believe in destiny, but how else can I explain the pull I feel towards these four, the way our lives seem to be inexorably intertwined?

A loud crack hits my window and interrupts my musings. Frowning, I carefully untangle myself from Zaiah, trying not to wake him. As I pad over to the window, I'm struck by how different I feel - stronger, more graceful, more aware. The Essence of Awakening that Zaiah gave me seems to have sharpened all my senses.

To my surprise, I see Zephyr and Corvus standing below. Zephyr tosses another small stone at the window. The courtyard below is shaded by the enormous trees overhead, and I smile and wave.

I open the window, leaning out slightly. "What are you two doing here?" I call down, not too loudly, mindful of Zaiah still sleeping behind me.

"Checking on you," Corvus says, his voice carrying easily in the quiet afternoon air. There's concern in his eyes, and I feel a warmth spread through me at the realisation that they cared enough to come. "Can we come up?"

I hesitate for a moment, glancing back at Zaiah's sleeping form. Part of me wants to keep this moment private, to stay in the bubble of peace I've found with Zaiah. But the concern in their eyes wins me over. "Okay," I say.

"Going to need more than that, princess," Zephyr says with a small smile. "Your tower doesn't like me."

"Likes me well enough," Corvus states and opens the door to step inside.

I giggle at Zephyr's scowl. "Yes, you can come up, my prince."

His eyes widen, and the smouldering look on his face makes me blush. "She's learning," he says and disappears through the open door, closing it behind him with a loud bang.

A few moments later, there's a soft knock at my bedroom door. I open it, and their eyes immediately land on Zaiah, still asleep on my bed. I see a flicker pass between them, but I can't decipher its meaning before they adjust their features.

"Come in," I say, stepping aside to let them enter. The room suddenly feels smaller with all of them here, the air charged with an energy I can't quite define.

"How are you doing?" Corvus asks, his voice gentle. "After last night, I mean."

I shrug, trying to appear calm even as I still feel a twinge of disappointment at the memory of not being chosen as House Captain. "I'm fine. Congratulations on becoming House Captain, by the way. You deserve it."

Corvus smiles, but there's a hint of concern in his eyes. "Thanks. But are you sure you're okay? We were worried about you. You seemed to take it a bit hard."

"Really, I'm fine," I insist, touched by their concern but also feeling a bit overwhelmed by it. "It was disappointing, but I'm learning that there's a lot more to all of this than titles and positions."

Corvus glances at his watch, his brow furrowing slightly. "We should go," he says. "Classes start soon, and we all need to get ready."

Time seems to move differently here at MistHallow, or maybe it's just the effect of being around these extraordinary beings. "Right, classes. That snuck up on me."

"Time does that here," Zaiah murmurs, clearly awake behind me now.

As Corvus and Zephyr leave, promising to see me later, I turn back to Zaiah. For a moment, as he looks at me, I see a vulnerability in his gaze that takes my breath away.

"Hey," I say softly, sitting on the edge of the bed. "Sleep well?"

He smiles, reaching out to touch my face gently. His fingers are warm against my skin. "Better than I have in a while," he murmurs. "How are you feeling?"

"Good," I say, and I'm surprised to realise it's true.

Despite the disappointment of last night, despite the confusion and uncertainty of my new life, I feel alive. Vibrant. "Different, but good. Strong."

Zaiah nods, his eyes searching my face. There's an intensity in his gaze that makes me feel like he's looking into my soul. "The Essence of Awakening is working its magick. Your abilities will continue to grow. Be careful, Adelaide. And remember, we're here for you."

With a final caress of my cheek, Zaiah rises. "I should go. You need to get ready for classes. But I'll see you soon."

As he leaves via the pocket dimension, I'm struck by a sense of loss, as if a part of me is walking away. The bond between us tugs at my heart, and I have to resist the urge to call him back. But I shake it off, focusing on getting ready for my first night of classes at MistHallow. I head upstairs to the bathroom and turn on the shower to let it heat while I strip off and change my tampon. I'm surprised to see that my period has stopped. "Well, I won't miss you if this is a vampire side effect," I mutter as I wrap it and bin it before turning on the shower.

The hot water cascades over me, washing away the last remnants of sleep. As I lather up, I replay the events of the past few days in my mind. The intensity of my connections with Zaiah, Corvus, Zephyr and Ignatius—although he is a tougher one to figure out. He isn't overtly interested in me, that I can tell. Not like the others. Maybe he is just looking for a friend. He definitely has one in me.

The last of the disappointment of not being chosen as House Captain washes away down the drain, and I focus on the strange new sensations coursing through my body as I finish up.

I step out of the shower and wrap a towel around myself, wiping the steam from the mirror. I gasp as, for a moment, nothing stares back at me, but then I see my face, ghostly pale, almost translucent. I hold my hand up to my face, making sure that I'm still corporeal. The illusion in the mirror is chilling. My eyes are bright red, my fangs are drawn, my fingers hooked into claws.

It's not a reflection at all, but it *is* me.

"Who are you?" I murmur.

"Crimson," she hisses back. "Crimson Sha—"

I leap back, stumbling over my piles of clothes, breaking the reflection. Gasping, my heart pumping, I look up from the floor to see the scary version of me is gone. "Fuck," I mutter, shoving my hands into my hair. "What the fuck was that?"

There is no answer, but I don't move. Not yet. I wait for my heartbeat to slow before I gather up my clothes and stand up. I risk a look in the mirror, but nothing stares back at me. "Well, I will miss you if this is a vampire side effect. My hair is going to be like a bird's nest for eternity now."

Sighing, I make my way back downstairs and attempt to get myself into some order. I dress in black jeans and a tee with a black cardigan over the top. Tying up my flat black boots, I see Orby whizz past me.

"You again. You're like a cat at a fair, mate."

He bobs up and down and nuzzles my cheek affectionately. I giggle and pat him. "We're going to have to head to the laundrette after class," I say to him. "I'm running out of clean underwear."

He jiggles from side to side in agreement, and I smile as I pick up my backpack. I don't have any supplies, so hopefully, these will be provided somewhere. In the meantime, at least I have my phone to take notes if it comes down to that.

Making my way downstairs, I cross the courtyard and see many other students doing the same—some in groups, others alone like me. I pull my schedule out of my backpack and see that my first class is Vampire History and Culture. This should be interesting and informative.

Orby seems to know where he's going, so I follow him through the corridors of the main academy building, excited but nervous. The hallways are filled with students of all kinds - vampires, witches, shifters, and beings I can't even begin to identify. The air is thick with the mystical, and I can feel it vibrating all around me.

I arrive at my first lecture, eager to learn more about this world I'm now a part of. As I enter the lecture hall, I'm immediately struck by the diversity of the students. I thought they would all be vampires, but Lyra is here—who is definitely not a vampire, although her status remains to be seen—along with a handful of other creatures that bear no resemblance to the typical vampire, who, by all appearances, looks human.

I was hoping Corvus would be here, but I'm guessing

he doesn't need this class, so I take a seat near the back, trying not to draw attention to myself as Orby settles on my backpack. A notepad and pen magickally appear on the desk in front of me, to my relief. When the professor begins to speak, I find myself leaning forward, hanging on every word. We dive into the ancient origins of vampires, the different bloodlines and their unique traits, and the complex politics that have shaped vampire society over millennia. The Sanguine family come up as a case study for ancient vampire families and their political affiliations within the vampire community. I get now why Corvus isn't here. Conflict of interest, or whatever they call it.

As the lecture progresses, I feel a strange sensation building. It's as if the knowledge isn't just entering my mind, but seeping into my being. I can feel my awareness expanding, my senses sharpening. By the time the class ends, I feel more like a vampire than I ever have before. Well, I assume that is what this is, not having much to go on.

Glancing at my schedule, I follow Orby, giving a quick wave to Lyra, who waves back and heads in the opposite direction. I wonder if I should have gone over and sat with her, but that is extrovert behaviour, and I am anything but that. I worry now that she has taken offence and thinks I'm avoiding her. I chew my lip and look over my shoulder, but she is gone, and Orby is racing ahead to my next lecture, so I forget it and race to catch up.

My next lecture is just called Blood Magick. I'm not sure why I'm here as Blackthorn said, I have no *powers,* only abilities. I assumed that meant I couldn't do magick.

As I enter the room, I see Corvus wave me over to an empty seat next to him. I smile, grateful for the familiar face in this class, which I'm pretty sure is a wrong assignment for me.

"How's your first night of classes going?" he asks as I sit down, his voice low and warm.

"Intense," I admit, running a hand through my hair. "But amazing. I feel like I'm finally starting to understand who and what I am."

Corvus nods, a knowing look in his eyes. "It'll get easier, and more complicated."

"Yeah." I glance around and then back at him. "I don't know what I'm doing here, though. I don't have magickal powers."

He frowns at me. "Yes, you do. All supernatural creatures do in some form. You, as a vampire, have access to Blood Magick."

"I do?" I frown back at him. Blackthorn told me I don't have powers. Then I recall his magickal ability. Was that Blood Magick? I have to assume so, but why did he tell me I don't have powers? Maybe he assumed such with me being only half vampire. But that raises the question of why I'm in this class then.

"You're overthinking something," Corvus mutters. "What's up?"

Focusing on him, I shake my head and force a smile. "Nothing. It's nothing."

We turn to the front as the professor begins the lecture, I notice a vampire glaring at me from across the room. His eyes are cold, filled with a hatred I don't understand. I try to ignore him, focusing instead on the intricate blood rituals we're learning about.

I get the impression I'm way behind everyone else in here. They seem to be taking in all the words as if they understand them, and I'm sitting here gawping like a goldfish, with it going in one ear and out the other.

"I can tutor you, don't stress," Corvus murmurs as he keeps his eyes on the professor as he calls for pairing off to practicals.

"Fuck," I mutter, looking at Corvus. "I don't know what I'm doing."

"I do. Don't worry."

"You keep saying that, but I'm going to fail."

"You aren't going to fail. Trust me. It's innate. You'll get it, and when you do, there will be no stopping you."

The professor has just finished demonstrating the blood-summoning spell, and now it is our turn to try. I prick my finger with a small, ornate dagger, watching as a bead of crimson forms on my skin. Focusing my energy, I begin to chant the incantation on the spell sheet in front of me.

At first, nothing happens. Then, slowly, the drop of blood quivers. It lifts off my skin, hovering in the air. Encouraged, I intensify my focus, willing the blood to move.

Suddenly, the droplet explodes into a scarlet mist. It swirls around me, responding to my thoughts and movements. With a flick of my wrist, I send the mist dancing across the room, weaving between startled classmates.

"Adelaide," Corvus mutters as he watches me.

But I ignore the warning in his tone.

As my confidence grows, so does the amount of blood I can control. More droplets rise from my finger, joining the swirling mist. It is exhilarating, feeling the connection between my will and the blood.

But then, something shifts. The mist pulses with a life of its own, growing denser and more agitated. I feel it pulling at me, draining my energy. Panic rises in my throat as I realise I'm losing control.

Just as the blood mist is about to overwhelm me, Corvus's hand clamps down on mine. His energy flows into me, steadying my power. Together, we rein in the wild magick, condensing the mist back into a single droplet that falls harmlessly to the desk.

Shaken, I glance up at Corvus, who gives me a small smile. "Do you see just how powerful you are now?"

"Wow," I breathe as the professor dismisses us, and we stand up to leave the lecture hall. "That was scary as fuck."

"Which is why next time I call your name, listen to me," he chides gently.

"Noted," I reply with a mock salute.

He chuckles, but it turns into a growl when the vampire who was glaring at me earlier approaches us outside in the corridor.

"Well, well," he sneers, his voice dripping with contempt. "If it isn't the newbie and her pet pureblood. How cute."

I tense, frozen, but Corvus moves smoothly, placing himself between me and the nasty vampire. The movement is casual, almost lazy, but I can sense the power coiled in his body, ready to strike.

"Back off, Asher," he says, his voice low and dangerous. "You're way out of your league here."

Asher's eyes narrow, a cruel smile playing at his lips. "Oh? And who's going to stop me? You?" He lunges at Corvus, fangs bared, a blur of motion and fury. But Corvus is faster, stronger. In a heartbeat, he has Asher pinned against the wall, one hand around his throat. The display of power is breathtaking and arousing.

"Yes," Corvus says calmly, as if he's discussing the weather rather than holding a snarling vampire against the wall. "I am. Now, have we got a problem here?"

Asher struggles for a moment, his eyes wild with rage and humiliation as the crowd of onlookers grows, some giggling, some growling, but no one else gets involved, thankfully. Then, slowly, he goes limp, admitting defeat. Corvus releases him, and Asher slinks away, shooting us one last venomous glare.

As Corvus turns back to me, I see a fire in his eyes that I've never noticed before. It's primal, possessive, and it sends a tingle down the back of my neck. Without warning, he pulls me close and kisses me.

It's passionate, claiming, and over far too quickly.

When Corvus pulls away, leaving me panting, I hear the hushed whispers around us.

"Are you okay?" he asks softly, his hand still cupping my face.

I nod, still a bit dazed from the kiss and the confrontation. "Yeah," I manage to say. "Who did that idiot think he was?"

"A complete arsehole who doesn't know when to quit," he snarls.

I nod, agreeing with the complete arsehole part. But while part of me is thrilled that Corvus staked his claim so publicly, another part worries about the complications this might bring. Have I made an enemy of this vampire who I've never even spoken to?

"What's next for you?" Corvus asks, interrupting my worrying.

"Uhm," I mutter, checking my schedule as Orby hovers nearby. "A break for an hour and then Vampires and Myths."

"Fancy a drink?" His hand finds mine as we walk, and I'm struck by how natural it feels, how perfectly our fingers intertwine.

"Yeah, I'm feeling a bit drained."

"I'm not surprised. You kicked butt back there."

"Hardly," I snort. "I lost control."

He snickers as we enter the dining hall to grab some synthetic blood. The hunger that's been gnawing at me since I woke is intensifying, and my stomach rumbles in protest.

Grabbing two to-go cups, we sip as we walk out into the courtyard, where we see Ignatius juggling balls of fire. The sight is beautiful and slightly terrifying, the flames dancing between his hands with a life of their own.

"Adelaide!" he calls, grinning as he sees us approach. "Corvus. How were classes?"

"Eventful," I say, watching the flames dance between Ignatius's hands. "I nearly lost control of a blood mist in Blood Magick class."

Ignatius extinguishes the fireballs with a snap of his fingers. "Oh?"

I shrug, still feeling uneasy about what happened. "It was more terrifying than impressive. If Corvus hadn't been there…"

"I told you, you're powerful," Corvus says, squeezing my hand. "You just need to learn control."

Ignatius nods, his eyes gleaming with interest. "I'd love to see what you can do sometime. Maybe we could practice together?"

"You do Blood Magick?"

"I do all magick," he replies with a smile.

"Well, go you," I giggle.

"What can I say? I'm an overachiever."

"And sweet with a cute accent, too. You're the whole package."

"Don't you forget it."

We laugh as Corvus watches this interaction with interest.

"Well," I say. "I suppose I'd better get over to my next lecture. Don't want to be late."

"I'll walk you," Corvus says. "If Asher shows up again, don't engage, okay? Walk away and tell me about it. I'll handle him."

"I don't need you to protect me from bullies," I mutter.

"I know you don't. But you will learn, Dollie, that I protect what's mine."

Sounds familiar.

I say nothing as we head to the next building over, hoping that this is a normal class without magick or bullies.

Chapter 35

Ignatius

The corridors of MistHallow are bustling with activity as I make my way to the Elemental Magick lecture hall, my last lecture of the night. Rounding the corner, the scent of autumn leaves and woodsmoke fills the air, the scent of the elemental magick that permeates this part of the academy. The stone walls here are adorned with intricate murals depicting the four elements - earth, air, fire, and water - intertwining in an eternal spire. It's breathtaking, and I slow down to admire the artistry.

Sensing a certain energy in the air, I half turn and see Adelaide is standing by the lecture hall door, looking slightly lost and more than a little overwhelmed. Her dark hair is slightly tousled, as if she's been running her hands through it nervously, and there's a crease between her brows that I find endearing.

"Adelaide!" I call out, picking up my pace to reach her. "Fancy seeing you here. Elemental Magick, right?"

She turns at the sound of my voice, relief washing over her features. The smile that lights up her face sends a warmth through me that has nothing to do with my fire magick. "Hey, firestarter. Yes, Elemental Magick. I'm not even sure why I'm in this class. I thought vampires were all about Blood Magick?"

I grin, falling into step beside her as we enter the hall. The room is circular, with workstations arranged in concentric circles around a central dais. Each station is equipped with various tools and materials - crystals, bowls of water, small potted plants, and curiously empty glass orbs that I suspect are for air manipulation.

"Ah, but that's where you're wrong, my dear," I say, guiding her towards two empty seats near the middle of the room. "Vampires, like all magickal beings, have the potential to tap into elemental magick. It's just not as instinctive for them as Blood Magick is."

"Well, I'm here to learn what being a vampire is all about, so I guess, hit me with whatever!"

"That's the spirit, Addy."

She grins as I shorten her name, and I gesture for Adelaide to take the seat by the window. I notice the way the moonlight plays across her features. She's beautiful, in a way that goes beyond physical appearance. There's a spark in her, a potential that's just waiting to be unleashed.

"So," I say, leaning in slightly, our shoulders almost touching, "How have your classes been so far apart from the Blood Magick incident?"

Adelaide groans, burying her face in her hands. I

have to resist the urge to reach out and tuck a stray strand of hair behind her ear. "Don't even with that. But the rest have been fine. No more magick and no more bullies."

"Bullies?" I ask harsher than I meant to.

"Ugh, some vampire named Asher. He was a proper arse."

"Hmm, yeah. He is out to get Corvus, so I guess you got caught up in the crossfire."

She glares at me. "Oh great, thanks for telling me that part. He failed to mention it."

I chuckle. "I wouldn't worry about Asher or Lucian. They're both idiots."

"Lucian," she murmurs. "He had a pop at me as well the other day. Zephyr dealt with him."

"Vampires are weird. I wouldn't worry about it."

"No shit," she mumbles.

Adelaide's eyes meet mine, and for a moment, I'm lost in their depths. The air between us feels charged, like the moment before lightning strikes.

Before I can respond, the professor enters the room, calling the class to order. He's a tall, willowy man with hair the colour of autumn leaves and eyes that seem to shift like quicksilver. As he begins the lecture, his voice resonates with power, each word seeming to vibrate with elemental energy.

I'm hyper-aware of Adelaide's presence beside me. The way she leans forward, hanging on every word. The little furrow that appears between her brows when she's concentrating. The way her hand occasionally brushes against mine as we take notes, sends little sparks of electricity through me each time.

Halfway through the class, the professor announces that we'll be pairing up for a practical exercise. "Today, we'll be focusing on fire manipulation," he says, his eyes glowing with an inner flame. "Nothing too advanced - just creating and controlling a small flame."

I turn to Adelaide, a mischievous grin on my face. "Well, well. Looks like you're in luck, partner. Fire happens to be my speciality."

"Guess it is my lucky day, or whoever got stuck with me would be sorely disappointed when I epically failed."

With a flourish, I hold out my hand, palm up. I summon a small flame, no bigger than a candle's. It dances in my palm, casting a warm glow over our faces. The fire responds to my will, shaping itself into intricate patterns - a blooming flower, a fluttering butterfly, a spinning galaxy of sparks.

Adelaide's eyes widen in wonder, the firelight reflected in their depths. "That's amazing," she breathes, leaning in closer to watch the display. "How do you do it? And how the fuck am *I* supposed to do that?"

"It's all about focus and intent," I explain, my voice soft. The proximity of her face to mine is distracting, but I push through. "You have to feel the heat inside you, the spark of life that burns in every living thing. Then, you coax it out, give it form and purpose."

I gently take her hand, guiding it to hover over mine. Her skin is vampire cool against my fire-warmed palm, but she doesn't hiss and pull away as I half expected her to. "Close your eyes," I instruct, my voice low and intimate. "Feel the warmth of the flame. Now, imagine that warmth spreading through you, from your fingertips to the top of your head."

Adelaide's eyes flutter closed, her face a mask of concentration. I watch, fascinated, as a faint glow begins to emanate from her skin. It's subtle, barely noticeable to anyone who isn't looking for it. But to me, it's like watching the sunrise. The air around us grows warmer, charged with potential.

"That's it," I encourage, my thumb unconsciously tracing circles on the back of her hand. "Now, imagine that warmth gathering in your palm. Give it shape, will it into being."

For a moment, nothing happens. Then, ever so slowly, a tiny spark appears in Adelaide's palm. It flickers uncertainly, barely more than an ember. But it's there, a testament to her untapped potential.

Adelaide's eyes fly open, a look of pure joy on her face. The spark in her palm grows slightly, fed by her excitement. "Wait! What? How?"

Her excitement is infectious, and I grin like a fool. "You're a natural, Adelaide."

"No," she says, shaking her head and staring at our joined hands with a fierce frown. "No. It's not me."

"What do you mean?" I ask, following her gaze.

Her eyes shoot up to mine, and she smiles stiffly. "Nothing," she says. "I'm just surprised."

"You know," I say, my voice low enough that only she can hear, "I meant what I said earlier. About practising together sometime. I'd love to help you explore your powers more if you're interested, that is."

Adelaide looks up at me with a soft smile. "I'd like that," she says finally, her voice barely above a whisper.

"Good. I enjoy spending time with you, Addy."

She ducks her head, focusing intently on the small flame in her palm. It grows then flickers out, and she sighs with disappointment. "I enjoy spending time with you too, Iggy," she murmurs.

Iggy. The way she says that sends my blood pumping straight to my cock.

The rest of the practice passes in a blur of stolen glances and lingering touches. Adelaide's attempts to create fire come to nothing, but she did it once, she can do it again.

As we pack up our things, I'm reluctant to let this moment end. The connection between us feels tangible, a delicate thread that I don't want to break.

"So," I say, trying to keep my voice casual even as my heart races, "what do you say to grabbing some food? I know a place that does a great rare steak."

She giggles, and it's the sweetest sound. "I'd like that," she says.

I grin, my heart soaring at her acceptance. "Let's go then."

As we leave the lecture hall, I place my hand lightly on the small of Adelaide's back, guiding her through the crowded corridors. The simple touch sends sparks through my body, and I have to concentrate to keep my powers in check.

We make our way across the moonlit courtyard. Adelaide shivers slightly, and without thinking, I drape my arm around her shoulders. She leans into me, her body fitting perfectly against mine.

"God, you're so fucking warm and toasty," she laughs, looking up at me with those captivating eyes.

"Comes with the territory," I murmur, hoping that I can pluck up the nerve to kiss her before the night is out.

We enter the busy dining hall, which never seems to stop buzzing, and I guide her to the food counter. She grabs a steak quickly, and I grab one as well, slightly more well done, and we sit at a table nearby.

As we sit down, Adelaide digs into her steak with gusto. I can't help but smile at her enthusiasm.

"Hungry?" I tease.

She looks up, a bit sheepish. "Starving, actually. I didn't realise how much energy magick uses up."

"It does take a lot out of you," I agree, cutting into my own steak. "Especially when you're just starting out. Your body's not used to channelling that kind of power yet."

Adelaide nods, swallowing a bite. "It's like tapping into something ancient and powerful."

"That's exactly what you were doing," I say, leaning forward slightly. "Magick is as old as the universe itself. When we use it, we're connecting to that primordial force."

She looks at me, her eyes wide with wonder. "It's intense."

"Very."

We gaze into each other's eyes, and I feel a slight ping that snaps against my soul. I half rise, my gaze still pinning hers, and I reach out to tilt her chin up. I press my lips to hers.

Adelaide gasps softly as our lips meet, her cool breath mingling with mine. For a moment, she's frozen, but then she melts into the kiss, her hand coming up to tangle in my hair. The spark between us ignites into a roaring flame, and I have to concentrate hard not to burst into a pillar of fire.

The kiss deepens, and I can taste the faint metallic tang of blood on her tongue. It's intoxicating. I pull her closer, my hand cupping her face gently.

Suddenly, Adelaide pulls away, her eyes wide and pupils dilated. She's breathing heavily, and I can see a faint blush creeping up her neck.

"I'm sorry," I say quickly, worried I've ruined everything. "I shouldn't have—"

"No," she interrupts, her voice husky. "It's not you..." She scowls and turns her head.

I turn too to see Asher and Lucian staring at us, flashes of triumph in their eyes. "Ah, fuck," I mutter. "I'm guessing they are going to go straight to Corvus with this."

"I wanted this kiss," Addy says. "Don't worry about them."

"It's not that. Corvus won't care that I kissed you. He will care that Lucian and Asher are interfering, and they will also maybe spin this, so it looks bad on you."

She sighs, and for a moment, it looks like she is going

to vamp out and go on a rampage, but then she smiles. "Whatever they say about me, I've heard worse."

My heart aches for her. She sounds so resigned, like she's used to being hurt. I reach out and take her hand, squeezing it gently.

"Hey," I say softly, "You don't deserve that. No matter what they say, you're amazing, Adelaide. Don't let anyone make you think otherwise."

She gives me a small smile, but I can see the vulnerability in her eyes. "Thanks, Iggy. I'm still trying to figure out where I fit in all this."

I nod, understanding. "It's a lot to take in. But you're not alone, okay? You've got me, and Corvus, and Zephyr, and Zaiah. We're here for you."

Adelaide's smile grows a little brighter. "I know. It's just complicated."

"Life usually is," I say with a wry grin. "Especially when you throw magick and vampires into the mix."

She laughs, the sound lightening the mood. "You can say that again."

We finish our meal, chatting about lighter topics, but as we're leaving the dining hall, I notice Asher and Lucian still watching us, their gazes cold and their expressions calculating. Whatever they are planning, it's not going to be pretty. Perhaps it's time the four of us took the fight to them and fuck the consequences. Addy is more important, and right now, she is a bug under their microscope. No way this ends well for any of us.

Chapter 36

Corvus

The Blood Bar is in half-light, the air thick with the scent of copper and iron. I slide onto a stool at the counter, my fingers drumming an impatient rhythm on the polished wood. It's been a long night, and all I want is a glass of the good stuff to take the edge off.

Grim, the bartender, approaches with his usual, well, *grim* expression. He shakes his head, a flicker of apology crossing his features. "No human blood tonight. Staff did a sweep for the start of the term. It's synthetic or nothing."

I groan, running a hand through my hair in frustration. "You're kidding me, right? Please tell me you're kidding."

Grim just shrugs, his shoulders rising and falling like the movement of ancient machinery. "Wish I was. Rules are rules, though. Even for a Sanguine. Give it a week, and they'll forget all about it again."

For a moment, I consider leaving. The thought of synthetic blood turns my stomach. I have tried it because Adelaide is drinking it. It's not pleasant, but the thirst is gnawing at me, and I know I can't ignore it for long.

"Fine," I mutter. "Give me the synthetic shit."

Grim nods, turning to prepare my drink. As he does, I let my gaze wander around the bar. It's relatively quiet tonight, just a few other vampires scattered about, nursing their glasses of synthetic blood. The start of term always brings a certain tension to the air, a mix of excitement and apprehension that even we immortals aren't immune to.

My thoughts drift to Adelaide, as they often do these days. The memory of our kiss in the corridor after the lecture sends a thrill through me. The way she looked at me, her eyes wide with surprise and something deeper, more primal is enough to make my cock hard,

"Here you go," Grim says, sliding a glass of dark red liquid in front of me.

I take a reluctant sip, grimacing at the artificial taste. It's terrible, a far cry from the real thing. Still, it takes the edge off the thirst, and for that, I'm grateful.

As I'm nursing my drink, the door to the bar swings open. I don't need to turn around to know who it is - I can sense their presence, as familiar to me now as my own shadow. Ignatius, Zaiah, and Zephyr make their way over, pulling up stools beside me.

"Corvus," Zaiah greets me, his voice low and serious. The tension in his posture sets me on edge immediately. "We need to talk."

I raise an eyebrow, taking another sip of my synthetic blood. "What about?"

"Adelaide," Zephyr cuts in. "And something else."

Ignatius leans in, looking serious as all fuck, which is the one thing that makes me pay attention. The other two can be drama queens, but Ig is a take-it-as-it-comes kind of guy. "Zaiah has sensed something. Something dark."

I set my glass down, all thoughts of my unsatisfactory drink forgotten. "Something dark? Like what?"

Zaiah shakes his head, his frustration clear. "I don't know exactly. But I know it has something to do with Adelaide. There's a shadow looming over her future, a threat we can't yet see."

A growl builds in my throat, low and dangerous. The thought of Adelaide in danger brings out a fierce protectiveness that makes me want to kill. The synthetic blood in my glass sits forgotten as Zaiah's words send a chill down my spine.

"It's like a shadow," Zaiah murmurs, his eyes unfocused, seeing something beyond the dimly lit bar. "A darkness creeping at the edges of my dreams. I've never felt anything quite like it before."

Zephyr's fingers drum an impatient rhythm on the bar. "Can you be more specific? What kind of danger are we talking about here?"

Zaiah shakes his head. "That's just it. It's not clear. Sometimes I see fire, consuming everything in its path. Other times, it's a flood of darkness, drowning out all light. But always, at the centre of it all, I see Adelaide."

"Is she the cause or the target?" Ignatius asks, his tone harder, more serious than usual.

"Both, perhaps," Zaiah replies, his voice barely above a whisper. "Or neither. It's as if she's a focal point. A nexus where all these dark forces are converging."

I feel a growl building in my chest, my fangs itching to descend. "And you're sure about this? It's not just some djinn hunch?"

Zaiah's eyes snap to mine, blazing with an inner fire. "Fuck you. This is real. And it's coming, whether we're ready or not."

"Then we'll make sure we're ready," Zephyr interjects. "We'll train her, protect her."

I nod, my mind already racing with plans. "We need to tell her—"

"No," Zaiah cuts me off. "Not yet. She's only just beginning to understand her powers. If we tell her about this now, it could overwhelm her, maybe even push her towards the darkness we're trying to protect her from."

A tense silence falls over our group. I can see the weight of this knowledge settling on each of us.

Finally, Ignatius breaks the quiet. "So, what do we do?"

I lean back, the decision already made. "We watch. We wait, and we make damn sure that whatever's coming, Adelaide's ready for it."

The others nod in agreement, and as we continue to discuss strategy in hushed tones, I can't shake the feeling that this is just the beginning of something much bigger than any of us could have imagined.

Zephyr nods. "She has power, more than she knows. I've felt it. We need to help her tap further into it."

He's felt it? That sends a pang of envy through me. I've tasted her power in her blood, but it's not enough to get a real gauge of it. Zephyr makes it sound like he knows exactly what she is capable of.

"I can work with her on her elemental magick," Ignatius offers. "She showed real potential in class today."

"What?" Zephyr says with a fierce frown. "She doesn't have elemental magick."

"She does, I saw it."

"No," he says, shaking his head. "That's not possible..." He trails off and chews his lip in an oddly nervous gesture for the cool Dark Fae prince.

"What are you thinking?" I ask.

He gestures that we leave the bar, and we follow him outside to huddle around in the oddly cold night. The hairs on the back of my neck stand on end, and now I totally believe that Zaiah is onto something. This isn't natural. It is supernatural, one hundred per cent.

"I'm sure we've all figured out by now what she is," Zephyr whispers.

I nod, and so do the other two.

"So you know that it's rumoured her kind can amplify powers, yes?"

"What of it?" I murmur.

"She amplified mine so we could win the scavenger hunt. It was... fuck... I've never felt anything like it."

"What's that got to do with elemental magick?" I snap, getting annoyed at the awed look on his face.

"Vampires can't do elemental magick," he snaps back. "Can you?"

I shake my head. "No..." A thought is forming in my mind, and I gulp back the concern that has burst in my chest. "Fuck."

"Yeah."

"Will you two stop with the cryptic," Ig growls. "She created fire. I saw it."

"From you. She took your power and used it," I state.

Zephyr nods in agreement.

Ig frowns and shakes his head. "No, that's not possible..."

"Pretty sure it is," Zephyr says. "We don't know much about her kind. We know practically nothing, and the others that exist right now, apart from her, are weaker. Randall Black sired her. That in itself is monumental."

"Fuck," Ig says, his shoulder slumping. "I mean... fuck."

"Precisely. If she doesn't know she can do this, which I'm going out on a limb to say she doesn't, that makes her—"

"Dangerous."

"Yep."

"Fuck," Zaiah says, who has been quiet while we discussed this. "That means I'm right in saying she is the nexus."

"But the nexus to *what* exactly?" I murmur.

"That's what we need to find out," he replies.

The memory of Adelaide's power during our practical earlier sends an icy snake of discomfort slithering over my soul. She'd been magnificent but terrifying in her raw potential.

"I'll take the first watch," I volunteer as our meeting winds down. "We can keep an eye on her. Lucian and Asher are up to something, and that just makes this even more dodgy for her."

"About them," Ig starts and then blushes. "They saw us kissing in the dining hall earlier."

I blink, and then smirk. "Go you. She is a great kisser."

"She is," Zephyr murmurs.

"Mm," Zaiah comments, and I chuckle.

It's strange, this unspoken agreement we have about Adelaide Black. We're so different, each with our own agenda, our own feelings for Adelaide. But in this, we're united. We all want her, and we will all get her. It's just a matter of time before she knows she can't escape us. It's fate. There is no other word for it, no other explanation.

The others nod their agreement, and we part ways, each lost in our thoughts. I take a deep breath, letting the scents of the academy wash over me. Adelaide is going about her night, blissfully unaware of the forces gathering around her. The urge to go to her, to see her with my own eyes, is almost overwhelming.

With a thought, I shift forms, my body shrinking and changing until I'm no longer a man, but a bat. My wings catch the night air, and I soar upwards, circling Adelaide's tower. The lights are on in her room, and through the window, I can see her moving about.

As I watch, she pauses, her gaze turning towards the

window. For a moment, our eyes meet, and I see recognition flicker across her face. To my surprise, she moves to the window, opening it wide.

"Corvus?" she calls softly. "Is that you?"

I hesitate for a moment, then swoop down, landing gracefully on her windowsill. With another thought, I shift back to my human form, perched precariously on the narrow ledge.

"Hey," I say, trying for casual and probably missing by a mile. "Lovely night for a fly, isn't it?"

She raises an eyebrow, a smile tugging at the corners of her mouth. "Can't say I'd know."

"Do you want to see if you can?" I jump on that as a way to spend more time with her, teaching her, protecting her.

She steps aside, and I leap into her room. "Do you really think I can?"

"Don't see why not. But we won't know unless you try."

"Good point."

The memory of our kiss in the corridor flashes through my mind, and I have to resist the urge to pull her close and claim her lips again.

"So," she says, crossing her arms over her chest. "To what do I owe the pleasure of this late-night visit apart from offers to turn me into a bat?"

I hesitate, unsure how much to reveal. The last thing I want is to frighten her, but she deserves to know that she might be in danger. "I wanted to check on you," I say finally. "After what happened with Asher, I was worried.

Also, Ig mentioned about Asher and Lucian seeing you earlier."

She raises an eyebrow. "Oh? And how do you feel about that?"

Her question takes me aback. "I'm happy that you two are getting closer. We are all connected, Adelaide. You can feel it. I know you can." Reaching out to tuck a stray strand of hair behind her ear, the simple touch sends a jolt of electricity through me.

For a moment, we stand there, caught in each other's gaze. The air between us is charged, heavy with unspoken words and unfulfilled desires. Then, slowly, Adelaide leans in, her lips brushing against mine in a soft, tentative kiss.

It's nothing like our kiss in the corridor. That had been all fire and passion, a public claiming. This is something else entirely. It's gentle, exploratory, filled with a tenderness that takes my breath away.

When we finally part, Adelaide's cheeks are flushed, her eyes bright. "I've been wanting to do that again," she admits, a shy smile playing on her lips.

"So have I," I confess, my hand cupping her cheek. "And so much more."

"I want that too," she murmurs, lowering her gaze before she pulls her tee off. Her skin is paler than before, which shows her vampire side emerging in force. She is stunning in every sense of the word.

"You're beautiful, Adelaide."

"Addy," she mutters. "Call me Addy."

I smile and bend down to kiss her again, wanting to

bite her, ravage her. My fangs drop and slice into her lips and tongue. She gasps but doesn't stop. If anything, it deepens the kiss, and my cock bounces to attention, pressing painfully against my pants.

"Addy," I growl and pick her up, slamming her against the wall of her room.

"Ah!" she cries out as my claws rip her bra away, marking her skin, drawing blood. I bend down to lick it away, and she moans, her head falling back against the wall. I trail kisses down her neck, savouring the taste of her blood, and she writhes in my arms.

"Corvus," she whispers, her voice breathy and needy. "Please."

I hear the desire in her voice, and I can't resist any longer. I flick open her jeans and lower her to the floor. She looks up at me with those big, dark eyes, and it's more than I can take. I drop to my knees and pull her jeans down. Taking off her boots and socks first, I then run my hands up her outer thighs. My fingers hook into her knickers, and I slice the sides away. I breathe in deeply but pause when I sense she has stopped bleeding.

Retracting my fangs and claws, I thrust two fingers deep inside her pussy, making her cry out in surprise and pleasure. She's so wet and warm, her pussy clenching around my fingers as I move them in and out. She is throbbing against my hand, her hips bucking as she tries to get closer.

"Corvus," she gasps, her nails digging into my neck.

I rise so I can kiss her again. I can taste her blood on her lips, and it only makes me hungrier for her.

"You taste so good," I growl, my voice low and rough. "I want more."

I add a third finger, stretching her wider as I twist them inside her, hitting that spot that makes her moan even louder. I can feel her getting closer, her body tensing as she starts to shake.

"Come for me, Addy," I whisper against her lips, my thumb finding her clit and rubbing circles around it. "Be a good girl for me and come all over my hand."

With a cry, she does, her orgasm washing over her in waves as she clings to me. I keep my fingers inside her, feeling her pulse around me as she climaxes hard.

"Fuck," she breathes, her eyes closed as she leans against me. "More. Corvus. I need all of you."

With a low growl, I unzip my pants and let them fall around my ankles. She reaches up and shoves my jacket from my shoulders, gripping the sides of my shirt and ripping it open with more strength than I've seen from her yet.

It makes my cock bounce.

"Fuck, yes, baby girl." I groan as I thrust my cock deep inside her in one swift motion. She's so tight, so wet, and she feels incredible. I grip her hips, pulling her closer as I thrust deep and hard.

Her nails dig into my back, her legs wrapped tightly around my waist as she moans my name. "Corvus, yes. Harder."

My movements become more frantic as I lose myself in the feel of her. She's so perfect, so beautiful, so fragile, and I never want this to end. I can feel myself getting closer, my orgasm building as I pound into her harder and faster.

"I want to feel you come on my cock when I bite into you, feed from you."

"Yes," she whispers, her voice strained with pleasure. "Bite me, Corvus. I want to feel you taking my blood."

I don't need anything else but that. I lean in, my fangs sinking into the soft flesh of her neck as I thrust even deeper into her. She screams, her body trembling as she comes apart in my arms when I suckle on her vein. The taste of her blood is sweet and intoxicating. It fills my mouth as I drink from her, my cock pulsing with release as I feel her orgasm around me. I groan, my hips jerking as I come inside her, filling her with my cum.

With my fangs still buried in her neck, her body pressed against mine, I swallow, drinking more than I should but unable to pull back.

"Corvus," she pants, and I force myself to withdraw, licking the wound to seal it. Adelaide's eyes are wide, her breathing ragged.

"Are you okay?" I murmur, gently pushing her hair back from her face.

"Yes," she murmurs, her voice husky. "Are you?"

I chuckle. "You have no idea, and never worry about me, baby girl. I've got you, not the other way around."

She stares into my eyes for a moment before she closes her eyes and leans back against the wall. My cock is still inside her, growing stiff again already.

She giggles. "Is that a vampire thing?"

"Most supes," I laugh back. "But vamps are extra speedy."

"Not complaining. I need more of you."

I grin, my fangs still out as I lean in to nip at her earlobe.

I move again, slower this time, savouring the feeling of her wrapped around me. She moans, her head falling back against the wall as I thrust into her. Her hips rise to meet mine, her body responding to me.

"You're so perfect," I whisper, my lips brushing against her neck. "I could do this forever."

"I want you to," she gasps. "I never want this to end."

"Don't worry, baby girl. I'm not going anywhere."

The bond between us tightens. I can feel her emotions and desires, and it only makes me want her more.

"Corvus," she whispers, her voice filled with need.

I growl and pull away from the wall, staggering to the bed when I let her go to remove the rest of my clothes. Her legs are open for me, and I drop onto her, my cock returning to her warmth as I thrust inside her sweet pussy.

"Can you bite me back, baby girl?"

Her eyes snap open, and she nods. "I can try."

"Do you want to?"

"Yes. But I don't know if I can."

"Bite me with your teeth first. The rest will come. It's natural for you."

She nods and presses her mouth to my neck.

I groan as I thrust deeper into her, feeling her body

respond to me. She bites down harder, and I hiss as I feel the sting of her teeth piercing my flesh. She hesitates, but I encourage her to keep going. "That's it, baby girl. Bite me harder." I whisper in her ear, my voice low and husky. She does as I say, and I feel her teeth sink deeper into my skin. It's a strange sensation, but it's also incredibly erotic.

I can feel my orgasm building again. I press down on her hips as I slam into her. "Feed from me, Addy."

She moans and suckles, her body trembling uncontrollably under me. It must be when my blood hits her tongue, her fangs descend, and I feel them slicing into my vein. I groan, and my cock explodes cum inside her as she drinks from me. I'm rock hard again instantly, needing every second of this time with her to count.

The room spins as Addy's bite heightens every sensation, every touch. I can feel her pulse, her heartbeat in sync with mine as we become one. Her nails scrape down my back, drawing blood.

She releases me, her eyes wild with lust and something more feral than I've ever seen. I roll us over, positioning her on top of me, her hair cascading around us like a dark curtain. She looks down at me with hooded eyes.

"Ride me, Addy."

Her hips rise and fall in a rhythmic motion that drives me wild. I can feel her claws grazing my chest as she teases me.

I grip her hips, guiding her movements as she grinds against me. I can feel her climax building, her body tensing around me as she nears the edge. I thrust deeper into her, my third orgasm about to burst.

"Corvus," she moans, my name a plea on her lips. With a final thrust, we both fall over the edge, our bodies convulsing together as our souls bleed into one another.

"Eternally mine," I murmur, my hand clasping the back of her neck tightly.

"Eternally yours," she replies with a slow smile as her eyes flash red and blood pours out of the sockets, stopping me dead in my tracks.

Chapter 37

Adelaide

As the words leave my lips, I feel a sudden, searing pain behind my eyes. The world around me blurs, and I'm gripped by an overwhelming sense of terror. Something is wrong. It's like a dam has broken inside my mind, releasing a flood of sensations and emotions I've never experienced before because they aren't mine.

"Adelaide?" Corvus's voice sounds distant, muffled, as if I'm underwater. I try to focus on his face, but my vision is clouded by a red haze. His features, usually so sharp and clear to my vampire senses, are now distorted, wavering like a mirage in the desert.

I blink rapidly, trying to clear my sight, but the red doesn't disappear. If anything, it intensifies, deepening to a crimson so dark it's almost black. A warm, thick liquid trickles down my cheeks. With a shaking hand, I touch my face, pulling it away to find my fingers coated in blood. The sight of it fills me with dread.

"Oh God," I whisper, panic rising in my throat like bile. "Corvus!"

This isn't some external force attacking me. This is coming from deep in my soul. It's me, and yet... not me. A door has been opened in my mind, revealing a room I never knew existed, filled with shadows and whispers and a power that scares the shit out of me.

A memory flashes through my mind, vivid and frightening - the bathroom mirror earlier with the reflection that wasn't mine. The woman, the vampire, with blood-red eyes and a cruel smile. *Crimson. Crimson Sha—*. It echoes in my mind, growing louder with each repetition until it drowns out everything else.

I can feel it now, pushing at the edges of my consciousness, trying to take control. It's like there's another person inside my head, clawing her way out. Her presence is both familiar and alien, like a half-remembered dream suddenly coming to life.

"No!" I yell, clutching my head. The pain is intensifying, feeling like my skull might split open at any moment. "No, no, no. This isn't happening. This can't be happening."

Corvus is saying something, his hands on my shoulders, shaking me gently. But I can barely hear him over the roaring in my ears. The room is spinning, reality seeming to warp around me. The walls of my bedroom stretch and contort, shadows dancing at the corners of my vision.

I squeeze my eyes shut, trying to block out the world, to focus on pushing back against this other me. But when

I open them again, it's like I'm seeing through a red filter. Everything is bathed in a crimson glow, pulsing in time with my rapid heartbeat.

"Adelaide, look at me," Corvus's voice finally breaks through the chaos in my mind. His face swims into focus, his expression showing his concern and fear. I've never seen him look scared before, and it only adds to my terror. "What's going on? Talk to me."

I open my mouth to respond, to beg for help, but nothing comes out.

Horror washes over me as I realise what's happening. I'm losing control, losing myself to this other entity. This vampire in the mirror. It's like watching myself from outside my body, powerless to stop what's happening.

"No," I whisper, fighting to regain control of my voice. Each word is a struggle, like swimming against a powerful current. "Corvus, help me. I can't... I can't stop it."

I feel like I'm being torn in two, my mind a battlefield between the two parts of me. Part of me wants to give in, to let this other, stronger version of myself take control. The power she offers is alluring, promising strength beyond anything I've ever known. But another part, the part that's still me, fights desperately to hold on. I can't lose myself. I won't.

"Stop what?" Corvus asks, his voice tight with tension. His hands are on my face, his thumbs brushing the blood away.

"I don't know," I choke out. Each word feels like glass in my throat. "It's—"

My words are cut off as another wave of pain washes over me. The blood flowing from my eyes intensifies, and I can taste it on my lips, metallic and warm. It should disgust me, but a part of me revels in it.

The soul seems to hold its breath, teetering on the edge of a precipice. One step, and I could fall into an abyss of power and darkness.

With a cry of defiance that seems to shake the foundations of the tower, I push back against the invading presence in my mind. "No," I growl. "Fuck off!"

The struggle is intense. It feels like my soul is being ripped to shreds and put back together. Every cell in my body screams in protest, caught in the crossfire of this internal war. The images that flash through my mind are horrifying and haunting. Battles fought in shadow, power wielded with ruthless perfection, a legacy of blood and darkness.

But slowly, painfully, I begin to regain control. It's like climbing out of a deep, dark pit, clawing my way back to the surface one painful inch at a time. The red haze starts to recede, the world coming back into focus. The blood flow from my eyes slows, then stops altogether. I slump, feeling his lips on mine.

"Addy?" he murmurs against my lips, his arms tightening around me.

"I'm okay," I rasp. The terror of what just happened is still fresh, leaving me shaken to my core. But I'm here. I'm me. For now, at least. The room stops spinning, the shadows retreating to their corners. But I can still feel this presence, lurking at the edges of my consciousness. Waiting.

"What happened?" Corvus asks softly, his hand gently stroking my hair. The tenderness in his touch is at odds with the strength I know he possesses, and it helps to bring me back to the present me, to remind me who I am.

"I don't know," I whisper, my voice hoarse. "It was like there was someone else inside me. Another version of me. Stronger, darker." I shudder, remembering the intensity of her presence. I try to gather my thoughts, to make sense of what just happened, when a sudden gust of wind rattles the window. The glass pane shudders violently. A vicious storm of thunder and lightning has suddenly descended upon MistHallow.

But this is no ordinary storm.

"Zephyr," I whisper, somehow recognising the unique energy signature of the Dark Fae prince.

Before I can move, Zaiah and Ignatius step out of the pocket dimension and into my room, with me naked on top of Corvus and covered in my own blood.

"Adelaide," Zaiah starts, his eyes darting between Corvus and me. "We felt something. Are you alright?"

I open my mouth to respond, but the words catch in my throat. How can I explain what I don't understand myself?

The window bursts open with a crash, and a whirlwind of leaves and shadow pours into the room. It swirls around us, a miniature tempest contained within my bedroom walls. As suddenly as it began, the wind dies down, merging into the form of Zephyr.

His purple and silver eyes lock onto mine. "What happened?" he demands, his voice as sharp as a blade.

I look around at the four of them - Corvus, Zaiah, Ignatius, and Zephyr - all gathered here because of me, because they sensed something was wrong. Their concern, their protection, is comforting but overwhelming.

"I..." I start, but the words won't come. How do I tell them about the presence in my mind? The blood, the visions, the terrifying power I felt?

Corvus, sensing my struggle, steps in. "Something strange happened," he explains slowly. "She was in pain, bleeding from her eyes. She said it felt like there was someone else inside her, trying to take control."

Zaiah's brow furrows, his ancient eyes clouded with worry. "Another presence? Did you recognise it, Adelaide?"

I shake my head, still unable to find my voice. The memory of that other self, so familiar yet so alien, sends a shiver down my spine. "No, and yes. It was me. It was another me."

I can see their confusion, but I have no other way to explain it.

Zaiah steps forward. "May I?" he asks, his hand hovering near my forehead.

I nod, and he places his palm against my skin. Warmth spreads from his touch, soothing and calming.

For a moment, I feel the djinn's power flowing through me, searching, probing.

His eyes widen slightly as he pulls his hand away. "There is something there," he murmurs. "A great power. It's dormant now, but..."

"But what?" Zephyr demands, his patience clearly wearing thin.

Zaiah shakes his head. "It's not a threat. At least not to Addy."

A heavy silence falls over the room. I can feel their eyes on me, filled with concern, curiosity, and something else. Fear, probably. All of this is not what they signed up for. Mind you, it's not what I signed up for either, so I can't blame them if they run and hide.

But when I look around at these four extraordinary beings, each powerful in their own right, each connected to me in ways I'm only beginning to understand, I feel a surge of emotion. Gratitude, fear, and something deeper, more complex because they aren't running. They are here with me, and they aren't leaving.

Corvus pulls me close, and I feel the others gathering around us. A circle of protection, a barrier against whatever darkness is trying to claim me.

But as I close my eyes, I know that this is just the beginning. The battle for control has only just begun, and the stakes are higher than any of us could imagine.

In the depths of my mind, in that dark room newly discovered, something stirs. Waiting. Watching. And I know, with a certainty that chills me to my core, that this is far from over.

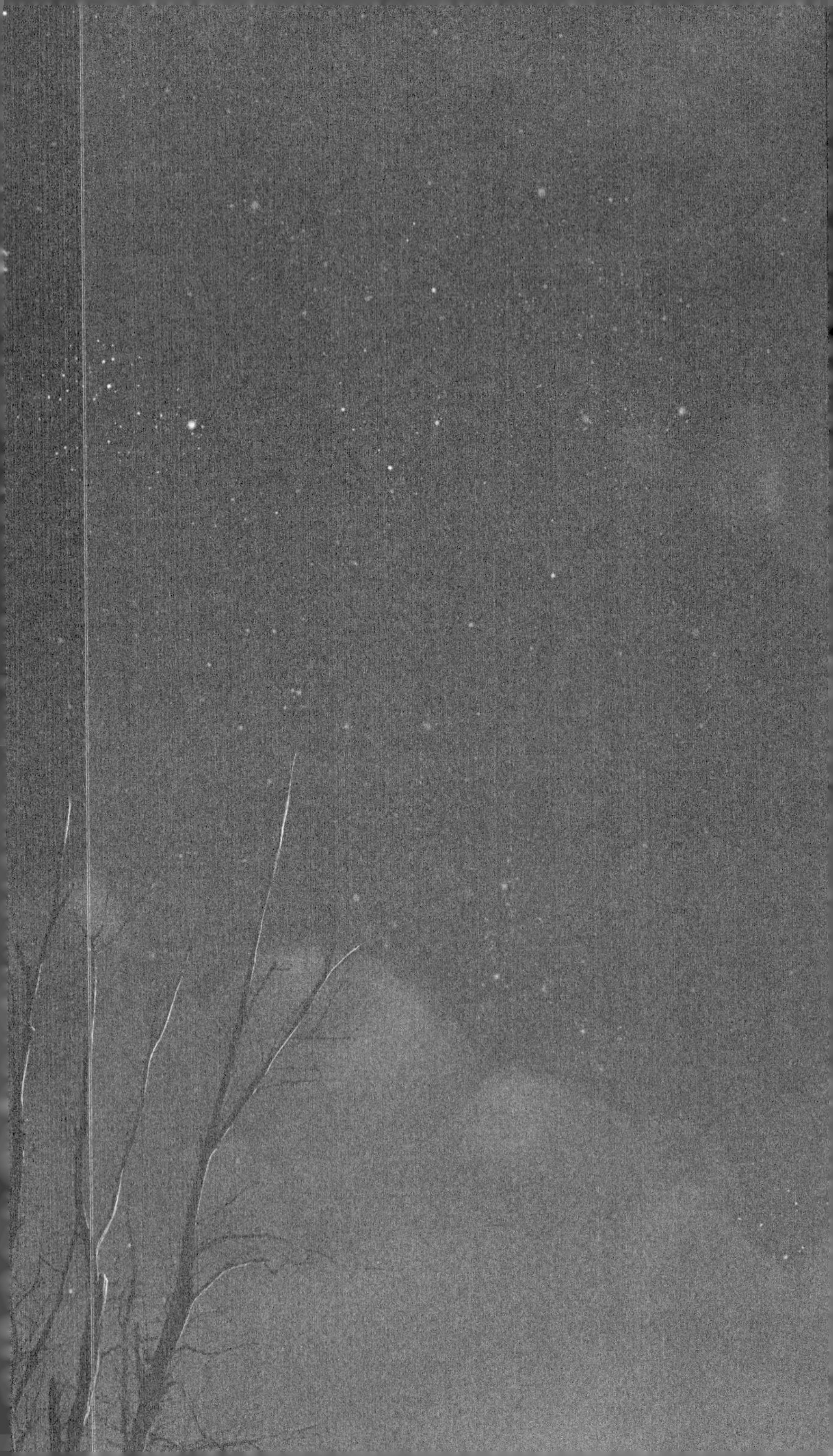

Chapter 38

Adelaide

The guys hover around me. Their concern is suffocating, even if I appreciate their intentions. I need space. I need to think. The room feels smaller with all of them here, their powerful presence filling every corner. I'm not used to this. I'm used to me and dealing with things on my own.

"I need you all to leave," I blurt out. I feel a pang of guilt, but I know it's necessary.

They exchange glances, clearly reluctant. I can see the worry etched on their faces, the tension in their bodies. They want to protect me, but right now, I need to protect myself.

"Adelaide," Zaiah starts, his white eyes filled with worry. "Are you sure that's wise? After what just happened—"

"I'm sure," I cut him off, perhaps more harshly than I intended. "Please. I need to be alone."

Corvus lifts me off his lap and pulls the covers over

me quickly. He gets dressed before he reaches for my hand. His touch, so comforting earlier, now feels like an intrusion. "Addy, we're just worried about you. What if it happens again?"

I pull my hand away, immediately regretting the hurt that flashes across his face. It's like a knife to my gut, but I steel myself. "Then it happens again. But I need to figure this out on my own. At least for now."

Zephyr, surprisingly, is the first to nod. "We should respect her wishes," he says. There's an understanding that I didn't expect in his gaze. Of all of them, he seems to grasp my need for solitude the most. That says a lot about him.

Ignatius looks like he wants to argue, his fiery nature is clearly at odds with the idea of leaving me alone. But after a moment, he sighs, the fight going out of him. "Fine. But promise you'll come to us if anything happens. Anything at all."

I nod, relief washing over me as they move towards the door. It's like the air is coming back into the room, allowing me to breathe again.

Zaiah creates a pocket dimension for himself and Ignatius, the air shimmering as they step through. Zephyr transforms into a gust of wind, his presence lingering for a moment before slipping out the window. Corvus is the last to leave, his eyes lingering on me. The intensity of his gaze makes my heart ache.

"Be careful," he says softly before transforming into a bat and following Zephyr out. It's only when I get up to close the window behind them, I wonder how they got in without me inviting them. Have the wards failed? Or do they just recognise my fated mates? Mates. Is that even a thing? I guess it is.

The room feels bigger now, less claustrophobic, but the silence is almost deafening. I can hear my heartbeat, steady but fast, like a drum in my ears.

I race upstairs to the bathroom, wincing at my reflection in the mirror. Dried blood cakes my cheeks, my eyes red-rimmed and puffy. I look like hell. Like I've been through a war. In a way, I suppose I have: an internal one for my soul.

I jump when my reflection turns back to that Crimson bitch, but I glare at her, my body primed.

"You," she hisses. "Will not last long here."

"And you," I hiss back, matching her cadence perfectly. "Will fuck off out of my sight right now before I smash this mirror with my bare hands."

"Go for it," she snarls. "I'm not going anywhere."

She does, however, vanish from the mirror, but I can feel her presence pressing at my consciousness.

Turning on the tap, I splash cold water on my face, scrubbing away the evidence of whatever the fuck this is. The water runs pink for a moment before clearing. As I pat my face dry, I stare at my reflection, half expecting to see that other face again. But it's just me—just Adelaide.

Or is it?

Am I even me anymore?

I lean closer to the mirror, studying my eyes. Are they a shade darker than before? Is there a hint of red in their depths? Or am I just being paranoid?

Shaking off the thought, I head back to my room and get dressed. The same old jeans and black tee I've been wearing all night and my combat boots. Minus any knickers. But it's practical. I'm ready for anything. Because, at this point, anything could happen.

I need answers, and I know just where to start looking.

Hauling up my backpack, I jump a mile when Orby zooms out of it. I'd forgotten he went in there during classes and seems to have been asleep this entire time. At least, I hope he was and not being a semi-sentient voyeur to me and Corvus. "Orby," I murmur.

He bounces around as usual, so I don't think he saw anything he shouldn't have. I'm going to have to remember that for the future.

Making my way downstairs, I cross the courtyard and head to the library. It's quiet at this hour, nearing dawn. Perfect. I don't need an audience for this. The smell of old books and dust fills my nostrils as I enter, a comforting scent that sets me firmly in reality.

I start in the vampire section, pulling out every book I can find on vampire lore and history. The weight of the old books is reassuring in my hands. Surely, among all this knowledge, I'll find something about what's happening to me.

But hours pass as I pore over dusty tomes and ancient scrolls, and I find nothing about any Crimson anything. My eyes burn from the strain, but I push on. I can't stop. Not now. Not when the answers might be just a page away.

Crimson. I search for any mention of the name, any reference to vampires with red eyes or blood tears. But I come up empty. There's plenty about vampires, their powers, their weaknesses. Stories of ancient bloodlines and legendary vampires. But nothing about whatever the fuck is happening to me.

"Fuck!" I exclaim, catching the attention of a vampire studying at a nearby table. He frowns at me, but then goes back to his work.

I read about vampires who can control minds, vampires who can turn into mist or animals. I learn about the politics of vampire society, the complex hierarchies and alliances. But nowhere do I find anything about a vampire with another presence inside them. A darker, more powerful self.

My frustration is ripping at my insides as I shelve the last book. I've been at this for too long, and I'm no closer to understanding what's going on. The sun is high outside, and I'm getting tired.

Sighing, I gather my things and head out. I need air. I need to think. Then I need to sleep and start all over again after lectures tonight. The stuffy atmosphere of the library suddenly feels oppressive, the weight of all that useless knowledge pressing down on me.

Leaving it behind, I aim for the forest at the edge of the MistHallow grounds. The morning mist clings to the ground, swirling around my ankles as I walk. It's peaceful, the sounds of the forest a welcome change from the stuffy silence of the library.

As I walk, my mind races. What the fuck is

happening to me? Am I going crazy? Is this some weird vampire puberty shit that no one thought to warn me about? Or is it something else entirely? Something older, more powerful, more dangerous?

I think back to the bathroom mirror, to the face I saw. It was me, but not me. Older, maybe. Harder. And those eyes... blood-red and full of power. It was like looking at a version of myself from a dark future, a path I'm not sure I want to walk.

Or do I?

I can't deny that the sheer power coming from her is alluring, tempting. It's calling to me, and I want to give in. It would be easier than to fight her.

Crimson. The name echoes in my head, but it is meaningless.

A twig snaps under my foot, startling me out of my thoughts. I've wandered deeper into the forest than I meant to. The trees are thicker, the mist heavier, the chill icy. For a moment, I consider turning back. This far from the academy, who knows what kind of creatures might be lurking?

But something pulls me forward. A feeling, an instinct I can't explain. It's like there's a thread connected to my very core, tugging me deeper into the woods.

I push on, the forest growing denser around me. The mist thickens, obscuring my vision. It's like walking through a dream. Shapes loom out of the fog, settling into trees or rocks before fading away again.

Suddenly, the trees part, revealing a small clearing. In the centre stands a stone monolith, ancient and weathered. It's different from the one I was in with Zephyr the other night. Symbols I don't recognise are carved into its surface, barely visible under years of moss and lichen. It feels old. Older than MistHallow, which is saying something.

As I approach, I feel a strange energy pouring from the stone. It's familiar somehow, like a half-remembered dream. Like the presence I felt earlier, but different. Older. More primal.

Without thinking, I reach out and touch the monolith. The moment my fingers make contact, a jolt of energy surges through me. Images flash before my eyes, too fast to make sense of. Blood. Fire. Shadows that move with a life of their own. Battles fought in darkness, power beyond imagination wielded by figures shrouded in mystery.

I try to pull my hand away, but I can't move. The energy builds, growing stronger, more intense. My whole body feels like it's on fire, every nerve ending screaming in protest.

Pain explodes behind my eyes, and I hear myself scream. The sound echoes through the clearing, sending birds scattering from the trees.

"Who are you?" I shout, my voice echoing in the clearing. "What do you want?"

For a moment, there's nothing but silence. The forest seems to hold its breath, waiting. Then, a voice. Her voice. My voice.

"I am you," it says. "And you are me. We are one, little bitch. Accept it."

The words resonate through me, shaking me to my core.

"No," I growl, fighting against the pain, the intrusion. "I'm Adelaide Légère. Adelaide *Black*."

Laughter echoes in my mind, cold and cruel. "Oh, little bitch. You have no idea what you are."

The energy surges again, and I fall to my knees, my hand still pressed against the stone. I can feel her trying to take control. It's like being torn in two, my soul splitting apart.

"Stop," I gasp. "Please."

"I can't stop," the voice says. "I am you. Your power. Your potential. Your destiny."

"I don't want it," I cry out. "I just want to be me."

The laughter comes again, softer this time. Almost sad. "Oh, Adelaide. You can't fight what you are. We are the shadow that walks in daylight, the power that flows through your veins. We are Crimson Shadow."

With a final burst of energy, the connection breaks. I fall back, my hand finally free from the stone. The clearing spins around me as I struggle to catch my breath. My whole body aches, every muscle screaming in protest.

As my vision clears, I see that the symbols on the monolith are glowing faintly. Red, like blood. Like her eyes. Like my eyes.

I scramble to my feet, stumbling away from the stone. My head is pounding, my whole body aching. But I'm me. Just me.

For now.

What the fuck was that? Who is she? What am I?

The questions swirl in my head, unanswered and terrifying. But one thing is clear: I can't keep this to myself anymore. I need help. I need to speak to Blackthorn, or maybe even Randall.

The forest seems different as I retrace my steps. Darker, more alive. I can feel eyes on me, watching from the shadows. But nothing attacks. Nothing approaches. It's as if the forest recognises something in me, something dangerous.

I trip over a tangled mass of roots and fall to the ground, my ankle twinging with pain. "Fuck," I growl as I sit up and brush my hands off on my jeans. "Fuck you, roots. Fuck you, forest, Fuck you, Crimson. Fuck everything."

Tears spring into my eyes, and I haul myself onto a fallen log, dropping my head into my hands as I cry for everything I lost, everything I thought I didn't want, but miss like crazy right now.

Chapter 39

Zephyr

The scent of damp earth and decaying leaves fills my nostrils as I slip through the forest, my footsteps muffled by the thick, dark fog that clings to the ground. This is unusual. It's like wading underwater, unable to see your hand in front of your face.

As I round a bend in the path, the fog clears, and I spot Adelaide. She's sitting on a fallen log, her shoulders slumped, and her head bowed. Even from a distance, I can see the tightness in her body, the way her hands are clenched in her lap. She looks so small and vulnerable, and it takes all my self-control not to rush over and wrap her in my arms.

Instead, I slow my pace, approaching her cautiously. I don't want to startle her or make her feel like I'm invading her space. As I draw closer, I see the faint traces of blood tears on her cheeks, and it freezes my already icy blood.

"Princess," I say softly, trying to keep my voice steady. "You shouldn't be out here alone."

She looks up at me, her eyes red-rimmed and haunted. "I'm fine," she says, but her voice is thin and shaky.

"I don't believe you for one second." I take a seat next to her on the log, close enough that our shoulders are touching.

"I don't care," she mumbles.

"Ouch. And here I thought we were coming to an understanding."

"Of what, exactly?"

"Of who you are to me."

For a moment, we sit in silence, listening to the distant sounds of the forest. I can hear the faint rustling of leaves, the lap of the water from the lake not far from here. It's peaceful, which is so at odds with Adelaide's anxiety, which is clawing at my insides, making me squirm slightly. I'm connected to her at such a basic level, if I stop to think about it too long, it scares me.

"What are you doing out here?" I ask finally, breaking the silence.

"I needed some fresh air," she says.

"It's dangerous."

"How is it any more dangerous than being in my room and being attacked by crazy, ancient vampire women?"

"Okay, but out here, more than crazy vampire women can get to you."

"You forgot ancient."

"Hmm?"

"Crazy *ancient* vampire women. And it's not even. It's one. One vampire."

Hearing the crack of a twig, I look up to see Christos approaching. I scowl at him. He is my cousin and my nemesis, if we want to get all super villain about it. I can't stand the arse-kiss, and I know he hates me just as much.

"What do you want?" I snap, causing Adelaide to look up.

"Ah, cousin," Christos sneers, his eyes glinting with malice. "Fancy seeing you here."

"What do you want, Christos?" I repeat, my voice low and dangerous.

He smirks, running a hand through his jet-black hair. "I saw our new girl sitting here all alone and thought I'd see if everything was okay, perhaps offer her some comfort."

"She's not alone."

"No, not anymore," he drawls. "More's the pity."

"Get out of here, Chris. You have seriously picked the wrong day to wind me up."

Christos glares at me, his magick sparking around him. He is looking for a fight, and I'm fully prepared to give him one. I rise in one fluid motion and grab his shirt.

"Back off," I growl. I can feel my magick swirling around me, a dark cloud of power and authority.

Christos tries to shrug off my grip, but I tighten it. I can feel his magick thrumming beneath his skin, but it's no match for mine. I'm the heir to the Dark Fae throne, and he seems to forget that.

"You don't scare me," Chris sneers.

"You should be scared," I say, my voice cold and hard. "Because if you so much as look at her the wrong way, I'll make sure you regret it."

"You think you can protect her from me? I know what she is, and she is about to learn that she doesn't get a fucking choice when it comes to me and the power I want."

Adelaide's harsh rasp as she takes that threat on board is a beautiful thing. I can feel the power in me rise up exponentially. She isn't even touching me, and yet she is boosting my power.

Suddenly, Chris lunges at me, his fists flying in a move I didn't expect. Physical blows are beneath us, usually. But if he wants to see that my father has trained me in *all* forms of combat, bring it.

I dodge and weave, my movements fluid and precise. I can feel the power of my magick coursing through me, driven harder by Adelaide's power. I land a punch, and Chris stumbles back, his face contorted in pain.

He summons a blast of pure energy that sends me flying backwards. I hit the ground hard, but I'm back on my feet in an instant. I can see the blood trickling down my face, but I don't care. "Oh, that was a bad move, cousin," I snarl, now more pissed off than anything.

He charges at me again, but I grab his arm, twisting it behind his back. He lets out a cry of pain, but I don't let go. I hold my hand up and slam him to the ground with my magick, crushing his chest with the weight of the power behind me as I crouch next to him.

"If you come within five hundred yards of her again, I will fucking smite you where you stand. The only reason you get a pass today, and I mean the *only* fucking reason I'm not slicing you up into tiny pieces to barbecue and feed to the wolves, is because I seriously cannot be arsed dealing with my father's lecture on family. Today. But don't make the mistake of thinking the same tomorrow, fucker. Got it?"

He glares at me, his eyes burning with hatred. But he has nowhere to go. He didn't expect it. We are not evenly matched at the best of times, but he gives me a good workout. He is no slouch being who he is.

"You're a fucking dick," he hisses. "Your father will hear about this."

"Oh, please. I beg you to inform him that you were about to attack and rape my future wife. I fucking dare you."

His face pales as he looks at Adelaide, and his jaw clenches.

"This isn't over. The Vesper is fair game. You might think she's yours, but no way in hell are you getting her."

"Excuse fucking you!" Adelaide suddenly exclaims, standing up and kicking Christos in the nuts so hard I burst out laughing. "I would rather gouge my eyes out with a blunt spoon than *ever* be with you. Fuck off. And if you come near me again, Zephyr will be the least of your worries, are we clear?"

Christos growls, and I let him up reluctantly. The beast inside me is screaming at me to end him, to rip his limbs off and eat them, but he is already gone.

I smile as I look up at Adelaide, my smile slow and predatory. Her anger satisfies something primal in my black soul. "You're mine, Adelaide," I murmur as I rise and go to her. I grip her chin, just this side of roughly. "Do you understand?"

I expect her to be angry, to push back against my possessiveness. But instead, I see a dark thrill in her eyes, an instinctual response to my words. She feels it, too, this connection between us. She's mine, and I am hers.

"What do you want, Zephyr?" she asks. "What do you want from me?"

"You. I want you, Adelaide. All of you."

"Zephyr," she whispers, her voice a plea, a surrender.

I lean in, my lips crushing hers. This time, the kiss is not soft, not fleeting. It's hungry, demanding, consuming. She melts into me, her body pressing against mine, her hands tangling in my hair. I growl low in my throat, my arms wrapping around her, pulling her closer. I can feel her desire, her passion, her need for me. It's raw, primitive, all-consuming.

My touch is rough, demanding, leaving marks on her skin as I strip her bare using magick for the trickier bits.

"Fuck, Adelaide," I groan, my voice ragged. "I need you."

She moans in response, her body arching against mine. I can feel the darkness in her, the savagery, and it calls to the darkness in me. I want more. I want everything.

"Zephyr," she gasps, her voice a plea. "More. I need more."

I growl again and push her onto her hands and knees in the middle of the forest where anyone could walk up and see us. My hands grip her hips, my fingers digging into her flesh. I unzip my pants and grab my rock hard cock.

"Is this what you want, Adelaide?" I murmur. "You want me to fuck you like an animal?"

"Yes," she moans, pushing back against me. "Yes, please."

I laugh, a dark, dangerous sound. "Such a bad, Little Dollie." I slap her arse and slam into her, thrusting deep with a low groan.

She cries out. She's tight, but she takes all of me, her body stretching to accommodate my throbbing cock. It feels so good, so right. This is what I've been craving, what I've been needing.

My hips move with a brutal rhythm, my cock pounding into her with a force that leaves her breathless. My fingers dig into her flesh, holding her in place, controlling her completely.

"Harder," she gasps, her voice ragged. "Fuck me harder, Zephyr."

I growl, my pace increasing, my thrusts becoming more forceful. I can feel the darkness in me, the savagery, the brutality rising to the surface and wanting to show her the real me. But she isn't ready for that. Not yet.

The pleasure builds, intense and overwhelming. I can feel her orgasm approaching, like a storm on the horizon, and when it hits, it's all-consuming, a wave of pleasure that crashes over her, leaving her shaking and breathless as her pussy clutches my cock possessively, letting me know that she is mine.

My cock pulses inside her, my body shuddering against hers as I unload into her with a grunt of pure satisfaction. I've never felt this way about anyone before, never wanted someone so completely, so intensely. But Adelaide is different. She's mine and she knows it. I'll do whatever it takes to protect her, to keep her by my side because I know that my life has changed irrevocably. I've found my fate, my equal, my partner in darkness, and I'll do whatever it takes to keep her safe, to make her happy, to give her the world she deserves.

Because this is who I am. This is my truth, my power, my destiny. We'll conquer the darkness, embrace the savagery, and reign supreme in this new world of shadows and desires.

"Fuck, Zephyr," Adelaide pants, still trembling from her orgasm. I smile at the sight of her, sprawled out in nature, with my cock still inside her. She's a fucking goddess, my dark queen.

I pull out of her, my cock still throbbing from the intensity of our fucking. I zip up my pants and help her to her feet, my hands gentle as I brush the dirt off her skin. She looks up at me with a small, shy smile, her eyes still full of desire.

"This is just the beginning, princess," I murmur.

She shivers at the sound of my voice, her body responding instinctively to the promise of more.

I lean into whisper in her ear. "I'm going to claim you, Adelaide. Every inch of you. You're mine, and soon you won't be able to live without me. You will need me, crave me, die without me."

She gasps at my words, her eyes widening in surprise and lust. "Yes," she breathes. "I want that, Zephyr. I want all of that."

I stroke her hair softly. "Good, Little Dollie. I will break you and put you back together so that no one else can have you except us."

She nods and leans into me with her eyes closed, and I hold her, knowing that now her secret is out, she is in more danger than she realises. But anyone who wants to get to her will have to go through me first, and I pity the arsehole that tries to get between me and the only creature that has ever made me want them this way.

Chapter 40

Adelaide

My skin still tingles from our encounter as I step out of the forest with Zephyr. The connection between us feels more substantial, more intense than ever before. His possessive words are wild at the same time as thrilling. *My future wife.* Is that really how he sees me? What about my say in this?

I glance at him as we walk, remembering the way his hands felt on my skin, the heat of his breath on my neck. The forest around us seems different now, charged with an energy I can't quite explain. It's leaning into us, following our path in a protective and approving way. It's weird, but that is precisely what it is. I can sense it all around me.

But as we approach the campus, a chill runs through my blood that has nothing to do with desire and everything to do with the fight with Christos. Those words echo in my mind now, cutting through everything else with a laser-like quality.

Vesper.

He called me a Vesper.

The secret I've been trying so hard to keep is out now. What does this mean for me? For my future at MistHallow?

I open my mouth to ask Zephyr about it, to seek some reassurance or explanation, but before I can form the words, chaos erupts around us. Students are running towards us, shouting, their faces contorted with fear and urgency. At first, I think it's some kind of practical class, but then I see the looks on their faces, the raw panic in their eyes. This is real. Terrifyingly real.

"Zephyr," I murmur, my voice trembling slightly, but he's already moving, pushing me behind him protectively. His body tenses, ready for a fight, and I can sense his power building, ready to be unleashed.

The students' faces are twisted with aggression I've never seen before. It's like they've been transformed into something else entirely.

"What's going on?" I shout over the growing chaos. The sounds of screams and running feet fill the air, creating a chaos of screams and panic.

Zephyr doesn't answer. His body is coiled tight, a panther ready to strike. "Stay close to me," he says, his voice low and urgent. There's a fierceness in his eyes that reassures but frightens me. This is a side to him that I've merely glimpsed, but now I'm about to see a whole lot more.

But before we can move, before we can even think about finding safety, the sky darkens. At first, I think it's a storm rolling in - the weather at MistHallow can be unpredictable at best. Then I see them, and my blood runs icy cold.

Strix.

Dozens of them, maybe more. Their massive wings block out the daylight as they descend upon us, turning day into an eerie twilight. Their talons gleam wickedly, their eyes fixed on me with an aggressive intensity that makes my skin crawl. I've never seen anything like it before, and I hope I never will again.

My breath catches in my throat, fear gripping my chest like a frozen hand. The supernatural assassins, deadly and relentless, are coming for me again, and I know this time they will get to me. They're terrifying in a way that goes beyond simple fear. It's primal, instinctive.

Zephyr springs into action, his movements a blur of speed, grace, and power. His face is set in a mask of pure ferociousness as he takes on the first wave of attackers. His power is breathtaking, awe-inspiring even now, when I should be running, instead I'm standing rooted to the spot like an idiot.

Shadows bend to Zephyr's will, lashing out at the Strix like solid weapons. It's like watching the beast of nature unleashed and on a rampage. For every Strix he takes down, two more seem to take its place. The air is filled with the sound of beating wings and inhuman screeches, a noise that sets my teeth on edge and makes my hair stand on end.

I want to help, to do something, anything. But what can I do? I have no powers, no way to defend myself or assist Zephyr. I feel useless, helpless, a liability in this fight that's all about me.

The first Strix dives, its wings cutting through the air like a blade. I duck instinctively, feeling the rush of air as it passes over me, so close I can feel the wind from its wings. For a moment, I think I'm done for. But then Zephyr is there in an instant, a dark blur of motion.

His hands, tipped with black claws, lash out, catching the Strix mid-flight, suspended with magick. With a brutal twist of his hands, he tears the creature in two, its screech of pain cut short as its body hits the ground with a wet thud.

But there's no time to take in the horror of the gruesome sight. More Strix are coming, always more. They're all around us like a plague, their cries filling the air like a chorus of the damned.

Zephyr moves like a dancer, his body a lethal weapon. He tears through the Strix, trying to get to me with a savagery that is beautiful and horrifying. Blood rains down, painting the ground in dark, glistening patterns. Feathers and flesh fly in all directions, the air thick with the coppery scent of blood and the acrid tang of fear.

Then, a flash of fire.

Ignatius has joined the fight.

"Get her inside!"

Zephyr's yell falls on deaf ears. There is too much action, violence and screeching for anyone to hear.

Get inside.

The voice resonates in my mind.

Move, princess, before there is nothing left of you for me to claim.

"Zephyr?"

Distracted, a sharp pain tears through my shoulder as a Strix sinks its talons into my flesh. I cry out, stumbling back, my vision swimming with pain. The Strix presses its advantage, its beak snapping mere inches from my face. I can see the hunger in its eyes, the promise of death.

Zephyr dives in my direction, his roar of fury shaking the ground underneath us. His eyes are fully silver now, black veins running under his pale skin. He tears the Strix away from me, his claws sinking deep into its flesh. With a brutal wrench, he rips the creature apart with magick, its body nothing but a bloody heap when he's done. In shock, I place my hand on my shoulder, but the wound has healed already.

He turns back to the oncoming horde. He is a force of nature, a god of war. He tears through the Strix like a whirlwind, his magick rending flesh and bone with ease. Blood sprays in all directions, the ground is soaked.

"Run!" Zephyr shouts at me. "Get inside, for fuck's sake!"

I hesitate for a split second, not wanting to leave him. The thought of abandoning him to face this horde alone tears at me. But I know I'm only a distraction, a liability in this fight. As much as I hate it, the best thing I can do for everyone right now is to get out of the way.

I turn and run, my feet pounding against the ground. The campus has become a battleground. Students and staff are fleeing in all directions, some fighting back against the Strix with whatever weapons or powers they have at hand.

But it's chaos, pure and simple.

I don't get far. A shadow passes over me, more significant and darker than the others. Before I can react, before I can even think to dodge, I'm lifted off my feet. Talons dig into my arms, enough to break my skin, making me bleed. The pain is sharp, immediate, and I cry out.

I scream, kicking and thrashing with all my might, but it's no use. The Strix is too strong, its grip unbreakable. It's carrying me away, higher and higher, into the sky. The ground falls away beneath me at a terrifying rate.

I crane my neck, trying desperately to see Zephyr and Ignatius. They're still fighting with Zaiah and other creatures I don't know. They're getting smaller, more distant with each beat of the Strix's wings. The distance between us grows with every second, and with it, my hope of rescue.

"Zephyr!" I scream his name, pouring all my fear and desperation into that one word. But my voice is lost in the wind, swallowed up by the vast expanse of sky around me.

The ground below becomes a patchwork of green and grey as we soar over the forest. My stomach lurches at the height, a dizzying vertigo that makes me squeeze my eyes shut. I've never been afraid of heights before, but this is something else entirely.

This can't be happening. It feels like a nightmare, but

the pain in my arms, the wind whipping through my hair - it's all too real. What do they want with me? Where are they taking me? The questions swirl in my mind, each more terrifying than the last.

I try to think, to come up with some plan of escape. But what can I do? I'm powerless, defenceless, suspended hundreds of feet in the air, with no way down except a fatal fall. I'm a Vesper, this supposed wonder of the supernatural world, but I have nothing defensive in my arsenal. Everything I have is passive.

That you know of.

"Not helping," I grit out loud, trying to find courage instead of fear. But it's not easy.

The wind whips through my hair, the growing fog hitting my face, chilling me to the bone. I shiver, from cold and fear. The Strix's grip on my arms is relentless. They've gone numb from the talons digging into my flesh deep enough to reach bone.

The reality of my situation hits me like a punch to the gut. I'm alone. Truly alone. Just like always.

No Zephyr, no Corvus, no Ignatius or Zaiah. No one to swoop in and save me at the last moment like in the stories. This is real life, and in real life, sometimes there are no heroes coming to the rescue.

You are all you've got.

I've never felt so vulnerable, so utterly helpless, but I feel the surge of useless anger rising. Whatever is happening, whatever these Strix want with me—or better yet, their master—I have no way of fighting back. I have no powers to call on, no tricks up my sleeve. I'm at their mercy.

The Strix carrying me, suddenly banks sharply to the left, and my stomach lurches violently. I can feel bile rising in my throat, but I swallow it down with difficulty. Getting sick now would only make things worse, if that's even possible.

We're flying over a part of the forest that is thicker, more dense, visible in the thinning fog. The trees here are older, darker, their branches twisting in ways that are unnatural. There's something ominous about them, as if they're watching us pass overhead with ancient, evil eyes. An endless sea of green, stretching out to the horizon in every direction.

I try to shift, to relieve some of the pressure on my arms, but its talons only tighten in response. I let out a whimper, but it's lost in the rush of wind.

"Where are you taking me?" I shout, my voice hoarse with fear and the effort of trying to be heard over the wind. But my words are whipped away the moment they leave my mouth, lost in the vast emptiness of the sky.

The Strix doesn't respond. Of course, it doesn't. If they even can speak at all, it's not their job to tell me jack-shit. Right now, they're simply instruments of my abduction, silent and implacable.

I close my eyes again, trying to think past the fear and pain. There has to be a way out of this. There has to be something I can do. I refuse to believe that this is how my story ends—just as I feel it's getting started—carried off by mythical creatures to who knows where, helpless and alone.

But before I can come up with anything, before I can even begin to formulate a plan, pain explodes in my head. One of the other Strix, forming a circle around us, has struck me with its wing, hard. The blow comes out of nowhere, sudden and vicious.

My vision blurs instantly, the world around me becoming a swirl of colours and shapes. Darkness creeps in at the edges of my sight. I fight against the encroaching unconsciousness with everything I have. I have to stay awake. I have to.

But it's no use. The darkness is too strong, the pain too intense. I feel myself slipping away, my grip on consciousness weakening with each passing second.

The world fades to black, and I'm falling, falling into an abyss of uncertainty and fear.

As consciousness slips away entirely, I feel a strange sense of peace wash over me. Maybe it's just my mind's way of coping with the trauma, but for a brief moment, I feel... safe. Protected. Something deep inside me has stirred, awakened.

"Crimson..."

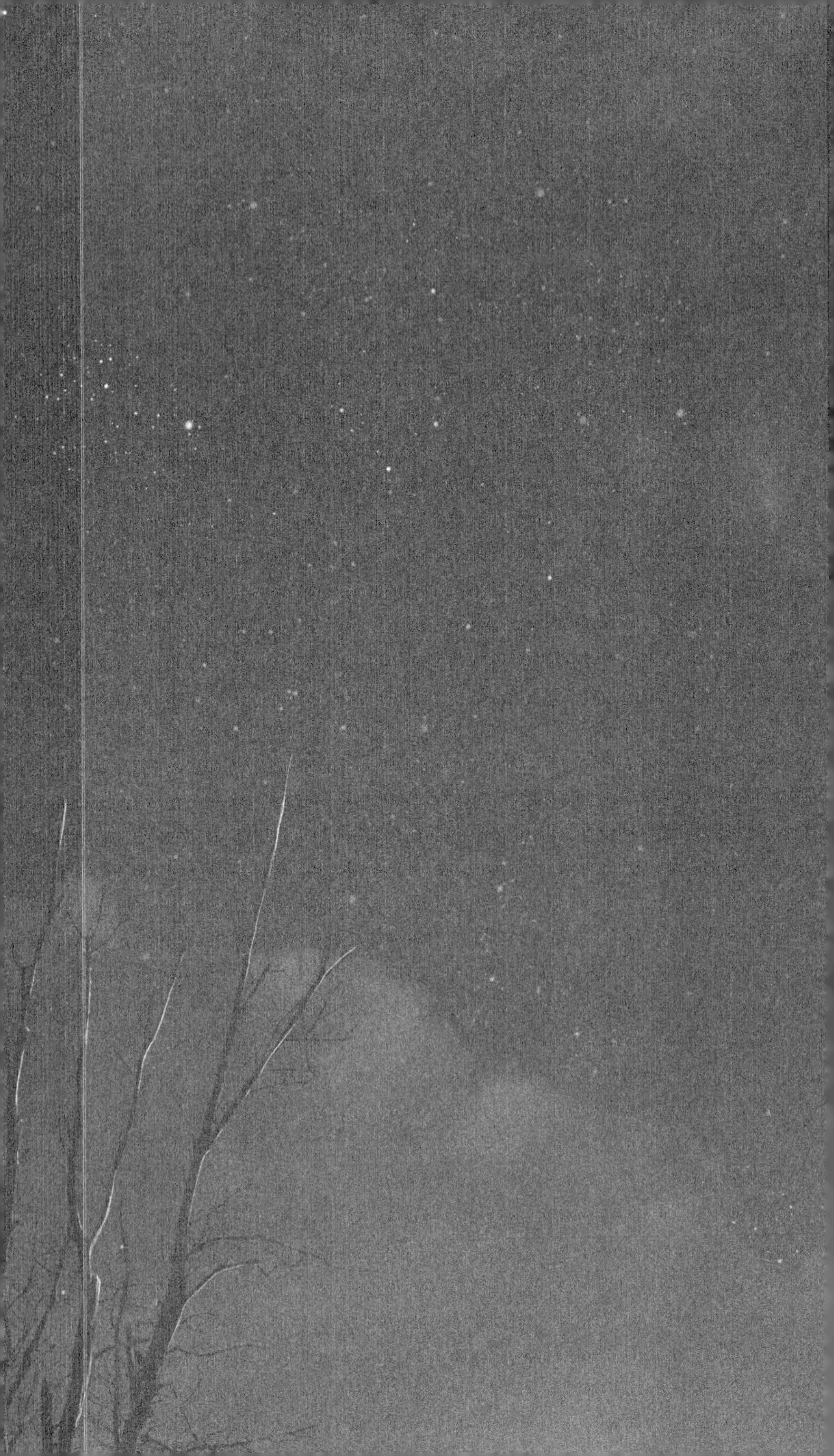

Chapter 41

Adelaide

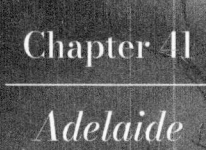

With my head throbbing, I wake up.

The pain is intense, pulsing behind my eyes and making it hard to concentrate. Everything's fuzzy. My vision is blurred, and I can't quite make sense of my surroundings. The world seems to swim in and out of focus, making me feel disoriented and nauseous.

Where am I? I try to move, but something's wrong. My arms and legs won't budge. There's resistance when I try to shift. Something is holding me in place. I blink rapidly, trying to clear my vision, but it's like looking through a heat haze. The air around me seems to shimmer and waver, distorting my perception.

Slowly, shapes start to form, and the sharp scent of nature hits my nose. The smell of damp earth, pine needles, and fresh air fills my nostrils. Trees. I'm outside in the forest.

As my eyes adjust. I see stones. A circle of them

surrounds me, their rough surfaces covered in moss and lichen. They're large, taller than a person, and seem ancient. I'm in the middle of this stone circle, lying on something hard and cold. The surface beneath me is unyielding, probably stone as well.

I look around, taking in more details of my surroundings, and my stomach drops as the realisation sets in. There are five points, strategically placed around me. Metal glints in the low light, and I can feel the cold touch of chains on my wrists and ankles. It doesn't take a genius to figure out that I'm chained to a pentagram.

Fuck. Fuck!

Panic hits me like a truck, a rush of adrenaline flooding my system. My heart rate skyrockets, and I can hear the blood rushing in my ears. I thrash against the chains, the metal biting into my skin. The pain is sharp, real. This isn't a dream. This is really happening.

"Help!" I scream, my voice raw and desperate. "Somebody help me!"

My voice echoes through the trees, bouncing off the stone circle and fading into the distance. No one answers. The forest around me is deathly quiet. Just the rustle of leaves in the wind and the distant call of a bird breaks the silence. It's as if the whole world has abandoned me.

I strain against the chains again, putting all my strength into trying to break free. But they're too tight, the metal isn't giving way. I can barely move an inch in any direction. The chains rattle loudly in the quiet forest, a harsh sound that only emphasises my helplessness.

"Adelaide, calm down." Professor Blackthorn's voice

cuts through my panic as he moves into view on my left. The sound of his familiar voice in this bizarre situation is jarring. He's standing over me, his face grim, his eyes shadowed. How did he find me? Why is he here? "You need to trust me, okay?"

Trust him? Is he fucking joking? "You abducted me and chained me to a pentagram!" I shriek at him, my voice high and hysterical. I'm driven purely by panic and fear, unable to process the situation rationally.

"Get away from her, Luke!"

I know that voice. I recognise it instantly, even though it's new to me.

My dad. Randall Black.

He's walking towards us, his footsteps heavy on the forest floor. He's holding something that glints in the low light. A knife? The sight of the weapon sends a fresh wave of fear through me.

Blackthorn turns to face him, his body tensing as if preparing for a fight. "You don't know what you're doing, Randall."

"Get away from her, Luke," my father growls again. "I'm not telling you again." His voice is filled with deadly aggression, a tone I've never heard before. Despite the situation, my stomach untwists slightly at the protective note in his voice.

"Not a fucking chance, Randall," Blackthorn retorts. Suddenly, fire erupts from Blackthorn's hands, the flames casting flickering shadows across the clearing. At the same time, shadows seem to bend and twist around my father, the darkness itself responding to his will. The air snaps with a magick so dark and powerful, I nearly vomit from the pressure of it bearing down on my soul.

I watch, frozen in shock and fear, unable to do anything but observe as these two men prepare to battle over me.

They clash. Trees splinter and fall as blasts of energy miss their targets, the sound of breaking wood echoing through the forest. The ground shakes beneath me with each impact, the vibrations travelling through the stone I'm lying on. The atmosphere is heavy, static, thick like soup. I can barely breathe, the air pressing down on my chest.

My mind races, trying to make sense of what's happening. None of this makes sense. Why are they fighting? What do they want with me? I pull at the chains again, ignoring the pain as they cut into my wrists. They won't budge, the metal as unyielding as ever. I'm trapped, forced to watch as these two powerful beings fight over me.

You're in for it now, little bitch.

"Oh, you can shut the fuck up, massive cunt," I growl at Crimson's voice in my head. Even in this terrifying situation, her presence is an unwelcome intrusion.

She laughs, the sound full of amusement while I'm chained to the ground in some kind of satanic ritual.

Don't be silly, girl. This is full-on witch powers. Pagan. The Satanists stole it.

"Gee, thanks for the fucking religious lesson, cunt. Got any ideas to get me out of here?"

She goes quiet, offering no help or advice.

"Of course," I mutter, not surprised by her lack of assistance.

The fight intensifies, drawing my attention back to the battle raging around me. Blackthorn hurls bolts of energy that light up the clearing like lightning, the flashes momentarily blinding me. My father counters with waves of darkness that seem to swallow the light, plunging the area into brief moments of total blackness. I can't tell who's winning. They seem evenly matched, neither able to gain the upper hand.

Light and dark.

Légère and Black.

I don't know what to think. My eyes dart between the two men, trying to find some clue on how to get out of here. But I'm helpless, unable to do anything but watch and hope.

As I watch them clash again, a terrifying thought hits me. No matter who wins this fight, I'm in danger. I will always be in danger because of what I am. This realisation settles over me like a heavy blanket, smothering any hope I had of things ever going back to normal.

A stray bolt of energy from the fight strikes the ground near me, showering me with dirt and small stones. I scream, the debris stinging my skin. I try to curl into myself for protection, but the chains hold me spread-eagled out on the ground, leaving me exposed and vulnerable.

"Stop!" I yell, my voice is hoarse from screaming. "Please, just stop!"

But they don't seem to hear me. Or if they do, they

don't care. They're too focused on each other, on their battle over me. My pleas fall on deaf ears as the fight continues to rage around me.

I strain my ears, trying to catch snippets of what they're saying to each other as they fight. Their words are mostly lost in the chaos of the battle, but I manage to catch a few fragments.

"This is—" Blackthorn is cut off as a bolt of magick hits him square in the chest. The impact sends him flying backwards, his body slamming into one of the standing stones with a sickening thud.

I breathe a sigh of relief as he goes down. Maybe now this will all be over.

Glancing up at Randall as he stands over me, I smile. A spark of hope ignites in my chest. "Thanks for the rescue—"

"I'm sorry, Adelaide," Randall interrupts me and then slams the knife into my chest, straight into my heart.

Read on with Midnight Reign, Book 2 MidnightReign

Join my Facebook Reader Group for more info on my latest books and backlist: Eve Newton's Books & Readers

Join my newsletter for exclusive news, giveaways and competitions: Eve Newton's News

Also by Eve Newton

https://evenewton.com

Printed in Great Britain
by Amazon